Dedicated to Dad

The Names We Go By

© 2021 Tyler Patrick Wood

Paperback ISBN: 978-1-66781-008-9
eBook ISBN: 978-1-66781-009-6

THE

NAMES

WE GO BY

A
WESTERN
NOVEL

TYLER PATRICK WOOD

TABLE OF CONTENTS

CHAPTER 1:

LOOT

HE WAS SET UP HIGH IN THE HILLS BEHIND THREE GRANITE boulders that tended toward pink in the sun. A small opening in the rock afforded enough space to manage the barrel of his rifle down the slope, gunmetal as still as the stones left and right. Someone was riding alone and deliberate up the trail to his cabin. He wasn't much partial to hosting company. Just a little longer and the lone stranger would know permanent the error of coming this way.

His repeater was cleaned from the night before and aimed at a point where anyone sticking to the trail would have to cross, maybe a hundred yards down. His gloved hand steadied the weapon while an unadorned trigger finger was bent ready and hard calloused. He heard a raspy voice calling, "Hey Loot! Loot Moreno! You up there!?"

As the rider below kept on, he let out a half minute's stored breath and allowed his body some slack. A familiar face passed by the gunsight. He got up slow and dusted off his heavy wool pants, steady and sure-footed around the boulders while high pines drifted back and forth under a sharp afternoon sun. Jasper Bedford was close now, struggling atop a horse appearing to match the rider for age. "When you going to learn to make yourself known farther down the hill?" asked Moreno. His throat caught as he tried to project. It had been a spell last he'd said so many words running.

"Your violence could never extend to me," Jasper announced, slurring his proclamation a touch as he eased back the reins. "Our rich history has taught me so, though I'm sure you'd jump to say otherwise." He gathered steam as he spoke and patted his vacant stomach. "Ah, lives such as ours can't be snuffed so trivially."

Moreno's voice was steadier and attained a sharper edge. "Point is, I don't know if it's friend or other. Holler sooner. My mutt blood doesn't come with the power to see past what is."

Jasper appeared ready to let fatigue slide him from his saddle as Loot neared. "I can't ever remember when I'm supposed to call out. Apologies. Confusing in a way, rocks and the trees. Everything out here tends toward sameness."

"I suppose."

"Don't be so disappointed in me," Bedford huffed. "I'm a top hand at finding the nearest saloon, regardless of orientation." Jasper's long bare chin was raised, trying to claim back some dignity.

"Well," said Loot, "that's got the ring of truth." He took the reins with his naked hand and ushered the gray gelding up a widening trail carpeted with brown tree needles to his home; just a little cabin, fashioned out from an indention in the mossy cliff-side. "All to say, if you're feeling unsure out here, early introductions are best."

Bedford sat high in his saddle before addressing Moreno with a formal bow. "Your logic is concise and unimpeachable, my friend."

"Get on down," Loot said, breath still quicker than normal. "Come inside and take coffee. Smelling whisky about, so I reckon you already got a jump on feeling warm."

"I did indeed," Jasper smiled tentatively. He was weary and near drunk by any reasonable standard. Coming up on Moreno's hideaway absent proper form was a good way to hasten St. Peter. He whispered a warning reminder to himself for next time, else it might be his last.

Loot moved fast to spell the horse its rider. "You've got a look like you might be about done in. Take my hand. I'll help you off."

"Cheers. My steed could be tuckered. A ghastly trudge to get up here." Jasper cleared his ragged throat and spit once his feet were under him. "More importantly, my procreative elements suffered greatly from this unforgiving saddle. The leather is harder than diamonds."

Loot patted the weary animal just above his drooping eyes. "A bettin' man might wager on your horse falling dead before too long."

"Oh," Bedford said, scratching his wrinkled brow in wonder, like Loot's assessment was a revolution in thought. "Losing Rocinante would be a dreadful loss. I really enjoy him, *despite* the deleterious effect riding has on my balls." He stood up on his toes a little when he said *despite*. It was a habit Moreno had noticed and tried figuring out for years. Bedford liked to get higher up to put extra heat to a word, but there was no telling when it might be or what word might command the honor.

"You're strange, JB, even for an old white man. Gonna get to what brings you?" Loot hitched the horse and opened the door to his little hideaway. It was a tidier situation than one might expect from the outside. A dry, single room setup that served mostly as surroundings for a large cast-iron potbelly stove. Transporting it up the steep hillside might've whittled years from a man less robust than Moreno.

"Yes, what brings me," Jasper said, removing a tan duster big enough to force Loot into assuming it was a borrow. He placed it on one of two chairs in the cabin and took to the other like he'd just endured all forty years of wilderness. "I know you don't love callers, but I felt duty bound to make the ascent."

Loot pulled the other chair near his visitor and sat himself. "Something's weighing heavy, enough to go through that flask more than once."

"No fooling you." Jasper was staring at the table, rubbing the sleeves of his wrinkled brown suit for warmth. "I always said you should've been a newsman."

Loot grunted. "Nothing against your trade, but I never myself understood the draw."

Bedford kept to the table, attempting to avoid the sober midnight blue of his friend's eyes. "Like I said, apologies for scaling Olympus. You value your privacy, I understand."

"Value might not be the right word, Jasper." Moreno kicked the dirt-covered stone floor with the heel of his boot. "People don't hole up like this without necessity hammering in some of the nails."

"Of course," Jasper smiled, patting the top of his glistening head. He was about the only "European" Loot had ever known that refused a hat. It didn't make much sense to him or anyone else, considering the nature of the man's hair. It was sparse and ragged and nonexistent saving the sides, the color of chalk or soot, depending on the spot. There was something to his looks, though. Bedford had forgiving brown eyes to match his suit and slumped shoulders that would rise to meet excitement or fall to share a burden. His was a posture of ready humility, always reacting and therefore always engaging. Most meeting the wrinkled writer gave over to his winning ways within minutes. In that regard, Loot, as much as he'd deny it, was like the herd.

"I understand it's not been ideal up here, but solitude sometimes is best society," Jasper said, all thumbs, trying to find the old feeling of familiarity with his host. It had been near six months since their last encounter.

"Best society. Is that one of your writings?"

"Hell no. It's Milton. *Paradise Lost*? Forget it. I was trying too hard. Foolish."

"*Paradise Lost*, huh?" returned Moreno. "Well, that's a title I can get my head around. The lost part, anyhow."

Bedford realized he was clenching his veiny hands with strength not called upon in many years. He wrenched them apart and used one to awkwardly smack Loot on the knee. "I've said it before, but a woman or two could really make time go faster. Isolation is fine, but life needs punctuation marks."

"You're saying what you're always saying? Saying it different?"

"Yes! Copulation, my good man. I can always hire a few discreet beauties to make you forget about things."

"What things in particular?" Loot would play along, seeing that it was helping to speed Jasper's recovery.

"Anything in particular. Anything in general. I find that in general, a little affection can cover a multitude of particulars."

"Same old letch, Jasper."

His shoulders were high as they'd go, a product of the lightened mood. "I won't prevaricate. You've always had my measurements."

"Don't know how you get through a day without paying for flesh."

"Me neither," returned the writer, now hitting Loot on the arm. "But," Jasper stopped, all of a sudden embarrassed. His hollow drunkard's cheeks turned ruddy, regretting the frivolous course the conversation had taken. There was hard truth on the docket and a swift tonal change wasn't the best way to go about things. Still. Enough stalling. Had to be done. He leaned in for the sharp bend. "I came to let you know, word from Thunder Hill was sent through on the telegraph. That's the machine, we've had one—"

"I know all about it. On and on about that damn thing each time seeing you."

"Of course," Jasper coughed, sitting up solemn as his back would take. "Anyway, word came down that Ben Laird's dead. Happened yesterday. I climbed Rocinante for this mountain the minute I confirmed the sad news."

Loot moved strange and turned his head as he took in Jasper's report, like dodging slow punches. "How?"

"Fever grabbed him up and didn't let go. Only took a week, start to finish. Something in the lungs. Said the last few days it was like he was breathing underwater." Jasper imagined a bought woman from the week previous, anything not to contend with the choking sensation presently gripping his throat. Fighting the urge to pull for his flask and shrink lower, he instead raised his bearing high to Loot. His friend was now standing over the homemade table, head almost forcing up the roof. Jasper'd never seen a man to match him on the frontier. A neck like a tree trunk. Legs bigger than the average westerner's waist. Hair black like coal ran south of his shoulders absent a hint of gray, despite a run of years now stretching well into middle age. Dark blue eyes didn't seem likely on a face with such uniformly olive skin, but you could trace that back to his unique extraction. Loot's mother was a white settler who'd come over with a big family from somewhere in the high climes of Europe with barely a nickel and barely a word of English. Jasper'd heard rumors of a scandal, some sort of affair with one of society's "undesirables." A young rider that caught her eye, apparently named Moreno. He was hanged shortly after Loot's birth, this unwanted horseman, part Mexican and part Indian. The only time Bedford spoke with Moreno about his past, Loot put on like none of it made a difference. No allegiance to any band of people or group had ever earned him a damn thing, he said. The only tribe he'd ever joined turned him bad and done the world wrong. He explained it vague, not enough to help Bedford make sense of it. Jasper found the parts he knew and the parts he didn't endlessly fascinating, but the writer made no more approaches toward it. He'd always respect Moreno's wishes, much as his inquisitive nature told him to do otherwise. In a wide-open country where the individual was a castle, Loot was a fortress on a hill too high for the clouds. Close as Moreno kept his own council, Jasper, without knowing exactly the reasons, knew the man cared a whole heap about very few.

One such was Ben Laird.

"Damn. Preacher Laird. Damn shame," Moreno said, setting down a shaky tin cup of coffee in front of his guest. "Should've had some more years left in him."

"I thought you'd want the news, bad as it is. And you don't have to tell me what it was... the connection and the like. I know I've asked b—"

Moreno covered Jasper's mouth. "You hear that?" he asked, hand still where he left it. It was large enough to cover most of the writer's face. "Twig broke. Sounded not too far off." Moreno listened breathlessly a little longer and sprang. With strange agility he grabbed his repeater and glided out of the cabin, down the hill to his spot behind the three boulders. He fell to his chest silently, just in time to catch sight of black hair coming across his field of vision. One shot. Before the smoke cleared, he knew he'd hit his target dead between the eyes.

"Should I ready myself?" Jasper yelled, doing a bad job of moving quickly down to Moreno on his skinny legs. Loot was leaning against one of the boulders by the time Bedford made his way. The newspaper owner was struggling to free his pistol from its holster and wiping sweat from his spotty forehead with a favored red silk handkerchief. The thin air wasn't helping his lungs to find respite.

"It was just a bear. Big for a black. Had a good summer of eating, looks like."

"That's nice," Jasper panted, still a little on edge from Loot's sudden dash.

"Not really. I'm fixed for meat."

"Why then did you fire?"

Moreno was a little embarrassed, poor decisions with a gun not being a common trait. "Didn't know it was a bear until I'd already fired." He paused abruptly. "Or maybe I did. Hell, thought someone might've followed you up here, Jasper."

"I'd never give away your spot, Loot." Despite his wily ways, Bedford could pull an honest face and mean it when the occasion called.

"I know it," said Moreno. "C'mon back inside and take a load off." He walked up and stood square to his friend. The sun was getting lower and his massive shadow was thrown up along the boulders behind. "Truth is, I shouldn't have shot. Didn't used to make mistakes. Not that kind."

"But your aim was perfect. I'm still trying to figure out how you heard it from the cabin."

It'd take more than a bit to describe being in tune with nature. Moreno chose a smaller explanation, one with a quicker exit. "Killing's not the hard part, JB. Deciding, choosing's the hard part. Either I'm old or Ben Laird's death has me jumpy." There was a solemnity in his voice the newsman couldn't recall hearing.

Once inside, Loot seemed unsure whether to sit back down, moving cautiously. He was somewhere else, even in the familiar confines.

Bedford had a sip of near tasteless coffee and coughed, saying, "Also wanted to tell you I was off to the funeral."

"Why?"

Jasper pulled out a flask from the coat pocket next to his heart and drank the coffee taste away. He'd done his sacred duty as the bearer of bad news. Now he could resume normalcies without feeling too guilty. "Well, I knew the man. And there's more than a few folks from Durington heading down."

Loot wasn't mad at the newsman. Just mad in general. People had every right to pay their respects to Ben Laird. And Jasper, he was the type that earned his keep and helped more than most would ever try. *Still.* "Sounds like scheming. You're wondering who'll show up. Write one of your stories on it."

"I don't have any malicious intentions," Jasper said pointedly. "But yes, I made plans to pen something simple to honor the good pastor.

Nothing beyond that." He rubbed at his thin salt and pepper mustache as it quivered from nerves.

Moreno's voice was a locomotive engine when he called upon it, arrestingly low and powerful, and he knew it. "Sorry, JB," Loot said, gentler now. "Anyway, Thunder Hill's a long ride. Day more than Fort Callaway, if you're really about your business."

"We've got three days until the service. They're holding off, presumably on account of all the people coming in for saying goodbyes."

"Best be on your way then," Loot said. His delivery was too flat and cold to be believable as an honest demonstration of his feelings; from years of conversations and searching questions, Jasper could discern that much.

"I'm sorry," Bedford said, standing up. "I really am."

"It's not your fault, Jasper."

"I know. But I'm wondering if I should've said anything. Obvious you're itching to go to Thunder Hill. Looks like you're ready to knock down a wall. Not that I need a demonstration."

"How could I? Too many gawkers. You know I can't risk it."

"That's precisely my point. Sticking my nose in." Jasper clenched his weathered teeth together after another stingy drink. "Anyhow, anyway, I'm truly sorry about your friend."

Loot stood up and signaled the visit's drawdown. "Appreciate you coming up here and giving me the news. No small favor. I'll be owing you."

Jasper took his mighty hand for a shake, having one last look around the cabin. Orderly as it might be, he felt for his friend. The thing Milton said about solitude and society felt like horseshit. As publisher of the *Durington Daily*, he was well-versed in the practice. A man could move a heap of nonsense with the right words. "It's me that forever owes. Be seeing you, Loot."

Moreno watched Bedford down the trail, one old horse on top another. He'd kept his calm through the visit as best he could, but his insides were suffering. He walked in circles over the flat ground in front of the cabin, shoving his hands into his trouser pockets, heart and head arguing the immediate future. If he could've taken leave of his body for a minute, he might've forgiven himself the turmoil to recognize the undeniable drama. In a life full of gunpowder and darkened decisions, Loot Moreno had only made a few friends that were worth a handshake. One was heading down the mountain, on his way to stand over the grave of another.

"No," he said, over and over, repeating the circle until his boots had cleared the pine needles from his path. A taste like iron and ash filled his mouth and nose. The past and all its leavings were pressing on his brain, coming to the fore, dashing what little peace he had like breakers against rock.

Finally, he stopped retracing steps and repeating words. Jasper Bedford was out of sight now, probably nearing the flats leading into Durington. The short walk back to his cabin was labored and panicky. Despite the brisk air swirling against the mountain, little circles of sweat were collecting underneath his rugged arms. *I'm just worried for the boy*, he thought, removing the single glove to look disdainfully at the top of his hand and the mark carved into the skin. He wanted to forget the time when he looked at it with pride. *Live with it like you have been*, he thought, arguing with himself. It wasn't an uncommon thing for Moreno, considering the isolated nature of his existence. This was different, though. This one-party quarrel was going somewhere. It was *about* going somewhere. *It won't hurt to go check on him. Ben's not around anymore. You can talk to Doc Rufus, make sure he's okay. Kip and the rest of the townsfolk of Thunder Hill will never know you were there. Same as it always was.*

This was the logic that led Loot onto his saddle and down the mountain. After packing enough provisions to quickly get there and back, he took the western hill trails that skirted Durington Valley and gave Fort Callaway an extra wide berth. It was a strain to put on Pecos, but Moreno knew how far and long to push the muscular quarter horse. Despite the roundabout route, they made it to Thunder Hill's vicinity ahead of the big party that set off from Durington. No surprise. He'd spent most of his days in a saddle, chasing or being chased. Putting himself out to pasture was a fairly recent development, compared to the whole of things. Not enough time to unlearn the ways of getting around fast and quiet over difficult terrain.

After sighting the town, he stopped just above the tree line on the mountains to the south. Thunder Hill was plumb center in a valley flat as a table, surrounded by cliffs and mountains on all but one side. There was no way to approach without being seen for miles. "We'll wait till dark," he told Pecos, patting his deep brown coat just above the shoulder. Loot could hear the sound of water nearby; either a little mountain stream or waterfall. "Let's get you a drink, brother," he said, walking Pecos along the uneven slope, taking his time. It was no use lunging about and turning an ankle. Although the two-day trip had been steady as she goes, he had a sense that getting hobbled could mean the end. Maybe it was the feeling that his sand was on the wane; he'd never speak it, but his legs and back were giving him little fits. Loot held the reigns and watched each step carefully as the sound grew in intensity. "Not much fun off the beaten path, brother," he whispered, guiding Pecos gently along. "Just a little farther and we'll take rest till night's black as coal. Moon won't be much. Then we'll go see Doc."

CHAPTER 2:

KIP

"THERE IS BUT ONE THING WE CAN SEEK WITH A MIND toward what matters. One thing that can't be moved when we strip it all away. The loves and desires of this world, enticing as they may be, are nothing compared to the Glory of God." Kip Laird believed what he spoke. He needed to. The only father he'd ever known was gone and there were secrets in his midst. A look down at Ben's bible gave him strength, but stubborn questions persisted. Getting on with the day was the goal. Then, getting answers.

Everyone packed in the humble church was transfixed on the young man behind the pulpit. Many of the females were quietly taken hostage by his bold green eyes and precociously handsome face; despite the worthy menfolk sitting in their midst, men they'd sworn to cherish alone. There wasn't much harm in it, one of those innocuous untouched understandings, like a thousand silent contracts folks strung together in community enter into without form or rancor. The entire congregation, young and old, couldn't help but admire Kip's humble passion and sense for the Good Book. His voice was fresh and eager. There was excitement in it, a signal to all that he loved speaking and hinted at an even stronger fondness for listening.

As adept as Laird could be at handling the Message and the wanting eyes and all the rest, now there was a new heaviness to hide in everything he said and did and everything that went on around him. His adoptive father's body lay still in the house next to the church; the man who'd preceded Kip in the running of the church and one of the founding members of the Thunder Hill community. Man, woman, and child alike did their best not to stir and cry at the thought of Ben Laird, stiff and cold, spirit already ascended, flesh prepared for the dirt.

It wasn't Sunday. The usual din of a working town drove on steady outside the church walls. Between needed words of hope and comfort, the congregation cringed hearing the sounds of the less devoted to God and His word.

"Ben built this house of praise and worship with his own hands and sweat, alongside many of you, when I wasn't even a pup."

As the older pioneers nodded and grumbled their agreement, solemnity was punctured by the tinny sound of a faraway piano and unfettered hollering from afternoon drinkers. Realizing the limits of their grace, many began turning toward the door to express disgust.

"C'mon now folks," Kip said, bringing the attention back his way. "That doesn't sound like Armageddon. More like a few wagonloads a'ranch boys blowin' steam before heading back out to it. Ben wouldn't judge those men, but I'll tell you what." The young preacher set down his Bible and stepped purposefully out in front of the pulpit. He stood quiet on sturdy legs straight and true, inflating his rugged chest and shoulders as a physical manifestation of spiritual strength. A tiny smile snuck from the side of his full-lipped mouth as he sunk his hands in his pockets and shrugged. "I think our Ben would want to be the center of attention, just this once."

The congregation laughed, pining after a collective moment of release. Not everyone packed into the pews believed the same things the same ways, but they were all there to pay an honest measure of homage or respect to Ben. Kip leaned slightly toward the attendees and forged ahead with his message, pressing across the battle lines and checking his swelling emotions. He wondered if they could sense the maelstrom breeding chaos in his soul. Like Mr. Caesar at Pharsalus, unsure of the outcome, but sure that ahead and head high was the only way. For now. A time for every purpose. *Lord, hand me down Solomon's inscrutable wisdom. I've need of it presently.*

Pieces of Kip's past had been revealed, whispered hot and sick in his ear by Ben Laird during those dying days. How many in his midst had been keeping the same secrets, and for how long? He snuck a glance at his family in the front row. His adoptive sister Elsie looked up at him with salt-burdened, loving eyes. As she cried pure tears of a grieving daughter, did she know? Mabel Laird, the woman he'd called mother since he could make words, freshly widowed, dignified and well-presented to the last—she had to know. Kip tried to imagine a scenario that ended with her innocence or ignorance on the matter, but none came to mind.

And now that he was privy, what good did it do? He looked at ruddy-cheeked Sydney, his mostly good-hearted but troubled older brother, puffy and usually ill-fitted to his surroundings. Syd could be awkward and inflame, though his recent enlistment as one of the young Thunder Hill deputies had helped even his keel. Kip thought perhaps he'd broach the subject of secrets with Sydney first. *Maybe today. Or not. Oh God give me a little strength, what to do? Handle your business first, remember? Honor thy father. Don't go pitching fits in holy hallowed moments.*

"So, let's not get too caught up attaching ceremony or tradition to this day. Pa wasn't about such things. I'm of limited years and limited wisdom, but I doubt there's many a man of faith that put less stock in all the 'nonsense' surrounding belief."

Another reference to the man they'd gathered for. It helped Kip recapture their attention and lent him a tick to put personal gripes on hold. *Remember your Solomon.*

"Nonsense," the young man declared, making bold gestures with his hands.

It was a bad impersonation, but they got the point. Ben liked to wave his long fingers in front of his face and say, "That's a hot pile of nonsense," never failing to follow the gesture with a tiny wink and a country-sized smile. Each attendee in the church had their own memory picture of the man, and in capturing them, they felt an impossibly pure mixture of grateful and sad; a formula rendered by looking back on a life lived right before man and God.

After a prayer and some grateful words amongst the family and friends, Kip walked over to the Laird house, no more than twenty paces from the church door. It was a sturdy affair with a neat little garden out front and yellow flowers underneath the windows. Not the biggest place in town, but it was looked after like new by Mabel and Elsie. Besides the steep green roof, the house was as white as the church that it sat next to, at Mabel's insistence. She said if God took up in a white residence, so should she. Like most things mentioned sidesaddle by a woman, old Ben accepted it as a joke and a threat, in equal portions.

Old. Ben Laird never really had the chance to be old. Kip lamented this truth as he stepped slowly up to the open coffin sitting in the front room. A man in a fine Chicago black suit with slicked-back tinsel-gray hair sat hunched on a little stool by the body. A stranger might think he was lost in prayer, but Kip knew better. He was holding his slender stomach, practicing a sort of exhalation ritual. "Doc Rufus," said the junior preacher. The three syllables cut through the whole house, powerful and unwavering. Kip couldn't bear to speak softly at present. He feared any cracks or gentleness in manner might turn him brittle to breaking. "Is that breathing some new technique for wrangling a hangover? Something from one of your New York medical journals?"

"New York? Medieval. Worse. Prehistoric. This country is behind. Sadly behind. If I could get some publications from France or England delivered to this backwater, maybe there'd be something worth reading."

"But?" Kip smiled.

"But I doubt that would even do me any good. We're centuries away from catching back up to the Greeks or Romans. Persians. They had fine physicians."

"The Persians," Kip crossed his arms. "You only bring them into your tirades after particularly long nights."

"Well, good reason for it. You do your part, youngster?" Rufus asked, rubbing the thick mustache that covered his top lip. He was proud of each and every whisker, as long as they remained dark. The doctor claimed his facial hair as proof that he was a man no older than thirty to any woman passing through town. It worked, generally, until he had to take off his bowler. Add all that up and the doctor got a fresh trim at Billy's Barbershop every morning and rarely went about head uncovered.

"I sank my heels in. Got through it. Getting through it." Kip accepted a sturdy hug as the older man rose to his feet. Doc Rufus was in his early 50s, near as tall and still strong as Kip, especially thick in the neck and arms. An embrace from the town surgeon required a little preparation or at least resolution. Rufus wasn't given to handing out quarter to those close to him. As they slapped each other's round shoulders Kip said, "You might've come in the church this once. Could've used the support. I know it's not your way, but heck."

The doctor grabbed his sheened lapels and looked down in self-defense. He wasn't ashamed or regretful. Something with more layers. Given his fondness for the kid and the setting and the circumstances, though, he'd let it go this time. A grunt followed by silence was his chosen course of action. Rufus understood the boy's burdened state of mind as well as anyone could. They were looking down at his closest friend: Elias Rufus had struggled and bled alongside the departed. They'd survived a war, cleared forests, fought off Indians, traversed a whole country together. That the doctor and preacher agreed on very little was a hard bit of philosophy for any youth to chew, even one as sharp and clear-headed as Kip.

"Sorry, Doc," Kip sighed, sensing he'd tread clumsy on proper etiquette. "I'm tired, I think. And it's more than that. More than this whole deal," he said, motioning toward the casket. The body was so strangely inert; the absence of life making it infinitely more dead than the box that contained it. The simple casket sat there on dusty sawhorses, waiting to be observed and inspected by morbidly interested townsfolk making their funeral faces.

"I can see you're full of complications," Rufus said with a playful bit of suspicion. His inquisitive icy blue eyes sharpened toward the young man and then relaxed again. "Are the rubes coming in, kid?"

"You can hear them out there as good as I can."

"Though I consider myself learned and fairly understanding of the human experience, this is one tradition I'll never apprehend." He pulled a leather flask from his back pocket. After a short taste he passed it to Kip. "What do the rubes get out of seeing a body? I can indulge a gathering, telling tales, remembering. But the spying of a breathless being, not even a being at all. The rubes are an astonishing lot."

The intake of liquor momentarily wrinkled the junior preacher's usually fresh face. "You're in here yourself, paying respects. Judge not, if'n you please. And what do you get out of calling everyone a rube? How and why you settle on these terms, it's quite astonishing."

Rufus beckoned the flask back with a hand thick from life's hard fight. "Me being *here's* different than being in the worship house. You've known that about me since you were knee-high." He gave the youth a hearty slap on the back. "I love you, son. But as for your astonishment, well, follow that river to its source. You'll find an almost incalculable lack of life experience at the headwater."

Before Kip could muster a response, the door swung open and Mabel walked in with typically short, determined steps. After a carefully muted cough the new widow turned back to the door and held out her hands, fixing a warm expression for the procession of people, prayers and personal messages to come. Her dark brown eyes, now observably swollen from grief, shot holes through her adopted son and turned with vigorous ire toward the silver-haired doctor. "I don't want you here, Rufus," she said, as mannered as she could. "Please find your way out the back. I'd appreciate you being quick about it."

Rufus donned his signature charcoal bowler without a word. He bowed in retreat to Mabel and gave Kip a wink. The doctor walked past the narrow staircase then skirted through the warm kitchen where he'd broken bread so many times before. Mabel'd been out those nights, nights with the women's church group or playing cards with the few ladies of Thunder Hill sharp enough to keep her interested. Ben's dinners weren't exactly a secret. The "rumor" was famous around town: everyone imagining Preach Laird, Doc, and Sheriff Cox all exchanging stories and whiskey over a warm dish. When Doctor Elias Rufus, as he liked to be called in public, was asked what they discussed, he would deny it outright or tip up the shiny brim of his hat to say, "Some things aren't for public consumption."

Mabel made sure she heard Rufus close the door then gave Kip one more look of admonishment before nestling her petite frame between his body and the casket of her late husband. She waved people in with the smallest dutiful smile on her trembling lips. "You shouldn't talk to that old heathen," she whispered between handshakes. The line was awkward, as people had to go out the way they came.

Between *God bless you*s and *thanks for coming*s, Kip whispered back, "I'm sorry, Ma. He was here paying his respects, just like everyone else."

"I know you've always been partial to him," Mabel said. "Heaven help me, your father was. Despite me. Maybe *to* spite me. I shouldn't have been so rude. Y'all didn't deserve it."

Kip draped a long arm around the woman who'd taught him devotion and wit as much as anyone else ever could. "This isn't a day you apologize for anything, Ma. I love you. Everybody loves you. Even that old heathen."

Mabel almost let out a defensive laugh. She bumped him with her hip as they kept coming, one handshake after the next. Otto Buchholz, the blacksmith, with his entire brood. The town surveyor and his wife. Lindy Samuels, with her fiancé. He was fairly new to Thunder Hill, working the town's first official bank. Kip had wondered if Lindy would show, hoping she wouldn't. He lowered his emerald eyes and accepted her warm little hand. She did a full curtsy that gave off not-so-subtle hints of flirtation. The obvious gesture riled Elsie; she was standing next to him now. Sydney sat on a windowsill in the corner, chewing on a toothpick and looking out the glass with a hangdog expression. He fiddled with his crooked short brim hat and rubbed his paunch, typically unable to summon the requisite patience for observing decencies.

More and more piled in. Kip tried not to wince as they scuffed up his mother's prized rug and filled the house with whatever smell they couldn't get off their clothes that morning.

Kip was reeling from the consistent sorrow that hung over everything. It was inescapable. The little draft that always managed to find a path through the house was stunted by bodies. A coat of sweat began to form on his normally pacific face. There was still the burial. More words. More thinking about Ben's dying revelations and pretending not to. *God help me.*

The crack of three distant gunshots sliced their way through all those thoughts. Everyone present stiffened and apprehensively turned their heads toward the noise outside. Sydney roughly pushed his way out the door and started running in the direction of the gunfire. "Syd!" Kip yelled, pulling his mother and sister close. "Keep them all here if you can. I'm going to see what that's about."

He didn't wait for a response. His father's Colt was in the study next to the stairs. He grabbed it and checked the load and action, spinning the oily chamber and snapping it closed again. Quickly he was out the back-door and around the front of the house, trotting heavy through the thick mud of Thunder Hill's main thoroughfare.

It didn't take long to see. Two men were down in the street, not moving. He recognized the Tollier brothers, sons of one of the county's prominent ranchers. Another man he didn't recognize was leaning against the hitching post in front of the saloon, bleeding in silence from a wound in the right leg. Sheriff Cox, Syd, and three others were training their pistols at the hobbled man, yelling with hammers cocked. Kip skidded to a stop at the periphery of the fracas. "Everybody, calm down," he said, gripping his dead father's gun tight in his right hand. He didn't have the weapon raised. There seemed to be enough of that at the moment. "The man's wounded."

"Back," the newcomer said, using the post to steady and turn his focus on Kip. He was a singularly large black-haired man who didn't seem too put out by the bullet in his leg or the numbers stacked against him. The newcomer started raising his pistol again but stopped, looking directly into the green of Kip's wondering eyes. The shouting continued from every which way and the big man appeared to be somewhere else all of a sudden. He dropped his weapon then slumped to the ground, wind gone from his sails. The young preacher was fixated on the face of the stranger. It was brown as treated oak, made darker by a layer of dirt caked across his cheeks and forehead. Only that wasn't what had Laird's focus captured. There were two vertical lines below the eyes of the wounded man where his skin was slightly lighter. He was crying. Without knowing a thing, Kip could tell that this wasn't the sort to go bawling over something as trivial as a bullet wound.

"Stay out of this, kid," Sheriff Cox said, slowly closing the distance to the shooter. "And stay still there, chief. It's a few fresh holes if you're thinkin' to reach back for that gun." The sheriff was lean as a bottleneck at the waist and taller than average, not to mention tough as a coffin nail. He had a flattened nose and dark eyes, carrying the focused aspect of someone you ignored at your peril. Cox wore the same style blue denim shirt and sheepskin-lined leather jacket every single day, on account of being superstitious. The lawman had faith in his skill and pride in the way he went about his part, but he also figured never getting shot besides once in the ear was based on some measure of plain old luck. He'd worn a uniform for the Union during the dark days of the War, and now he wore another. Cox had no inclinations toward changing his ways as long as intransigence kept him above dirt. "Back away!" he commanded. "All of you!"

Everyone obeyed. Kip was confused and angry. Selfish thoughts flooded his mind. His father still needed burying. He still needed his answers. Had to have answers. *There hadn't been a shooting in Thunder Hill in ten years. Now two bodies in the street. This odd figure at the center of it.* Kip looked at the gun in his hand and turned his head toward the church. He forced himself into returning to a dutiful mindset. The spiritual torch had been passed down from Ben; there were no more comers. Duty bound or not, Kip didn't want to go back still unsure of who he was. Every step through the stubborn muck of the road seemed a mile. Ma to take care of. The church to take care of. The faithful. The flock. Elsie, that was a knot that needed a man's work. It was all on him, and he wasn't even sure he was a man. Only one thing was certain. He couldn't go forward in earnest until he knew exactly where he'd come from.

CHAPTER 3:
CARRYING ON

KIP SAT AGAINST THE WALL IN HIS ROOM ABOVE THE GRIMES General Store, heavy-eyed but unable to catch a wink. Something about the big stranger in the street had him riled bone deep. He needed to know more about the man, but presently he was miles short of his best. After the excitement of the shootout and the unremitting pain of returning his father to the dust, he'd taken more whisky in the last twelve hours than the whole of his life. Ambrose, a three-year-old golden retriever, made a whimper and set his pointy nose on Kip's legs. The dog lifted its head and brought it down again and again.

"You understand me, don't you boy?"

For a moment Ambrose stopped and looked at his struggling master. Then he yawned and licked his chops. "Or, more likely, you need to eat and do your business." Magic words. The retriever's tail began wagging furiously, thudding against uneven floorboards every three or four cycles. "Fine," he said, peeling himself slowly from the floor like he'd been stuck there for years. The movement set off little demons of pain throughout his body until they all seemed to run at once toward his head. "Mother of mercy," he groaned, afraid to even rub his temples. Despite the human's condition, Ambrose was encouraged by the simple fact of progress and started scratching at the door. "Let me get the leash, Ambs." He tied the rope off short and tight; no choice, living on the town's main thoroughfare. Too much length and his excitable friend could wind up trampled by horse or carriage. "Hold on, now," he said, finishing the knot, fighting off the throbbing above his eyes. He held the homemade dog collar with one hand and pulled on the rope hard but not enough to see Ambrose choke. It seemed in good order. "Try not to explode on the front walk, will ya?" The suggestion was met with another happy lick of the chops and rhapsodic wagging.

Before he could reach the knob, two gentle knocks were followed by a small, familiar voice. "It's Lindy. You around, hun?"

Ambrose looked up at his suddenly paralyzed owner. A few whimpers from the dog forced him into regaining his senses. Kip opened the door and secured his pet. "Hey there, Miss Lindy. Sorry," he stopped, imagining the sight and smell he was presenting to the lady. "We weren't expecting." Ambrose scratched his hind parts. "Guess that's obvious."

She was smiling sympathetically and trying in vain for sad eyes. They weren't at all convincing. Lindy danced through life. No time for sadness when you're dancing. Wouldn't even be appropriate. "How you faring, handsome?" she asked, letting her fiery hair spill down with the removal of a pin and shake of the head.

"I'm well enough. Maybe didn't acquit myself too heroically in the wee hours last night, but okay." He barely lifted his head as he spoke, letting his sandy bangs fall over his eyes like a wave.

Without a lick of time or added ceremony, Lindy Samuels was across the threshold, kissing him on the mouth wet, all sorts of angles and intensities. Her tightly gloved hands wrapped sure around the back of his neck as she pulled him down to stay the embrace. Kip eventually surrendered a hand for the small of her back. His lips met the tightness of her uncovered shoulders. There was familiarity to the exercise. Shame too.

"C'mon now, Lindy," he said, pulling away just enough for breathy words. The contest between heart and head was no small thing. Something so sweet only seemed right after the bitterness of the last few weeks—that is, he wished it seemed right.

Lindy wasn't stricken by any such contest. She wouldn't let go. Never did, really, once she got her hands moving. She loved to play with his thick hair, separating the darker roots from the lighter ends with her dainty fingers as she whispered lecherous. He didn't know what was so interesting about hair or the great need for such talk. This time, unlike the other times, he wasn't pretending to indulge what he couldn't understand. "Don't push me away, Kip Laird," she said. *So dramatic. Uses both my names for some dang reason.* As always, she was unrelenting, turning his already disheveled mane into something more confused. "You need me right now." One of her wild hands found comfort below his waist.

"I need you to go," he pleaded, guiltily looking right and left like his home was a train station platform. "Somebody could've seen you come up here. We've spoke on this."

"Who cares?" Her hand remained tightened with intention.

He made a guttural sound at the touch that meant a million things but mostly just one. "This ain't Chicago. It's a small town and people are gonna talk."

"Let them," she whispered, fingers making things tumble.

"You're getting married. Dang, Lindy. If the banker fella finds out, I'm more than likely to take a bullet in the back."

Her face was no more than an inch away and all parts of their hips and legs were tangled up. Kip felt convicted and drawn back in, depending on the second; every time they kissed it was Hell and Heaven. He understood his dalliance with Lindy was a simple sin of the flesh, base and low. But that wasn't the whole of it. He did feel for her. A substantial portion of him wanted to close the door behind and spend the day in her enthusiastic embrace, laughing and carrying on like consequences were mere myths. But not now. *God help me, not ever again.*

And so, after a few more minutes of mumbled deflections, he was able to steer her back and out the door. She said something about it not being over while he repeated *fine, fine, fine,* all the time trying to keep her hands off his britches.

* * *

He slid down the door and listened to Lindy descending the steps. Ambrose sat in front of him, mouth closed and completely still. The animal looked disappointed at his master. Kip almost laughed at the idea, but it wasn't that funny. What did he know, anyway? Maybe Ben and Jesus and all the saints and angels were behind that dog's messy eyes, using Ambrose as a vessel to witness the messy destruction of a young soul. *I might still be drunk.* "Come here, boy," Kip said, holding his hand out while Ambrose lowered his ears and gave over for a good hearty petting. "Just a few seconds more, pal. Got to space out departures, in case anybody out there's by the door."

The dog wagged his tail and plopped his rear back down, craning his head forward to make sure the petting kept on without interruption. Boy and dog enjoyed a few moments of peace before Kip could will himself back to his feet.

As he reached for the knob, three sharp knocks sent him reeling backwards. "You in there?" Another female voice, but not Lindy.

Remnant head pain and lingering agitations gave Kip notions of playing silent, but Ambrose was reaching a breaking point and had been the good soldier long enough. "Yeah," he coughed to clear his throat. "Yeah, Elsie. Coming out." He wiped his face wildly with the back of his hand and forearm then opened the door quick and nonchalant, playing for regularity. His sister was on the landing, looking fit and proper in her black dress and tilted silk-lined hat. Twisting rivulets of blond fell down in carefully executed chaos over her porcelain forehead.

"Aren't you gonna put something on?" she asked, aiming her tiny purse at his barrel chest.

"I'm wearing things, Else," he said with a contained smile. "And we're not traversing the Himalayas. My boy needs his time in the sun, is all."

"Alright, feller. Only, conventionally some type of shirt is placed *underneath* the suspenders. Forgiveness if I'm being a little lady about things."

"Else," he said, unhid irritation in his voice, trying to control Ambrose down the steep, narrow staircase. His place had its own door, right next to the store entrance. That was the good news. Bad news was the stairs; a boot wrong and it'd spell curtains.

"I'm sorry," Elsie said, following him down with royal composure. If he was holding on for dear life, she was floating like a feather and making a show of it. "And since you asked so politely, I'd be happy to walk with you and Ambrose."

Once outside, Kip struggled to find a point ahead and stick to it, still battling the headache. He was experiencing a good old-fashioned hangover. The prospect of ever drinking again seemed worse than death, but he had a feeling a lot of full-time drunks fostered similar thoughts after their first hard stint with the bottle. "I think I'm dying, Else."

"All things pass," she said weightlessly. "Besides, I think it's best to save the drama for your sermons."

Elsie placed a guiding hand on his back and took the rope as they nodded past Mr. Haines the butcher and Mrs. McCarthy, the recently widowed schoolteacher. "We're heading out back, Ambrose," she said, moving the party along with a sudden vivacity, "but you hold steady until we've got some privacy." A quick look behind at Kip. "Can't have you adopting your master's manners."

"Hilarious, Else."

She didn't respond to his jab, instead walking head high with Ambrose, long skirt swishing against the tall yellow grass behind the store. Kip leaned against the back wall of the building. A hazy minute or two went by before Elsie handed back control of the dog. "I understand the impulse to tear yourself asunder, but it's past midday."

Kip bent over, hands gripping his knees as he fought the urge to vomit.

"Unfettered and unseemly isn't your style, feller."

"It's past midday," he reasoned, kneeling down to pet his dog. Ambrose was calmer now, but still hungry. "Not two years from now. A little repose is all I'm asking for."

"Alright," Elsie said, realizing Kip wasn't in fighting shape. She leaned in and whiffed his breath. "But what you need is a repast. Something to lock horns with that presence. I'll go back up and grab you a shirt, feed the dog."

"You don't have to." There was *too much* decency in her offering. Maybe she knew about Lindy Samuels and was granting calm before the storm. Could be he was thinking too much? Or not at all. *Damn that whisky. Damn.* Sneaking around like the most pitiable sinner, lying by not telling the whole truth. His people deserved more. Especially Elsie and especially now.

Finally, he threw up.

"There," she said, reclaiming the leash. "After you're gathered, go *place* yourself out front. My guess is you'll put the other town beggars out of business by the time I get back from feeding the boss here."

"Always funny, Else." He was talking to the ground, talking to her.

"Wherever more than one is gathered, somebody has to be wittier."

"It never stops."

"Never will." She winked as he rose up, meeting his pain with a sweet surprising smile of understanding. "Meet you out front."

Five minutes later, Elsie emerged on the orderly little boardwalk outside Kip's apartment. He was sitting with his long legs dangling over the side, sleepy again now that his stomach was calm. She threw a black shirt over his back along with a gray bandana. The cheerless colors crushed his heart all over. Making a show of mourning seemed an extra dose of cruelty to the ones needing comfort and the ones doing the comforting. No matter. Conventions.

After getting up and tucking in, Elsie asked him to wait a tick. She slid back inside the door and emerged with a fresh towel and washbowl full of clean water. "Figured you'd cleanse up before we adjourned."

He was grateful to dunk his head. The idea of baptism struck him. *If ever he needed another one.* "Suppose you're right," he said, rubbing off the stink and sick from his hands. "Probably needing a scenery change. Three little kids started poking me with a stick before you got out here."

"You possess an indelible gravitas," she said, holding her arm wide for him to escort her. "Even partially adorned. Fully adorned—well, you're positively magisterial."

They walked slow and silent in and out of the overhang's shade, grateful for a cool mountain breeze dancing down from the mountains. Crossing two streets of hardened clay, they arrived at The French Café. Only people that made Thunder Hill home used this appellation. To those passing through, it was simply *The Café.* Understandable. They served nothing French. An ancient named Beckett French owned the place, is all, and despite the lack of international cuisine, it was the best joint (out of three) in town.

Though swollen with customers, several parties stood up and offered their tables when the Lairds entered. Conversations about crops and cows and yesterday's shooting skidded to a stop in every corner.

"Oh no, fellas. We couldn't," Kip said. Simple deferential instinct.

"Thanks, George. Wilson, thanks so much," Elsie followed, happy enough at taking the first seat offered. Before he could object, the young preacher could see a chair and a clear place set in front of him. He began to mumble something like an argument but found himself cut off. "Just pipe down and accept some courtesy. Let other people take care of you. Stuff that mule obduracy."

"I'm only—"

"Nope," Elsie said, holding up the little menu in front of her comely, heart-shaped face. Kip looked around and realized that elbow-to-elbow in the busiest spot in town was no place for an argument. He took his medicine and began to brood in silence, still wearing the weight of Lindy Samuels around his neck. Little Cara, French's youngest granddaughter, came by with water. Kip ventured close to swallowing the glass whole. *Drinking the wrong thing makes you thirsty. Perhaps the start of a sermon.* Cara immediately came back and refilled his glass, big honest eyes and honest innocence. *Probably best not to do a sermon on debauchery's aftermath.*

"Thank you, Cara," Elsie said, rolling her eyes like she was witness to his thoughts.

"You're handling this like a Spartan, aren't you?" he asked, immediately wishing he hadn't.

"What's that supposed to mean?"

The only thing was to continue. If he went another direction she'd train him back. Since he was aware of the world, there was Elsie, made sharp by God. He'd speak his piece and follow it out. "Pa's dead, is what I mean. We're sitting here wearing black and people are looking at us queer. Not a lick of it seems to stick to you, though. Just chin up and crack wise, like always." Due to the close quarters, Kip's analysis was hardly above a whisper. Still, Elsie felt the intended bite.

"I'm away from Mama for twenty minutes and," she stopped abruptly but not emotionally, gaining composure. "Is this going to be our midday meal? If so, I'll go invite myself to sit with the boys from the Thompson spread."

He turned around. Elsie wasn't threatening idle. Thompson's cowpunchers were indeed seated in the corner. "You're not going over there," he said, squaring back up to the table. "They've been whispering things unsavory."

"I heard a little. Nice to know my curvatures can't be 'hid by no lady-like adornments and my backside is just the right size for grabbing hold.'"

He was brimming. Playing into her. "Don't with that."

"Why not? I bet they'd enjoy my company."

"I reckon they'd do more than that, if you open the barn door."

A scowl like he'd never seen came across Elsie's unblemished face. Her dimpled chin was protruding as she bit down on what she wanted to say. Her eyebrows, darker than her golden hair, were crooked and bent in more than one direction. Elsie's natural good looks made it worse when she turned them against you. "I'm sorry," Kip said. His hands were in the air to signal apology and surrender. He really did regret his behavior, from after the burial and on. Elsie wasn't supposed to be caught up in his backslide. She was good and right most all the time, and it was nice of her to check in on him. Nice to take him to French's. Their routine. Heaven knew she *almost* had the same heap piled on her shoulders, what-to-do's and won-derings. He stopped thinking of his damned thumping head and gathered his hands together, like offering a prayer. "You know what I'm thinking... I shouldn't be acting like this."

The gesture seemed to have a disarming effect. Elsie rolled her shoulders back and let the seat catch the nuances of her frame. "You've got a lot on your mind," she said, "more than just Pa. Something specific that won't just go away."

"That's right," Kip said, fiddling with a fork that looked like it pre-dated the word *antique*. "But how'd you guess that, Else? In a rush you've moved from insightful to clairvoyant."

"You were on about something the other day. I couldn't make heads or tails of it…"

Kip thought back through the vicissitudes of the last week. It was fog. Was it possible that he'd broken reticence and offered up the secret to someone who could understand? Was Elsie playing coy, just pretending she wasn't already privy to the things revealed to him by Ben? Add to that, he still didn't know if she was feigning ignorance about Lindy.

Damn. Had the haze and crushing confusion caused some sort of fevered state of forgetfulness? Surely not. Even she wouldn't be able to cut jokes pulling the same insufferable freight. Then again, she was a powerful, beautiful bird. His *sister.* "So," he said, toeing for solid ground, "we *haven't* talked about it…"

"Not in any good order. But whatever it is, I can handle the reins. God, give me something else to think about." She almost laughed, then caught herself. Pining for diversions wasn't proper public form. Elsie knew it, yet somehow, she knew the desire to be inevitable. At least for her.

"I'm not your brother."

She was still as stone, deciding from many options on which way was best to go. "I'm aware of that. We've *talked* on this. I mean, you know what I mean."

"I'm not putting it in the bullseye."

"Try harder, then."

"Before Pa passed, he told me some things. Elsie, he said who my real parents were. How I ended up here at all."

Elsie leaned forward and said, "Mama and Pa always said you were left on the steps of the church." She took the fork from his hand and gripped his thick fingers lightly. "So, this is what you were getting your mettle up to talk about the other day. Before you just faded off."

"If you say so. I was here and there, truth be told."

"Well go on and finish, because I didn't get the whole of it. Whatever *it* is."

"My parents—my *other* parents were killed when I wasn't much but a baby. Pa got to know the man who brought me. They kept in touch over the years. Said it was Loot Moreno."

* * *

The din of dishes and conversation dropped away as Elsie's hazel eyes went narrow and turned from green to gold depending on the spot.

"I know what you're gonna say," Kip continued, "but this came out of Pa's mouth straight as Gospel fact."

"But c'mon, feller. He was uttering all manner of nonsenses those last few days. Think of the state the man was in. Loot Moreno? He's a make-believe monster. Heaven's sake, they still tell stories about him around campfires to scare runts."

Elsie wasn't saying anything he hadn't already run through, but he trusted her enough to disclose the rest. "I might've just let it be…"

"But?"

"But then I set eyes on the man yesterday, the one in the shootout. Call me crazy, but I think that's Loot Moreno."

"I'm calling you crazy," Elsie said, crossing her arms. "And how'd you come to this conclusion?"

"A couple things Pa said about him. His gun. Heck, you didn't see him. Unique, to say the least. Then his hand when they were dragging him away. He had this one glove that fell off. A strange mark. A circle with two lines. I've heard about that mark."

"Let me guess. From Pa."

Kip couldn't help but smart from the incredulity. "No. But a few other places."

Elsie had every reason to throw water on whatever his brain was cooking up. He was talking myths and legends and the fevered last words of a dying man.

And his head was killing him.

And the man who raised him was gone forever. "Hey, Preach," said Andy, Beckett French's son, coming by in his trademark grease-stained apron to get their order. *Preach.* It was a strange thing to hear. Ben Laird's title since the founding days of Thunder Hill. Someone had to be the first to say it. A rather inglorious passing of the torch. Elsie could see the awkwardness bubbling underneath Kip's placid visage.

"Hi there, Andy," Elsie said, smiling wide up at the waiter, calming the chaos of his day with her orderly teeth and playful, shrugging shoulders.

"That was a nice service yesterday," Andy said, wiping his hands as a way to deal with the clunky nature of decency. "I'm sure gonna miss Ben. No finer fella around. Anything we can do, don't hesitate. People are being polite sometimes, but I mean it true. Glad you came in today."

"Thanks, Andy," Kip managed, "kind of you."

"Y'all want to order?"

Yes, Kip thought. *I want to eat and quit all the talking.* Elsie went ahead with her order as Sydney barged in the café, ungraceful as ever. His backside and belly knocked every dish, chair or person down or to the side. When he docked with their table, Elsie stood up gasping. "Syd! What happened to your face?"

Sydney asked a speechless Andy if he could get him a chair and stood rapping dirty knuckles on the table as Elsie looked him over and examined his wounds with her hands, trying to do too much with them in the absence of proper medication and dressings. Kip let her chide their brother for getting hurt and left it alone. The moment was all too revealing. He couldn't believe that before today he'd thought to confide Ben's deathbed confessions to Sydney. Trouble stuck to him like he was bred for it. Much as Kip loved him, his brother rarely made things better.

"Really, Syd. How'd you come by all that?" Kip finally asked, patting his arm on one of the few spots not ruined by blood or muck.

Sydney answered like a cannon shot. "The damn crossbreed put the boots to me is what happened. Took four of us to get him in the cell yesterday, even with the bullet wound in his leg."

"But I saw you yesterday," Elsie said, thinking he might need sewing up, "You seemed to come out all right."

"No, little sister. This was from today. He near escaped on the way back from seeing the judge, clattering all of us with them irons. I'm telling you, that mutt bastard is a ruffian of the highest order. Devil's spawn, I'm thinking. Scary sumbitch is what I'm saying."

Everyone in French's was looking at their table now, silent and attentive. Elsie and Kip might've been a heavy presence in the room, but now, with Sydney there, the Lairds were center stage with a spotlight beaming down.

Andy came back with a chair and Syd collapsed into it. He took a drink of water from Elsie's glass and left blood on the rim from his split lip. "What's this fella's name?" Elsie asked softly, eyeing the room, serving everyone notice to go back to their own doings.

"Calhoun. Brandon Calhoun. Son of a damn gun, I think he broke something in my chest. I better get on and see Doc Rufus. Hope he's not too drunk yet."

Syd looked first at Kip and then to Elsie. It was an expectant face, that said *help me up here, dammit.*

Kip did the lifting and told his brother he'd be checking on him later.

"Always with the courtesies," Syd said, rubbing Kip's dense hair with a mixture of condescension and acceptance. "I'm off then."

"Why didn't you go straight through to Doc's?" they asked, almost in unison.

"I was walking by and saw you through the window. Can't a man talk to his family? Just wanted to check in's all I'm driving at."

"You wanted to let Betsy Taylor get a look at you all rough and law-man'd up," Elsie said with a tiny smile and flared nostrils.

"Ain't she working?" Sydney asked, suddenly a little spryer in his boots as he torqued his head back for a last survey.

"Afraid we haven't seen her," Kip added. "Just little Cara and Andy running the tables."

"Damn shame. She's developing into quite a sight."

"You're incorrigible," Elsie whispered harsh. "Thrashed and all, still the same."

"Pretty girl, all's I'm trying to tell you. No sense hiding intentions under my hat."

"There's wisdom in that," Kip said, sitting back down, forced to smile at Syd's unchangeable ways. "Before you leave—that prisoner, are you sure he's giving you the right name?"

"What do you mean?"

"I don't presume to do you fellas' jobs, but that didn't look like any Brandon Calhoun I've ever slapped eyes on. Assumed it was something a little more mysterious."

"Nothing mysterious, little brother. Don't go making it a something. I know you're boiling cause Pa's peace was interrupted, but it won't matter come a few days."

"How's that?"

"I mean Brandon Calhoun's gonna hang. Judge sentenced him this morning. That's why I got this face. He wasn't taking too kindly to it. Figured on you doin' the math."

Elsie gave her goodbye as Sydney lumbered out of the café. Kip wore a pensive look that had her worried. "Whatever it is, best you stop rolling it around."

"I don't know, Else. The whole thing is off. And hanging…"

"You've got your principles." She gripped his hand. "But he did shoot down those Tollier boys. You've got nothing to say for it. Justice isn't pretty."

The crushing headache was starting to dissipate, leaving space for confusion, doubt, and shame. Though the young pastor opposed executions, he wasn't upset about hanging *in general*, as was most likely Elsie's point. His problem was specific. He needed some answers. Answers beyond the words of his dying father.

He rubbed her fingers, amazed at the softness. Elsie was near a miracle. He still needed to come clean about Lindy and what he'd been up to, almost as much as she deserved straight shooting. It would have to wait a little longer.

Kip raised his hand to flag down Cara or Andy. He was about finally getting some lunch.

Then, he needed to go to jail.

CHAPTER 4:

WAITING FOR THE WANTED

"YOU BOYS GET DOWN OFF THE WAGON NOW." THE MAN SERVing instructions was calm, hunched casually on a bulky mount. His red and gray-bearded face was barely visible to the two men driving the stage. "The ones inside, come out showing hands."

"Who the hell are you supposed to be?" asked the fella riding shotgun. He was ill-groomed and short for teeth, as was the driver.

"I'm Fallstead. United States Deputy Marshal Fallstead, if you're hard for credentials."

"Seems awful steep demandin' for someone set by his lonesome," growled the driver, spitting tobacco juice down his scraggly chin. "You just get on out the way before we get angry."

The wind was pushing a cloud of dust down the narrow road. The deputy marshal shielded his slender eyes by turning away from the stage and lowering his old tan bowler to his meager eyebrows. It was hard wrapping their heads around this obstruction; out on his own, showing his back without hint of caution. They scratched at their spotty beards and tensed their muscles and tried thinking if they'd heard tell of this lawman.

He turned back slowly after the air cleared. "Tell your boss to come on out that carriage. Needin' to wrap this up and get back to town."

The driver and his companion exchanged bewildered looks and started busting their underfed guts. The door to the wagon opened and a tall man rigged in a striped three-piece suit stepped out. He was a dimpled picture, tailored head to toe. The tips of his fingers glinted in the sun as he extended his hands outward. "What can I do for you, Marshal?"

"Called on to bring you to town. Got a warrant signed by the judge in Boyd City."

"You didn't even ask who I was."

"Don't need to ask. Seen you before, Mr. Trill. You know, 'round."

"I don't recall meeting."

"Never said we'd met." Deputy Marshal Fallstead slowly lifted the short brim of his hat and looked hard at the three men before him. "Y'all put down any weapons, and I'll ride you into town living as is. Fair dealing. Sure it'll get worked out."

"What's the charge?"

"No charge yet. Suspicion of murder. Couple of folks that worked your ranch haven't been heard from. Two negroes and a half-breed."

"Doesn't ring a bell." Trill pulled off his velvety top hat, allowing his shining black hair a breathing. He was proud of his pretty. "Three creatures. Not even people. Hardly worth coming out here."

"Don't much care one way or the other about them or you. Clear it up with the judge." The lawman sighed audibly and said *guns* like it wouldn't be said again.

"You've got a hell of a lot of nerve." Trill seemed taken with himself. "Don't you have any cohorts?"

"Yep. Got one cohort. Not necessary for you. Last chance, now. Goes for the slinger that's still holed up in that wagon, too. So we're clear."

"You must be about the most impetuous son of a bitch I've ever had the bad luck to meet," Trill said, putting his hands on his hips. Fallstead looked at the ranch owner's rig. Polished like new. Probably never been fired but to show off to some purchased company.

"Alright, then." Fallstead showed no tells. Most men would tighten up or, at the very least, change their expression. Not so with the veteran marshal. He reached across his body and pulled his pistol, killing the dirty man with the shotgun before he even knew a fight had commenced. The driver was dead before his pal hit the dirt. Both headshots. Fancy Mr. Trill was struggling to pull, but he was pulling. *Idiot.* Fallstead winged him in both arms and once more in the shoulder. Trill looked like a puppet on a string, gyrating back and forth before falling to the road in agony and then shock. He'd live. *Maybe.*

"You wantin' me to let you reload?" The question came from inside the wagon.

"Nope," Fallstead answered, holstering and finally getting down from his steady mount. "I saved the one."

"You gonna shoot me before I get the chance to set my feet?"

"If you make me."

"Alright then." The man inside came out the same door as Trill. He stepped over the moaning cattleman with his head held high, sporting a weathered look of unflappable confidence.

The two had about fifteen yards between them. The man from the carriage was staring holes at Fallstead through the smoke of spent cartridges. The marshal wasn't so keen as his opposite, looking only as much as he had to.

"There is a resemblance," Fallstead said, hardly loud enough to reach the other.

"What's that?"

"I met your brother in Boyd City, Mr. Rade. That's how I knew you were coming this way."

The gunman's symmetrical face took an odd shape. "Not possible."

"No?"

"Picker'd never sell me out to no tin star."

"Picker didn't want to." Through all the talking and shooting, the marshal's face still hadn't changed. Rade the gunman was put off. The "tin star" seemed lifeless. Plain old-fashioned bored.

"You trying to say you beat it out of him?"

Fallstead didn't answer, but he took note of Rade, lowering his arms little by little.

"You trying to say he's dead?"

Again, no answer.

Time and silence were enough for the gunslinger. He went for his right hip and came near to clearing the pistol from its holster before Fallstead's final bullet blew a wide hole through the back of his head.

"Let's get you up," he said, walking calmly over and kicking Trill lightly in his boot sole.

"You're a lunatic," the ranch owner cried. He didn't look so prim anymore. The only parts of him not covered with dirt were soaked through with blood. "You can't just kill everyone."

"You're still alive," the marshal said, stolid to the bone, voice rough from use but still even. "C'mon. I didn't shoot you in the legs."

Fallstead had a quick look at the scene and started shaking out his gun hand. Trill was still jabbering, but the marshal had tuned him out. Despite a thousand cries and protestations, the tortured suspect found himself tied from his wrists to Fallstead's saddle horn. He was made to see nothing past the anguish, running alongside the lawman's apathetic horse as they worked their way back to town. Every so often Trill would surrender footing and find himself dragged and stomped by the animal's hind legs. Mr. Trill's piteous five miles back to Boyd City was as bad a journey as one would dare consider. By the time they arrived, he was parched all the way through and busted up all over. One of his shoulders had gone wayward, and an ankle'd gotten broke. Not to mention the exhaustion. Not to mention the three bullet wounds giving way to unnatural colors.

Boyd City's sheriff was sleeping in the jailhouse when Fallstead walked unceremoniously through the door. The prisoner was unconscious, slung over his shoulder. "Sheriff Utterly, get yourself roused," the marshal said. Utterly was unmoved. Grumbling, the marshal set the cattleman down on the floor and kicked the sheriff's chair hard enough to tip it over. The town's leading arbiter of justice found himself waking up next to the dirt-ridden, bleeding body of Mr. Trill.

"Jesus Jupiter!" the sheriff said, popping to his feet, reaching for his gun out of instinct.

"Nope," Fallstead said, flat and hard as a mesa top.

The sheriff slapped himself and postured up a bit. "Oh, hey there, Holt."

"I've got a gun. No need for pulling yours."

"'Course not. I didn't know you was here. There."

"Normally you take sleep on the job?"

"It's been trying times, Trill and all that goes with it."

Fallstead looked right through the pudgy excuse of a man. No wonder he'd been called in to apprehend the rancher. Utterly was wholly unsuited for sentry duty, let alone rounding up villains. "Well, there he is."

Sheriff Utterly gave Trill a poke with a single fat finger. "Is he dead?"

"I reckon no, but if you don't raise the sawbones, he's gonna end up that way directly."

"Too right," Utterly whispered, running a hand through his tousled hair. "I'll go get the doc."

"No."

"No?"

"First I get the money."

"Oh yeah. S-sure. The money."

Utterly shuffled behind his desk and pulled an envelope from one of the top drawers, handing it to Fallstead like feeding a hungry lion.

"Okay," the marshal said, turning to leave.

"What about the rest of his people?" the sheriff asked reluctantly. "Trent and Saul, they weren't angels, but them boys weren't all bad."

Fallstead turned back but didn't speak. The jailhouse was thick with the smell of Trill's blood and shit and Utterly's general odor. He needed air, freedom from these little men.

"So, they didn't make it?"

Now the marshal answered quick. "No. Trent and Saul didn't make it. They threatened an officer of the peace. Made their intentions clear."

"Made their intentions… ok then. Just…" As that last searching word escaped his quivering lips, Utterly was cursing himself for not leaving the intimidating marshal be.

"What?"

"Oh, ah, nothing at all. Everything's great. Really appreciate you coming and helping out the county."

Fallstead stood straight. He wasn't the most physically imposing man, but the adjustment rattled his spurs and caused the sheriff to shiver. "If you're thinking this might'a been some sort of overreaching justice… well."

"I didn't say that!" Utterly whined. "I did not say that. At all, Marshal. You've done a fine job here. Above reproach. Beyond reproach. Irreproachable, all accounts."

"Good luck to you then," Fallstead said, no less hasty than before. It'd been a long ride to Boyd City, and he'd kicked up a good bit of dust in the matters relating to Mr. Trill and his gun thugs. Stepping out of the jail, he looked up and down the town's main thoroughfare. It wasn't a vista that inspired; Boyd City had but one passable hotel and a few other fledgling businesses. The lone corner cantina was in a sorry state, half adobe and half rotten timbers. Fallstead found himself headed there all the same, brown leather duster flapping behind from a welcome night breeze.

The marshal could hear the rumblings of a fracas as he neared. He walked up crooked steps and positioned himself to the side, between the door and the cantina's lonely little window. Inside things were boiling over, but he made no move for his gun. Fallstead took off his gloves and fished out a pouch of tobacco and papers from an inside coat pocket, getting fixed to roll a cigarette. The marshal practiced tedious care with his cigarettes, especially now that he was getting on in years. He limited himself to three a day and intended on enjoying the whole process, every time through. The goings-on in the bar were confined to the background; for the moment, Fallstead was solely focused on a good smoke.

"Best you come here and learn your place." Inside the shabby establishment, a brutish, middle-aged man with a large purple birthmark on his right cheek was winding up tight as a spring. His ire and want for sexual gratification were going the way of a pretty young woman leaning on the bar. Whatever his will, she didn't seem inclined on bending to it. The lady took a quick shot of whisky and kept her body square ahead, looking manifestly unimpressed.

"Predictability is a powerful force," she said, staring straight at the modest array of watered-down bottles behind the bartender. For all the disinterest in her manner, there was youthful eagerness in her voice too true to mask.

"What's that?" the man asked, all bluster and malformed thoughts. Every second served to rile him more. He was stroking his mangy chin hairs with one hand and hiking up his saggy wool trousers with the other. "You're the one first looked at me, little girl."

She smiled and tapped the top of an empty shot glass gently with her gloved middle finger. The barkeep, tired and oily from too long a day, poured her another and withdrew. She threw back the drink with the same quick form as the first. Every man in the cantina had a head turned her way; she was wild-haired, blond and brown streaks flowing and colliding down the halfway of her back. She wasn't tall, but her portions were presentable in all the right places, made more inviting by her vestments. She wore leather britches that clung tight to her skin, square-tipped rustler boots and a thin flannel shirt tucked in tight and unbuttoned low enough to show off more than a trifling tease of her breasts. A fancy man might find fault with her shoulders; they were rugged for a lady. Then again, she presented as something more than just some lady. "I looked at you because you're about the ugliest son of a bitch I've seen in a spell. Creation gone awry. I picture a wagon overturned, something like that. What's your name, specimen?"

"Tim. And you're fixin' to be sorry for taking tones. Thinkin' I might give you a good ride before I cut you up." Full of confidence, he gave the room a round look of sinister satisfaction before returning his attention back to the girl.

She didn't move at his heavy step. Her seeming lack of fear stalled his approach. He licked his teeth and played some more with his whiskers, eyeing her backside. The other men in the room inched away and exchanged looks of worry and wonder. They all knew getting in Tim's path was a dicey proposition when his blood was over the lip.

"So, you're *thinking*," she said, still fixed forward at the bottles. "That's a dangerous line to take, Tim. Sort of a baby with dynamite, I'd reckon."

"Enough!" he roared, lunging forward wildly. She quickly ducked under and took several short steps away from the bar. Tim crashed over two rickety stools and into the skeletal drunk that'd been previously stationed to her right. As he turned and regained his bearings, he stared at his prey, breathing angry and deep as a bothered bear. This time, she had a pistol drawn, steady at the hip.

"You gonna kill me, little missy?" Tim asked, stumbling away from the bar in her direction.

She drew back the hammer with her thumb. "Closer and I'll be obliged to shoot your pecker right off."

Tim stopped his advances and looked around the room one more time. He saw nearly familiar images swaying all around, the way one does after too much time inside a bottle.

"Take it easy, ma'am." The suggestion came from the darkest corner of the cantina, in the smoky shadows to her left. "Tim, you back off. She don't look like she's messing about."

"Stay on out of this, Jay," said the drunk, refusing to look off the girl.

"Can't do it. We need to be getting back. Mr. Trill's expected."

"I reckon you're gonna be disappointed there," she said, eyeing the second man.

"What's that mean?" he asked.

She kept her attention on Tim and snuck another glance at his companion. They were opposites in disposition and appearance. As he stepped slow from the corner she could see he was kept up proper, slender and in possession of a handsome face.

"Boss Trill's either dead or locked up, is what I mean," she said, dispassionately and demonstrably returning her pistol snugly to its holster.

"That's not possible," replied the dapper gent. The other patrons continued parting to the few peripheries the little joint provided. Outside, Fallstead was down to about a quarter of his cigarette. The girl saw the smoke drifting into the cantina and smirked before her attention was forced back to the fracas.

"I'll show you what's possible." Tim had lost the last of his meager cool. He reached for his gun, but she was far too quick; as promised, she fired a .45 caliber slug into his privates. As blood began spraying a wide pattern, the patrons and bartender ducked and dove in random directions, disoriented by the volume of the shot. The only one not stumbling about was poor Tim's compatriot, the handsome buck named Jay.

"Jesus," he said, moving over to check on his wounded friend. "Who the hell are you, lady?"

"Apologies. Name's Sybille." She took two steps back toward the entrance to make certain no one could flank or sneak up on her.

"You *duurty bitch*—" Tim cried, holding his wound and trembling. He repeated it over and over until it was barely audible.

"Don't bother helping," Sybille said, addressing Tim's bereft friend. "He'll bleed out in a minute or two. Die a woman."

A few breathy insults later, she was proved right. Jay closed the brute's eyes with red hands and stood up seething. He was bent knees and balled fists, like springing to action was the next thing.

"So ends the life of Tim. Not the brightest star. How about you, Jay?"

"What about me?"

"Just that I noticed you pulling the hammer back on your sidearm when you knelt down. You lookin' for vengeance?"

"Wouldn't be fair. You've already drawn."

"I can remedy that," she said, darting her eyes around the smoky room. "As long as everyone in this shithole makes it clear they witnessed a fair fight."

Nothing but a few indiscernible mumbles.

"I'll take that for affirmation." Sybille slowly slipped her revolver back in its place.

"I don't want this," he said.

"Okay. Expected as much from the associate of a man threatening to take up with an unwilling woman. From a man who works for a no-good murdering son of a bitch."

"That's enough."

"Enough's the right word. You're played out, mister. No job, no friends, no backbone." She let her gun hand dangle and gave a long breath. "Guess I'll be seeing you boys. Or we can do it the old way."

"The old way. What's that mean?" Jay asked, shiny teeth grinding.

"It's simple. Both of us take a chair. Set a candle in between. When it burns down to nothing, we draw. Never even have to get up. You slump to the afterlife real cozy."

"You're crazy."

"So that's a no then." Sybille turned and walked out to the street without looking back. Hopping down to the hitching post, she heard a gunshot and the thud of a man falling behind her. Calmly adjusting her saddle, she said, "Guess that's all of 'em."

Marshal Fallstead tossed his cigarette and kicked Jay to make sure he was out of print before walking deliberate toward her. His legs didn't pick up as light as they used to. Not after a long day. "You asking to get killed, Sybie?"

She made her eyes big and pleading. "I knew you were out here smoking. Saw it rush through the window, just like you wanted me to. What's the big deal?"

"Deal is I don't want you getting a bullet playing some game. It's damn stupid."

"Sorry, Pa." She turned from her horse to give Fallstead a kiss on his rough cheek. "It is better when you shoot them, though." A group was starting to form around the body, but not a soul ventured toward the marshal or his daughter. "He was a bad guy, and you handled it." She chanced a smile. "Your badge makes witnesses less prone to revising their stories." A kiss on his other cheek. Fallstead smirked and ran his hand gently through her wild hair. Despite the soft spot she was exploiting, a degree of irritation never fled his countenance.

"Trill's in jail," he muttered, noticing a few of the Boyd City townsfolk walking up to learn what consequences the shooting had produced.

"The rest?" Sybille asked. She looked up and saw a faraway thought behind her father's gray eyes. It was all the answer she'd need. "It's for the best. Not like you killed a wagon train'a nuns."

Fallstead left her for the fresh body still leaking on the cantina porch. Sybille could tell he was more cross than usual, but she wasn't worried; she had news in the offing. After grabbing her pale curved straw hat from her saddle horn, the lawman's daughter moved around her horse and took to a knee. She brought out her pistol and used the butt to draw a circle in the dirt with two horizontal lines, looking over to make sure Fallstead wasn't watching. After saying a few words under her breath, she looked to reconnect with her father. "Any problems?" she asked.

Fallstead looked expectedly at Brad Utterly, waiting for him to answer his daughter's question. "No," said the sheriff, standing over the body with his hands on his hips. "I suppose there ain't."

"That's good to hear," Sybille said. The townsfolk jumped a little every time she moved, hands always near her gun belt. Her energy was untamed and unpredictable, and them that hadn't witnessed the speed of her pull had learned about it by now. "You run a real tight outfit, Utterly."

"Well."

"Sorry, Sheriff. Excuse me one sec. Pa, can I get a word?"

"What is it?"

Sybille nodded him away from the crowd, close to the window where the deputy marshal watched her stirring trouble. "I've got something. Before you showed, I overheard some boys talking in the cantina. Three or four counties over, there's gonna be a hanging in a few days."

Fallstead looked down at his firecracker daughter and started groping around his tattered jacket on a quest for tobacco. "I'm gonna smoke another."

"Pa..."

"You made me shoot more people than I planned on today. Don't go heavin' judgments."

"Fine. Anyhow, one of these boys works in the telegraph office. He was telling the other fella."

"Who's the other fella?"

"It doesn't matter. The other fella ain't a factor in the telling."

"Go on girl. Putting your nose in."

Sybille propped her hat up to make sure he could see there was no fooling in her eyes. "The telegraph man said the hanging's over in Thunder Hill. A shootout or some such. Man shot down two or three others in the street. Took a bullet himself in the fracas."

"Waiting for why you're telling me." His scratchy voice was growing louder. Again, a long day.

"There was a description of the man that went to law across the territories, in case he was wanted on anything else. Guess he seemed the type to merit inquiry. Anyway, I listened to the telegraph man's description. Sounds like a gent I've heard tell about."

"Who?"

"Loot Moreno."

"No." Fallstead's answer was strident. He wasn't blind to his daughter's unending desire to see him in hot water, to see what he'd do. He wished he'd never told her word one about the past.

"Description fit. The few that know are talking like it could actually be the damned legend himself."

"People talk nonsense, Sybie. Nothing but, most times. Didn't think your ears were inclined toward hearing it."

As he started to walk away, Sybille pressed. "This man for the gallows, the one *not called* Loot Moreno—has a mark on the top of his hand. You need me to describe it?"

Fallstead stopped and lit up the cigarette he had in waiting. "It can't be him. He's dead. Everyone said he was dead. I made sure… everyone said."

With all that had taken place, Sybille was still light on her feet. She slapped her father's thick shoulder like she was fixing to mount up and the only thing for him to do was follow. "Yeah. But they said the same thing about you, Papa."

CHAPTER 5:
DODGE CITY

"IF Y'ALL ARE NEEDING ANYTHING ELSE, LET ME KNOW. DON'T you hesitate on account of… just don't hesitate. I'll be praying hard on it."

"You're a goodly lad Kip," Mrs. Bristol cried, English accent heavier than usual in her sadness. "And I'm sorry we missed *yur* pah's wake. Of all *tings* to miss."

"Don't say that. With all you're going through." He took her cold hands to stop them shaking. "Don't say that."

They were standing in the muggy air near the bed of the struggling Mr. Bristol. Doc Rufus was kneeling toward the old man as he tried to speak through cycles of agony. A brutal cough and fever had latched hold of the shop owner; he was in a bad way. Doc set a cold cloth on his patient's forehead and whispered that he'd be back to check on him in a bit. As he fastened up his medical bag and walked by Kip, he offered a sideways look absent much hope.

Kip's heart sank as Mrs. Bristol grabbed his hand again. He thought highly of the Bristols and wished to God he could answer her grasping with something more. It was impossible not to think of his father and how quickly strength could be taken from the strongest of men.

"Be with him," said Kip. "Never seen you two as quitters." They weren't just words. The Bristols were proper in their manners and bearing, but somehow suited to hard frontier life. They'd lost three children in their days as young adults and decided to start afresh across the Atlantic. Theirs was a successful business, one of the first to find home in Thunder Hill. Kip put an arm around the portly, red-faced Mrs. Bristol and gave her a gentle squeeze. She seemed to curl up inside his rangy embrace. He almost fell asleep on the padding of her shoulder. The days had taken a toll on all there present.

"Come here then lad," Mr. Bristol wheezed. Finally, the cough had let up enough to allow him an audible thought. Kip sat down next to the bed with caution, hoping not to break the momentary peace. He could feel the heat and sick coming off Bristol's body. "Had a… good enough run," he said, sputtering his way through the syllables.

"Don't be talking that way, sir. You still got acres of work here on this plane. Wouldn't bet against it. Rest up and do what Doc Rufus says."

"Never mind that, boy." Bristol's hand found a new grip. He raised his head until it touched Kip's. His milky eyes were pinned as he spoke. "There's darkness, boy. Watch. Don't wish for it. Finds you eventually. Comes from places you can't imagine. From nowhere it comes."

He'd heard people say crazy things before under fevers. They usually did, in truth. Mr. Bristol's declaration wasn't particularly eerie, but there was a clarity in the delivery that caused a lump in Kip's throat. "You rest now, Mr. Bristol."

The old man sputtered and nodded. The young preacher took a spare cloth from the bedside and wiped away spit running down deep wrinkles. Brave suffering was dreadful. Like any decent churchman, Kip felt burdened by this part of the Call. The Lord's work felt more work than Lord sometimes. Still, there was strange comfort in doing his part, keeping away from the mysteries and suspicions of the previous week. "I'll be back to look in on you both. Get some rest now." After patting Bristol gently on the arm and giving his dutiful wife one more tender hug, he walked softly out of the bedroom, head down and solemn. He found Rufus waiting with his arms crossed, leaning causally on the front doorframe.

"Talk with me a minute?" the doctor asked.

"Of course," Kip said, squinting into the waning light of dusk as they exited. His visit with the Bristol's had not been brief. "What's wrong?"

"Nothing's wrong, per se."

"Please Elias," he said. The lively green of his eyes was more like red from fatigue. "Just tell me what's needling."

"Worried about you, is all, huffing and puffing your way out of the café yesterday." Doc set down his bag and took measure of the young man. "Darting across the thoroughfare toward the jail, no doubt on some crusade. Question is, a crusade of what nature?"

"I wasn't on a *crusade*. And I know you're mocking the faith. Close-mindedness and melodrama aren't *requisites* for all our conversations. Maybe pa being gone's given you more sand."

"Watch it, son." The flint in Rufus' warning was something he couldn't recall hearing.

"Sorry." In an instant Kip was turned back to a boy.

"Then there's the drinking," the elder continued, close enough for Kip to go lightheaded on his shaving rum. "I might not be the best medical man this side of the Mississippi, but I can certainly tell and *smell* when someone's been down the whisky hole a few days. How's that head, besides mostly empty?"

"Better," Kip said, smiling a little with a charming, embarrassed look on his face. Rufus wasn't one to let a mood keep sour for long. He was grateful for that. "I've only had a swig or two since yesterday."

"Good lad."

"Why'd you have to turn me from the jail yesterday?" It had indeed been a sudden interruption, and they hadn't had a moment alone away from the Bristols to discuss it since. Kip felt the question still merited asking.

"Did you happen to slap eyes on the dying man in there? It's your job—calling. You send the rubes off packing with a smile, I try to keep them on the mortal coil."

"Snatching me from the street? Mr. Bristol is a long way from his last breath."

"Shall we trade professions outright, then?"

"Rufus?"

The doctor seemed to look everywhere save the younger man's eyes. It was uncharacteristic. Rufus was inveterately unashamed, deliberate in speech and action. "No idea what you're jabbering about. It's been a hard time, I know. Perhaps the notion struck me, you gettin' to your job."

"By expediting the prospect of looming death in my face? We'd buried my father the day before."

"That's actually not a terrible point," Doc Rufus conceded, scratching the round top of his hat. "It's possible that I was a little off the target. Salubrious aims don't always pan."

"Hope you're treating everybody else in town with the same deft perception and skill. We'll all live forever."

The doctor took up his old boxing stance as a tease. "You've got a lot more cheek than your father, young Laird."

"Yeah, well. Might be we had a lot less in common than you'd imagine."

The doctor bent his thick eyebrows and ceased the playful gesture. He didn't like the tone or the implication.

"Let's speak later, Doc. Nothing but long days lately. Best be off to check on my family."

Kip offered a hearty handshake and allowed Doc to yank him tight for a hug. He accepted it in kind and with no delay, like the two hadn't spent the last few minutes lashing each other.

"Give your mother my best," Rufus said with a wry smile, pulling out his flask and marching with proud strides in the direction of his house.

He can't help but be himself, Kip thought, taking the opposite direction. He adopted a route through the narrow alley between the Bristol's shop and the newspaper office which opened up onto Thunder Hill's Main Street. Activity in the town was beginning to ebb as folks made their way home for supper. Laird found a few moments of relative peace, concerned as he was with the Bristols and the odd behavior of Doc Rufus. Casually walking along the boardwalk, he did his best not to let the clanging commotion of the saloon break his tranquil state. Parts of him wanted to belly up and spend the night getting dead drunk, but he dismissed the thought as quick as it came. The town's sole preacher couldn't be seen assenting to too many fleshly habits, no matter the desire for escape.

Stepping off the boardwalk, he heard a coarse voice coming from the door of the saloon. "Hey, Kipper! C'mon over here!"

He squinted toward the call and spotted one of Thompson's hands that'd been lunching in French's the day before. "Hey there," Kip said, changing his posture from lazy to alert. "It's Valentine, right?"

"You know damn well it is, *church boy.*" Valentine seemed convinced he'd found the pinnacle of all insults. He laughed hysterically and put on a sloppy show of swagger as three more of his associates tumbled through the saloon doors like cars from a derailed train. Each man looked sweaty and wound up from hours of typical day-off carousing.

"I'll be seeing you gents. Bless you now," Kip said, sensing no good from more conversation.

"Hold on there," Valentine returned, "I ain't done talkin' to ya."

"Probably because you're yet to say a dang thing." Doc Rufus was right; Kip did have more cheek than his father.

A cacophony of mocking and slander went Valentine's way via the mouths of his buddies. They were having quite a laugh, the way followers usually do when their leader is knocked down a peg.

"I'm sorry," Laird said, sensing that he'd caused more damaged pride than intended. "Gonna go home, see my family."

"Your sister there? I might myself come a callin'."

"Yeah, she's a pretty piece." One of the others was chiming in, shorter and even less presentable than Val. "A real shapely, pretty piece. I think we get a taste of her before it's back to the stead. Looks bred for passing around. What u thinking, boys?"

"That's about enough," Kip said, rolling up the sleeves of his mourning shirt, aware of the incongruity. He was tired and at sea but talk like that was more than petty wind. Too much for turning cheeks. "Come on. Let's get it over with."

As they dropped off the end of the boardwalk onto the road, little puffs of dust sprang up from the concussion of their boots. Each man fanned out in a slightly different direction, creating a semicircle around their prey. He didn't see any guns and didn't suspect there'd be any; Joey the bartender was a bruiser and intractably consistent in confiscating all firearms once his patrons were sufficiently soused. These boys had hit that mark and then some.

"Don't worry, Preach," Val said, fists clenching. "After we beat your ass down, we'll take care that sister plenty good. Your purty mama too. She's gotta be getting lonely by now."

Kip had tussled and roughhoused all his life, no different than any other boy trying to find his place, but this was the first time he felt propelled by proper malice. Without a word he took two hefty steps forward and slammed a rugged right fist into Valentine's mouth. Crooked teeth went sailing. Val was felled like a tree long in need of an ax.

Everything seemed silent, like justice was taking a moment for itself. The three remaining cattle hands were stunned at first. So was Kip. His first coherent thought was one of concern. "Sorry," he said, holding his hands up apologetically to the others. Bending over the downed Valentine, he tried to summon him back to consciousness.

They weren't having repentance. A boot from Kip's left found a way to his ribs. From the right a fist cracked him across the jaw. The pain was blinding until the short mouthy one came over with an empty whisky bottle and smashed it over his forehead. For a few seconds he felt nothing, careening between the present and darkness.

Then they really started in, going like hyenas as he rolled around next to the sleeping Val in hapless defense. Inside a growing cloud of dust, the beating only grew more ferocious.

When it looked like the three drunks would never part from their task, two shots rang out. An older man in a traveled three-piece suit stood just away from the fracas, lowering his smoking pistol from the sky to the group's general direction. "I think it's time for a cessation. That boy had his fill, Jesus H."

"Who the hell're you?" the short one asked, snot dripping from his cracked lips.

"I'm not sure that's relevant, vagabond."

"You ain't relevant, dude."

"That's … clever, I suppose. My name is Jasper Bedford. Not from here." The stranger tried to straighten his saggy frame and cocked the pistol nervously using two hands. "I implore you gentlemen. The outnumbered party has benefited from whatever lesson you meant to teach. Find respite. Elsewhere, please."

A crowd of around thirty people was now watching the scene from a distance. The previous day's shooting had the citizens of Thunder Hill skittish but nonetheless curious, wanting to know the situation but not wanting to engage. The questions and grumbles were fairly uniform throughout the gathering.

It's got to be the boys from the Thompson place. Stirring up trouble's common as breathing for those fools.

Who's the old fella doing the gun-toting? Didn't he come in town the other day? What's he still here for?

Is that Kip down there in the dirt? What in God's name is he doing getting mixed up in such foolery? Shame on him. Like Mabel doesn't already have her fill.

Where's Cox? Sheriff, ain't he? What are we paying him for? This town is startin' to look like Dodge City.

It seemed the brief stalemate might fall apart between Bedford and the three brutes until Cox thundered his big spotted horse down the street to quell the situation. He fired a few warning shots in the air with his oily Winchester, holding the reins with his non-trigger hand.

The lawman pulled up behind Jasper Bedford and threw a leg over his saddle, sliding off the horse smoothly. His rifle was pointed and clenched with stiff purpose at the short man standing over Kip.

"Sheriff. Ain't nothing."

"Shut your mouth, Stevie. Damn half-formed drunk."

"I—"

"I'll plug you finished, swear to God. Pulling this. Like I don't have enough on my plate." The sheriff chambered a round in the Winchester. The large barrel was roughly twenty feet from the three men, more than close enough to put fear in their addled heads.

"Out of the way! Let me go!" Lindy Samuels emerged from the crowd after escaping her blustering fiancé's fervid grasp. As she offered Kip tears and succor, the witnesses' chatty concerns turned hell for leather into whispery gossip of the lewdest order.

Cox was standing beside Jasper Bedford, just a few feet away. He ordered the old newsman to holster his weapon with one wag of a finger. Bedford did it immediately and without question. The sheriff kept up his intensity and focused on seeing the dust settle. "You boys get. They'll be nothing more on it if you do."

"No jail?"

"Not even to sleep it off. You start running back to Thompson's right now, and my word's good."

The three looked down at Val and Kip, then at each other. A kernel of sense was taking root.

"The deal ends in five seconds. Start running." Cox pulled the rifle butt tight to his armpit. He had no intention to fire, but he couldn't let them know that. Not with Val and Kip bleeding in the dirt. Not with Miss Lindy mixed in the workings and her banker dandy seeing red.

"Let's get," Stevie said, running crooked with his friends down a narrow alley out into the prairie land that led to the Thompson's. Cox let out a deep, silent sigh. He told the crowd to get back to their business and rolled a pair of angry eyes at Jasper. The writer let his shoulders sink in embarrassment and cleared himself from the scene, allowing the shifting group of spectators to envelop him.

"Go fetch Doc Rufus," Cox said roundly, figuring someone would take up the task. He bent down with a long sigh and started slapping Valentine lightly on the face. "Jesus, Kip. You really gave him a walloping." He lowered his thin gray eyebrows at the youngest Laird. The two young men were almost on top of each other, faces covered in blood and clothes made brown by the dusty road. Lindy Samuels was close to coming apart, holding Kip's head in her lap. Over and over she kept kissing the top of his head, repeating something the sheriff couldn't quite make out. Cox didn't know exactly what her involvement was, but exact wasn't needed to whiff trouble coming down the line.

As Val finally came around, Rufus arrived. Cox exchanged a loaded look with his old friend and stood up to give him room. The sheriff backed up and onto the boardwalk, watching the crowd from above. Mabel and Elsie Laird had just rushed to the scene. Mother and sister wore very different expressions; Mabel was concerned, asking her loopy son questions. Elsie wasn't asking anything. Her generally welcoming eyes were fixed and hard. *Trouble coming down the line*, the lawman thought again.

Rufus ordered everyone away and enlisted Cox to help. He was clearly irritated and had already put in a long day with the Bristols. "Lindy, Mabel, get on back," Doc barked, whisky on his breath. "Boy," he said, pressing lightly on Kip's sides, "does it hurt bad to breathe?"

"I'm sorry about this. Tell the sheriff. Is Val okay?"

Rufus took Kip's hand and pulled him up to a sitting position. He checked his arms and hands for any breaks. "Val's fine. His smile's been permanently altered, but I'm not discounting the possibility of improvement."

"I'm sorry," Kip repeated.

"Enough with the sackcloth, kid. Save the apologies for the rubes. They're gonna be restless having an amateur pugilist for their holy man."

The remark almost made Kip smile through the pain. He asked for help getting to his feet. His rugged body was battered, but he'd recover. The worst was his hand; Val's flat face turned out to be hard as granite. He shook it out and patted Rufus on the back, offering him thanks.

"My pleasure," Doc smiled wryly. "A real exclamation mark to the day."

"Hey."

"What?"

"Later on, you need to cough up why you were really keeping me from the jail. I ain't letting go of it."

The doctor fiddled with his gray hat and checked his pocket watch, doing a bad job of feigning indifference. Kip caught a glance between Rufus and Cox. The sheriff clutched his rifle and looked off down the road. "We just went over this," Rufus said. "You're still a little punch drunk maybe, not remembering things."

"I remember it not being settled proper."

"Better set your mind somewhere else. That'd be my advice." The physician held out his hands and waved them around, clearly indicating he was talking about the town and everyone in it.

"Owe you my gratitude, Sheriff," Kip said, walking toward the left-over crowd and his mother. She started to wipe the remaining blood from his face, but he stopped her. "Don't go ruining your fancy garments."

"You could always ask Lindy for a swath," Elsie said. She was standing next to Mabel, arms crossed indignantly. "Seems she's more than happy to lay down vestments at your altar."

"Elsie, I'm sorry." Kip was singing the same song, and it was a song nobody wanted to hear. Sorry for being a house built on sand, *everyone*. Sorry for taking up on the sly with a betrothed woman, *Elsie*. Apologies for scuffling with the dregs and miscreants that I'm supposed to be ministering to, *God*.

Kip wanted his senses stripped. Val was still prostrate in the dirt, moaning intolerably. Lindy was casting a Gorgon-like stare in his direction. The mutterings and whispered bits of gossip from the onlookers were ants on his skin. He just wanted to get away and wash it all off. He met his mother with a trembling kiss on the forehead and told her that he was going home for the day. I want to go with you, make sure you're okay, Mabel said. I'm fine, just a few scrapes and bruises, he answered, lying straight to her loving face.

Lowering his head, he walked slowly through the crowd and across the road, heading gingerly toward his place above Grimes General Store. No one would bother him there. His mother was the only one in town maintaining unflappable support, and she'd be turning in after an hour or so, early as always. He'd knock on Mr. Grimes' door and procure a bottle of whisky and some bandages to wrap his sore ribs. Change his shirt and wait for night to come in earnest. Banged up or not, he still had things to do.

CHAPTER 6:
MR. CALHOUN & MR. MORENO

"YOU HUNGRY THERE, JAILBIRD?"

No response.

"Fine then, Calhoun. I wasn't getting you anything no how. Just be a waste anyways, considering where yur a-headin.'" Deputy Elbert Rooker threw his feet up on the sheriff's desk, wiggling his toes inside a pair of silver-tipped boots. Rooker was fastidious about his appearance; he wore a dark suede hat along with a gray silk vest and tailored black pants made from the finest wool a fella could pick from a merchant catalogue. It didn't do him any favors. Folks in town figured the clothes as compensation for his naturally unpleasant looks. He leaned back in Cox's desk chair, feet up, chewing on a toothpick. The prisoner sat heavy and hunched on the bed of the cell farthest from the entrance, long hair falling down and around his head. It was his only way to hide. There was no partition or privacy. The Thunder Hill Sheriff's Office and Jail was essentially one large room. A few old desks, a gun rack on the wall opposite the front door, and two cells. The ceiling was unreasonably low. The prisoner couldn't have stood up straight if he wanted to.

"When's Cox going to be back?"

"I ain't his keeper. What's it to you anyhow, Calhoun?"

"You're a bother."

"Well I'm sorry," the deputy said, drawing out his words for a full helping of condescension. "Maybe should've thought about that before you plugged them two boys. The Tolliers were friends of mine."

"I should've smacked you harder then," the prisoner said.

Deputy Rooker snarled and rubbed near the bandage on his nose. "You won't be throwing insults when you're roasted up in hellfire."

"You've got the measuring of things, I guess."

"That's right, jailbird," Rooker said.

"Don't know why I bother to say, but those friends weren't the kind worth having. I'd know something about that."

Rooker spit on the floor and took a dramatic pause before responding. "You don't know nothing."

"Firstly, I know them *boys* were going gray in their beards. Thirty at least, both of 'em."

"Murder's murder. Reckon the sight of the noose will take away some of that bluster."

"Murder my hide!" Calhoun roared, stomping the floor with his good leg. The force of it shook the building. The bolts holding the bars together rattled from the test.

The sudden outburst caused the young deputy to swallow down his toothpick. "Ahh, dammit," he hacked, smacking the flat of his bony chest, trying to cough it back up.

"Only way that's coming out is from the other end," Calhoun said, taking small pleasure in Rooker's new affliction.

As the deputy continued to demonstrate stabbing pain, Cox entered quietly and stopped cold. "What the hell is this?" he asked, watching his subordinate grab at his throat like a bad actor portraying a poisoning.

"You've got some real hard men here," Calhoun said.

Sheriff Cox yanked Rooker's shiny boots from his desk and ordered him gone. "Come back tomorrow with your head on straight." He pushed the gagging greenhorn through the door and locked it behind, standing silent for a minute, continuing to face the door. He shook his head and stowed his rifle before hanging up his duster and hat. "Where'd I keep it?" he mumbled, rummaging through the desk drawers.

"It's in the bottom left. Under the papers," said the prisoner.

Cox lifted some old wanted notices and sure enough found what he was looking for. "Thanks Loot," he said, taking down a healthy dose from an old whisky bottle. "You want some?"

"Be obliged. Talking to that kid of yours has me reminiscing on my years of seclusion with favor."

Cox smiled just enough to show his worn teeth as he walked the bottle over. He stuck it through the bars and gave it a shake. Loot stood up to answer the gesture, making sure to keep his head tucked down and most of his weight off the wounded right leg.

"What's all the ruckus? Somebody out there shooting, no doubt."

"There was some shooting, sure enough. Your buddy."

"My buddy?"

"The old newspaperman. Jasper Bedford."

Moreno almost spit up his whisky. "You're fooling."

Cox shook his head and took the bottle back. "Nope. And if that's not strange, the shooting was on account of him stepping in to help Kip Laird."

Moreno's dusky face was full of confusion. "The kid's okay though, right? And Jasper?"

"Everything is fine. Reckon Ben's boy is a little at odds. Blood's up, lost control with some of the town yokels. Out of the ordinary, but not completely surprising. Death of a parent and all."

"Yeah."

"Well, you know what I mean," Cox said, turning a tinge red in the face. The sheriff was good enough at orders and straight talk but nibbling around edges was a skill he'd never refined.

Moreno returned to his bed. It sank under the weight of his bulk.

Two knocks on the door. "It's Rufus. Let me in, Amos. I need to—hell—check on the prisoner's wound."

Cox got up and opened the door. "No need to put on airs, Doc. It's just us in here."

Rufus tipped his cap and walked in, holding the lapels of his long black suit jacket as he came to a stop in the center of the room. "How you doing, Loot?"

"I've been worse."

"Well, damn sorry to hear that," the doctor said, smiling wide and pointing to the sheriff's bottle. "Glad to see I'm not the only one drinking though."

"What's the kid doing? Getting into some scrap I hear?"

"Nothing to worry about. The honorable Cox stormed the battlements and quelled any escalations."

The sheriff crossed his arms. "I didn't do much. Battlements? How much you been drinking, Doc?"

"There may be another problem," Rufus said, ignoring Cox's inquiry, knowing the familiar lawman wouldn't fuss over an answer.

Moreno stood back up and grabbed the bars. "Tell us, Doc."

"The young squire was heading over here yesterday. I more or less diverted him, but he's kicking at sleeping dogs."

"How could he know?" Cox asked, looking from Rufus to Moreno. "What could he know?"

"It doesn't matter," the doctor said. "Another day of rest for that leg and you'll make your miraculous escape."

The laconic sheriff nodded and put his hands in his pockets, pacing around the little space. It was a right mess he was in, but he wasn't about to let an old friend hang for defending himself against the Tollier brothers. According to every honest set of eyes at the scene, the drunken troublemakers had forced Loot's actions, drawing down and cornering him outside the bar. Despite the testimonials, the city judge was quick to fix him for the gallows; he was a crooked old bastard. All he could see was a big mixed-breed from out of town and two dead sons of a local rich man. Stacked, sideways jury. Case closed.

"So damn dumb, me coming here," Moreno said. "Think it best to just let me swing. Us three here know it's been a long time coming."

"That's not a situation I'm comfortable living with," Rufus answered. "You've done penance a hundred times over." The well-dressed physician walked over and put a hand through the cell, patting Loot on his burly shoulder. "Hell, it'd be wasted work, the number of times I've patched you up. I can't see you in the noose."

"Me neither," Cox said, standing resolutely by his desk. He wished Loot hadn't come to Thunder Hill, but Ben Laird's death had thrown everybody's senses astray. "You don't hang. That's not the way."

"Gentlemen." Kip was standing in the open doorway. Rufus had forgotten to lock it back up. The older men were frozen in place, as if playing possum was a viable solution to their sudden problem. "Mr. Calhoun," Laird said. "Excuse me, Mr. Moreno. It's nice to meet you." Kip closed the door deliberately, keeping his actions and movements minimal, like drawing out a moment at the pulpit to add tension.

"How much did you hear?" Cox asked.

"Pretty much everything you've said since Doc came in. Not intruding, am I?"

"You know damn well you are," Rufus said. "And that's about all you know. I advise caution here, son. You reversing course might serve all parties. Before things get beyond control."

Kip's laugh was the mocking kind. "Kinda funny, Rufus, being called son. The word seems out of place aimed in my direction."

Moreno, Rufus and Cox traded loaded looks before Kip continued.

"Ben told me the truth… before he passed on. Some of it, anyhow. Been meaning to confirm the story, but dang if it hasn't been an eventful couple of days." A few renegade tears streamed down his smooth face. He wiped them away with the inside of his shirt sleeve and jumped at the sound of pounding on the door.

"Sheriff, I forgot something. Just take a second."

It was Rooker. Kip saw an unprecedented amount of worry ruining faces of men he'd grown up respecting as giants. He knew his presence was for them a complication, but Rooker showing up had them at odds like he'd never seen. Their familiarity with Moreno was about the biggest itch he'd ever needed scratching. He figured the high road for now. "I'll go out the back," he whispered, making sure to look at each of them as he stepped across the floor. "And later you can explain the coziness." He opened the backdoor while Rooker continued rapping the front. "Also," Kip said, "I'm eager hear about the jailbreak. That should be an adventure."

CHAPTER 7:
EXPOSED

AFTER THE SCUFFLE IN THE STREET, ELSIE LAIRD WENT BACK home and had herself a cry, not that she'd ever be admitting to it. The house was uncomfortably quiet as she cleared the table of a half-eaten meal; she and her mother had been in the middle of a roast left by some parishioners when one of the boys came by to report Kip's latest travail.

Following their return, Mabel gave her a war-weary hug before going to lie down. That left an emotional Elsie fetching water, tidying, and stoking the fires proper to last a frigid night. Summer was beginning to loosen its grip in earnest and Thunder Hill sat in a high valley.

"It's coming. He left me, and it's coming."

Elsie shrieked fierce at the voice and almost took a burn from the kitchen stove. Turning around she nearly shrieked the same; her mother looked *natural* and undone in a way that was as startling as her words. Gray-blonde hair fell randomly past her shoulders. Her nightclothes were crooked and hanging funny. A ragged homespun blanket was wrapped around her shaking back and chest. "It's coming. He left me, and it's coming," she kept saying. Little bits of light from the lantern and the stove were barely combating the dark. A bit more crept in from the big room in the front and the office that led out to the back porch. Mostly though, night prevailed. The dancing shadows made gothic twists and turns on the walls, but Elsie didn't deem it proper for being skittish as she was; they'd lived there for most of her twenty years, goodness sake.

"It's because he's not here," Mabel whispered.

Her mother wasn't speaking sense, but she could feel the meat of it involved her departed dad. That calming considered presence, forged by a thousand losses and thousands of prayers and starts and stops. Elsie felt exposed in her own home; she wasn't the intrepid autonomous woman projected to everyone in town. That personality was luxury afforded by the stalwart presence of her father and steadfast love of her mother. Now half her support was gone. Strange how losing half could make a person empty all the way.

"Can I get you something, Mama? It's late for coffee, but maybe something with a bite." Elsie was desperate for anchoring. Desperate for the both of them.

"Fetch that bottle of whisky from the top cabinet," Mabel said, glassy eyed from tears past or tears coming. "Let's hope your brothers haven't staked the entire claim."

"Yes ma'am," Elsie said, smiling a little while her mother took a careful seat at the kitchen table. The matriarch was moving slowly, like the last few weeks had shaved away years. The daughter figured it would pass. Hoped maybe, more than figured. The table helped. Thousands of chips and scratches in the wood signaling time and familiarity.

With two cups poured and the bottle between them, Elsie asked, "What'd you mean just then? What's coming? What did he leave you with?"

Mabel took a drink and lingered over the taste. Her affinity toward spirits was stronger than she was likely to concede. Ben had teased her on it enough to realize teasing was a bad idea. She didn't indulge too often and mostly had enough sense to know when to put the cork back in. Tonight, though, Mabel wasn't sure her footing was firm. Wasn't sure she cared, either. "An old woman rambling, Else. Rambling around the house one room to another, rambling around in my head."

"I feel wayward the same. Is it more than that, though?" Elsie didn't want to push too far or retreat too easy. She took a sip of whisky and waited. There was duty in enduring the silence.

Finally, Mabel answered her lovely daughter. "I can't tell you exact. But when your dad passed, holes were left open. This town, this county, he was sort of a center. There were things. Things he did for people."

"I know that," Elsie said. "Of course, I know that. He was the best man in the world. Girls always say that about their dads, guessing, but I mean it."

"I know *you* do. And girls don't often say that about their fathers." Mabel smiled enough to show she wasn't all sadness. It spurred hope inside Elsie. "Wouldn't catch me saying that about your grandpa. Man was a stump in a tended field. Never had a place and took it out on everyone in his path."

"You've said."

"And said. And said again. Suppose I've become a curmudgeon, or suppose I never wasn't one. What say you on that matter?"

She cleared her throat of the liquor sting. "I think *both* my parents are exemplars. Peerless pedestaled paragons."

The widow sighed dismissively and tapped the table with her cup. "With all you and Kip's fancy schooling, sometimes I get jealous. Rufus and those lessons he fed you. Talk runs so fast I can't keep pace."

"Sure you can. And do. Stubborn in admitting it is all."

Elsie finished her cup and allowed herself a generous refill. Mabel didn't even notice. The social graces and proprieties of days ago were being overlooked. Perhaps this would be the way for the short run, Elsie thought. Or perhaps everything had splintered off for good. Irrevocably changed. It was either the best time or the worst time to bring up the thing heaviest on her mind. "Mama?"

"What's bothering?"

"My bother that obvious?"

"Know my daughter's ways better than she thinks I do."

"Not sure the wisdom of letting out this horse. You may never speak to me again."

"Ahh. So that then." Mabel was all mother again.

Elsie sat up a little. "What do you mean *that then*?"

"Kip. You've been in love with him since y'all could speak proper. Before that, probably."

The word *proper* wasn't emphasized, but it's the one that stuck in Elsie's mind. Her alabaster cheeks turned ruddy, obvious even in the fitful yellow light.

"Don't get overstrung. There's nothing wrong with it. Some ways, nothing could be more right."

"I'm not sure," Elsie said, reaching across the tabletop to clutch her mother's hand. "He's my brother."

"He is," Mabel said, rubbing the smooth tops of her daughter's fingers. "And he isn't. Something to reconcile or not. Nothing simple to it."

"Lord, I'm far from swift," Elsie said, embarrassed for old reasons and new. "This whole time I thought I was keeping this grand and awful secret, but it was news to you like the sun rises in the east."

"It'll be a little more complicated. But women and men throwing themselves together is always complicated." Mabel wrapped the blanket tighter around her body as a cool draft slithered through the kitchen. Her daughter was rare beautiful, clever and still very young; sometimes a perilous combination. Still, there was no sense getting riled over something that at its heart was good. Not with all the darkness out there in the world and no Ben to help her face it. "You've always gotten on, you and Kip. There's no denying it," Mabel continued, surprised somewhat by her own advocacy but glad to be speaking on a worldly subject. "In a way, Sydney never quite found his place. Less a Laird than our adopted." She looked flush into her daughter's changeable eyes for the first time in the conversation. "But those few years Syd has on you, they were tough. They did something to his soul. The dark, the outside world can seep in. Find a way of manipulating a child's constitution to trouble. From their young days to their last."

A stronger draft followed Mabel's statement. The lantern on the edge of the table flickered. Mother and daughter heard the front door close sharply and heavy footsteps coming closer.

"I saw the lights on." The sound of Kip's voice put Mabel a little more at ease and Elsie a little more on edge, but there was something right about him being there with them in the kitchen of the family house. Especially now.

"The lights? That so?" Elsie said, keeping her flushed face from the full glow of the lantern. She didn't want to betray she'd been crying.

"What's going on, son?" Mabel asked hard. "Scuffling. Trouble. It's not you. Never has been. The town won't forgive forever."

"I'll be right back, Mama," Kip said, walking demonstrably loud up the stairs. Mabel and Elsie looked up at the ceiling, listening to a series of thumps and scratches. They traded a few more sips of whisky before he was back in the kitchen, holding a set of dingy little books in his hand like they were the source of all knowledge.

"And how can you say that I've never been trouble? You don't know all of me, do you?" Kip's asking wasn't aggressive, but he was acres from polite.

"What's that supposed to mean? I'm your mama."

"Oh, of course you are." Kip leaned over the table, waving dusty pages. "But you're also not my mama. And we never talk about it, or maybe we have, once or twice throughout the spread of my whole life. I'm to be grateful and that's the beginning and end of it." He was sweating. Sore in body and spirit. Dragging his whole perforated essence around town, one location to the next. The waving of pages stopped. "And, of course, I'm grateful. Yet still, it's going to eat away at my soul until I get the whole story."

"I can't tell you what I don't know."

Elsie sensed Mabel holding out. The woman that had just been so open and honest with her about Kip was new, suddenly indifferent as stone.

"I'll start with this," he said, holding up one of the little books higher than the rest. It was a dime novel with an amateurish illustration titled, *The Three-in-One Gang*. "I'd almost forgotten I had a secret trove of these hidden in my room upstairs. Trash, admittedly. Violence and tall tales. But that seems akin to what I've been told about my past."

"Don't chew raw with me, boy. You're taking leave of your respect."

Kip paced the table and surveyed Elsie and Mabel, letting his thoughts stack up on each other as neatly as could be arranged after such a day. Tending to the Bristols, brawling in the streets, girl trouble, more drinking, and his latest episode at the jail. The young man was beyond his natural limits. The situation before him would require delicacy; a lightness that could only really come from strength. Were he wise, he might understand. But he was barely a man. A sort of noble desire for the truth was tangled up with a selfish duty to himself.

"What is that?" Elsie asked, pointing to the wrinkled little books. "What is it to do with you?"

"Just some stories. Fictional, supposedly. But turns out one of the main players is in the jail down there. Met him myself about ten minutes ago." Kip leaned closer to his mother. "Funny thing. Seems there's a whole team that already knows him. Betting Mama's a member."

Mabel's head was down. Elsie stood up and slapped Kip. Whatever his problem, he had no right to take a nasty tone with the woman that loved them most. "What's wrong with you?" she blared.

"Loot Moreno. Are you in on this too?"

"Not again," Elsie said, moving over to put an arm around her mother. "You've taken too many hits. More likely it's just the drinking. I thought you were a better person."

He heard every word but decided they weren't worth his time at present. "I just met him over at the jail, Else. Mr. Calhoun is Loot Moreno of legend and lore."

"Get out. And stop bothering Mama."

"I'm just trying to *talk* to Mama. You're not on my side. Fine. You're only about what you want, Elsie."

She'd shown her heart too bold in the street. He saw her judging while he recovered from the fight. Judging him for taking Lindy's help. For letting her cast spells. "Not right now, Kip. I won't be stepping there."

His voice grew louder than he wanted but he made no attempt at calming. "You're needing more from me than I got. Sorry, Else, but it may never be. God knows I love you, but everything... it's crazy."

"Please stop talking. C'mon, Mama."

"It's Loot Moreno," Mabel whispered, clutching her daughter's slender arm. "He's right. It's all coming. And he left me."

Kip knelt down and tried to capture his mother's focus. She stared without a goal. Too much whisky and grief. *Maybe too many lies.* The thought came and left Kip's consciousness in a second's time. His mother wasn't nefarious. More was going on. He could see it in her overtaxed expression. It wouldn't do him any good to go stomping around the garden. Enough was enough for one night. "I'm sorry, Mama. God, I'm so sorry. We can talk about this later."

"Come here," she said, letting go of Elsie to hold out her arms. Kip fell into her embrace. *My beautiful boy*, she thought. *My beautiful baby boy. Found on a church step. God's sweetness ever since.*

Kip stood up and received a kiss on his forehead from Mabel. She bid them both goodnight and gently made her way to bed. Elsie looked up at him and asked, "What was that?"

"Maybe you hate me right now, but take my word as a preacher. That was someone trying to wrestle a burden off their chest. A piece of one, anyhow."

"Loot Moreno," Elsie said. Mabel had spoken the name. He was real to her now. "It doesn't make any sense. If he's not just a story, then he's really a killer. Unless you're saying just the bad parts of him were a legend."

Kip winced from his ribs and held up the little paperback, hitting it against his head. "Mama's weary. Spying on the jail only yielded more questions. I was forced away from their gathering when Rooker came back."

"So Rooker doesn't know?"

"I don't think many do. A small club I've got intentions to join. I'll start with these."

Elsie looked hard through the dim and read the author's name. *Jasper Bedford*. "Who's Jasper Bedford?"

"He seems okay. Stepped in when those boys were taking the boots to me earlier."

"That old twig in the wrinkled three-piece wrote the book you're holding presently?" She was incredulous.

"There's lots going on, I'll admit." Kip took a big breath. "And I came in too hot for what mama deserves. Or you." His head slumped. "It's been a long one."

"I'd say. Hard to reckon how those feet are still holding you up. Beat to a pulp is the phrase that comes to mind... maybe you should get Lindy Samuels to nurse you back to health."

Kip scowled but held his tongue except for a tortured goodnight, dragging his battered body toward the front door. Sydney was standing there, hands on his hips, having just entered. He looked like a substitute gatekeeper, disheveled but hell bent on standing his ground. "Where you goin' in such a huff, youngster?"

"Did you know?" Kip asked. "They forgot to mention it at the jail, whether you were involved."

"What are we talking about?" Syd said, donning a weird smile that was more than a little irritating. "You need to get it together, if you get my meaning. Whole town's talking. Leave the roughhousing to the men, little brother. Word of advice, all's I'm saying."

"Don't bother, Sydney," Elsie said, walking into the room, arms crossed. "Kip always does right. Historical fact."

"Ah, both of you can shut your traps. I'm beat up and sick a—"

Sydney sunk a fist flush against Kip's already injured ribs. He fell to his knees, gasping. Another punch. Syd's meaty right across his jaw. "You want another or are you done mouthing?"

More gasps.

"Best apologize to your sister. Do some praying for forgiveness while you're down there, do you some good. By God. What would Pa say?"

The question hurt more than the punches. Sydney rarely landed anything square, be it blow or word. Tonight, he was filling up the bull's eye.

Kip held up his hands, coughing on the pain. "I know who Calhoun is, Sydney." Kip gathered himself back to his feet but couldn't quite stand straight. It put him at eye level with the stockier Laird.

"No idea what you're about. Man's gonna hang is all I know. Sent out the telegram to the surrounding counties and everything."

"Why?"

"Because that's what we do when there's 'bout to be a hanging. In case he's suspected of crimes anywhere else. It's standard. Besides, I don't tell you what to preach."

Oh no. "Did you tell Cox about the telegram?"

"The hell difference does it matter about the telegram? No, I didn't tell him, but he's been busy."

"What'd it say?"

"Description. Name. The day of the hanging. Standard."

"Description," Kip winced, "did it include that mark on his hand?"

"Sure. Be strange leaving it out. Didn't write a poem though. They charge by the letter with them things."

Oh no. Kip brushed by his brother and staggered out toward the saloon. He had to find Jasper Bedford. Had to tell Cox and the others about that telegram. It could mean trouble. More than likely meant trouble. Trouble could get in the way of his answers.

It wasn't to be. The cumulative effect of getting beaten and brained, the nonstop pace of the day, those final two punches—it all climbed on his back at once. He tripped on a rock in the road and hit the muck. The young man was asleep almost instantly after impact, backside in the air like the top of a Sioux tent. Kip's long day had come to a dirty and ignominious end.

CHAPTER 8:
ON THE WIRE

"YOU BEEN SEEING MY BROTHER THIS MORNING?" SYDNEY Laird asked, clapping his thick hands to get Deputy Rooker's attention. Elbert was in his normal state, overdressed and underprepared, nodding off and sagging in the boss' chair.

"Who's all there?" Rooker asked, coming to and groggily grabbing at his hip. If not for Sheriff Cox's *Hang Up Your Guns* policy, he might've woken up shooting off his own leg.

"Sheriff's gonna whoop yur ass again, ER," Syd said, heavy eyes moving toward the prisoner. Moreno was standing still as sculpture, staring straight back at him. It wasn't a threatening glare, but still the meager bars seemed absurd, a straw cage for a lion. And there was something else in the prisoner's look Laird couldn't put his finger on. Getting riled by the strange silence, Sydney told "Brandon Calhoun" to stop gawking before passing his overwrought attentions back to Rooker. "Well? Have you seen Kip?"

"Is he not at home?" The question came from the doorway. Sheriff Cox was stepping in, having made his morning walk around town. His neck was red and raw from a shave just earlier and he smelled like two pots of strong coffee.

"No sir," Sydney said, "but it's not for you to be bothering about."

"Personal matter then," Cox grunted, hanging up his ancient duster and sweat-stained hat. He kept his pistol belt fastened. The firearm policy didn't apply to the man in charge.

"Right," Sydney said, trying to sound normal. "Personal matter. Anything kicking up out there?"

"All's quiet," Cox answered. He'd almost perfected the art of speaking without opening his mouth, but it meant in conversating the other was forced more into listening. "Hopefully it'll remain so. One day of normal would be nice."

"How's it coming with that scaffolding?" Deputy Rooker asked. He was on his feet, stepping about in his silly spurs while trying to assert himself by throwing a verbal jab at the man in captivity. "They better fashion it extra sturdy for this go-rilla. Double the nails and such. Thing's liable to come tumbling down before it gets the chance to snap his go-rilla neck."

"You made the same joke yesterday, ER," Cox said, wiping off his desk chair before finally sitting. Rooker had that effect; like everywhere he went was a little dirtier for it.

"Hey in the jail!" The voice was loud and clear, followed by two knocks on the door.

"Who's there?" Sydney hollered back.

"It's Patrick Hudson, Syd. Sheriff Cox about?"

Cox stood up and told Sydney to open up the door. "C'mon on in, Patrick," said the sheriff, shaking the broad-shouldered newcomer's sturdy hand. It was dirty and fresh blistered, but the man showed no feeling of pain.

"Good to see you, Amos," Hudson smiled, removing his wide-brimmed hat. It was made of dark fine leather and had a gentle curve to it, though it looked like it'd recently been through the wars.

"You two head out and ride the valley," Cox said, nodding at his deputies. "Go about it safe. Try not to get yourself killed."

"Reconnoitering the range," Rooker muttered.

"Reconnoitering the range," echoed Sydney. The deputies gathered their gear and made a quick exit, bowing at Cox and his acquaintance like nervous stage actors.

"Seems like you've got the troops in lockstep," Hudson said, smiling warmly. He was one of the only black businessmen to make it in the valley. A special tolerance for asshole types and general winning ways seemed to do the trick. His was a growing outfit, honest and fair as any Cox knew of. The two had met on a battlefield in Virginia during the War when their regiments got tangled up by the Rebs. They'd known each other as fair dealers ever since that bloody day.

"Lockstep," said the sheriff, almost forced into smiling. "If that's how it looks hope you keep the memory close. I ain't holding my breath for repeat performances."

"Oh, they're young yet. Don't be too much with the rod."

"What brings you, Patrick? The freight business?"

"It's good enough," said Hudson, grimacing a little after wiping caked dirt and sweat from his forehead. "Me and my men were gonna pass straight through this morning, but a wheel went real bad. Had to pull in full stop and have your smith take a look."

"What'd he say?" Cox asked, squinting with interest.

"Says I'm held up for the day. Be tomorrow morning earliest before we can venture."

"That old cuss ain't much for manners, but he's good for the trade. Reckon it's a sturdy appraisal. He's the sort that hates everyone the same, color not figuring like it does with some." Cox hated having to say it, but Thunder Hill was no more perfect than the rest of the world. No help pretending otherwise.

"I got that sense. Hopefully we can get some rooms squared away for tonight. I hate having to go idle, but fate says stop. No sense bucking."

"I'll do what I can for an old friend. Give a word at the hotel." Cox put a hand on Hudson's shoulder. The freighter was one of a handful that could pull warmth from the generally stoic sheriff.

"I appreciate it, Amos. Heck, it's good to see you. Almost takes the edge off my travails." Hudson smiled and shook the lawman's hand one more time, overdoing it the way people do when there's mutual admiration. Hudson took a quick peek over Cox's shoulder at Moreno. "Mind if we step just outside the jail for a second?" he asked.

"'Course," Cox said.

With the morning sun on their faces Hudson asked, "When's that hanging happening? I'd like to have my crew out of here by the time the proceedings are underway."

Sheriff Cox didn't answer right off. Just crossed his arms and leaned in curiously. "Hoping to have the matter done and dusted by tomorrow at noon."

"Okay. I'll throw a few extra coins at your smith, try to get us out of here way ahead of it."

"Uh-huh," Cox said, still more than a little confused.

"Hell, Amos. Just that I got some men on my crew on the younger side, really no more than boys. Not sure I want them seeing that kind of thing. Lord knows if we're still around, they'll be insistent. Most these tads are all the way green."

"Being a little protective?" Cox asked. He was starting to see Hudson's angle and had no reason to quarrel with it. Still, the man was acting strange.

"My son's on the crew, Amos. A good boy, sixteen, but he's never had view of the things we had to endure. Maybe I mother him a little too much since she passed, but I'd like to keep him innocent long as possible. Probably sounds daft, but there it is."

His son. Now it makes more sense. Men were complicated about their sons. "Ain't for me to tell a man the rights and wrongs for raising up their own."

"You've always been a fair man, Amos. Tough and fair."

"Don't know about all that," Cox said, spitting and looking at his boots, old and comfortable as his ease with Hudson. "So, you saw the gallows coming in, I reckon. I hate those things, myself. Always did give me a chill. Big reminder that someone's about to get sent up. Building it right in front of where people do business and get about their lives, one of the stranger institutions we got."

"Oh," Hudson said, "have they got the scaffolding built already?"

"It's getti—" Cox caught himself. "The hell else would you know about the hanging?"

"We heard about it last night, on the road from Briggs Creek. Couple of riders said people were talking about it in the saloon."

"Briggs Creek?" The sheriff tilted his head as the lines on his face grew deep from concern. "How in Jesus are they talking about it there? That's twenty miles saying it's good weather."

"More like twenty-two," Hudson answered. He knew distances as good as any man in the territory. Business depended on it.

"Somebody sent it out on that goddamned wire. Probably word's around from here to Timbuktu."

"I assumed. Another reason I had for pushing through. This kind of thing attracts the morbid. Queer pull a dying man has… folks are starved for entertainment, suppose. Or maybe that's the way it's always been. Every time I think people are stumbling toward basic decency, something like this. Yanks me back to cold realities."

"Son of a bitch," Cox growled. He hadn't heard a jot of Hudson's last rumination. "I got to go, Patrick."

"What's wrong. Anything I can do?"

The sheriff actually considered the offer for a few seconds. Hudson was one of the only people he trusted whole for a gunfight. *Nah. His son.* "No. I'm just needing to pistol-whip one of my deputies."

"Okay, then. G-good seeing you, Amos."

"Yessir."

CHAPTER 9:
SENTINEL CREEK

THEY'D TRIED TO FIND A BETTER OPTION, VENTURING MILES down the west bank of Sentinel Creek. It was almost midday when Sybille came charging back, shaking her head while her young mount blustered and backed up a little before settling from the hard ride. "Nothing for us that way either, Pa. Creek my ass. This here's some big water."

"Warm summer. Melt ain't let up." Fallstead was rolling a cigarette, using his other fingers to shelter the operation from cool wind coming down off the mountains. The geography was relatively stark. Not a lot of trees to block the weather.

Sybille spanked her curved hat against a thigh to rid it of dust. "Right here's our best option. Otherwise it's another fifteen miles out of the way. We ain't got that kind of time."

No response.

"Pa," Sybille said, pulling her horse around next to his. She almost had to holler to be registered above the rushing waters. "This is where we go."

He looked up from lighting his smoke and saw her nodding toward the water. "This is the place, huh?" he asked, casting gloomy circumspection.

"What's the matter?" Sybille couldn't understand what she was seeing. Her father was never the demonstrative sort, but he'd been more or less anemic since hearing the news about Loot Moreno. Up until now, she'd let it alone.

"Nothing's the matter," he said, huffing down his cigarette and wheeling his horse toward the water. "You say it's the way, let's go on and cross."

"Okay," she said, still trying to figure his bearing. She watched him plunge into the swollen stream. *Now he's too fast. Away from me or toward Loot Moreno.*

Sybille buried her thoughts deep and took a heavy breath, kicking forward into the charging water. It was passable if everything went right and the bottom dropped at a predictable rate. Nothing they hadn't done before, but man versus nature was never a sure bet. Both their horses were on the big side, trusty and true, but soon the animals were almost up to their necks in the cool water. It was murky and uniform in its procession, an unrelenting river more than a lively creek. "How you doing?" she asked, leaning against the force of the current and spurring her horse.

Fallstead was only two or three feet away, but now the noise was overwhelming. She took a short glance at her father and then back over her shoulder. They were at least halfway out. No going back. Her animal was breathing hard and manifesting a little moodiness but didn't show signs of buckling. *We'll be fine*, she thought, realizing the creek was starting to shallow. Sybille started thinking of the fire they'd build in a few hours. The crackling and the glow, wet duds drying out over the flames. The empty nothing out past the tiny lights of night, accepting that none of it was under control and therefore none of it mattered the way most folks thought.

Too many ideas. A common mistake made by people in dangerous situations, letting the mind wander outside the fence. She shook her head in self-admonishment.

Her mind wouldn't have made much difference on what happened next. Marshal Fallstead's horse lost footing from a slippery rock on the creek bed and bucked just sharp enough to send him crashing backward into the water. Sybille didn't waste time saying anything; instead, she got moving to shallower water so her horse could take easier strides. Her rope was out and, after a few quick overhead swings, the line was around Fallstead's head and underneath one of his armpits. When it caught, the force almost pulled Sybille in, but she'd prepared for it, transferring her weight expertly to the right side of her body. Long experience in the saddle made her as confident and prodigious as any poke on the range, but still it would take a fulsome effort and shredded hands to get her father reeled back in.

As Sybille moved toward the new shore, she started yelling out. By now, he should've been trying to stand up. "Can you pull yourself in?" she called, sure that he could hear her over the water.

He gave her a strange look. It only lasted a second yet scared her through. Dancing eyes, fear like a common man.

Sybille couldn't believe it. He turned away, pulled his knife and started cutting into the rope. "Are you crazy!?" she screamed. No time to wait for an answer. She yanked her pistol and shot the knife from his hands. No small task considering all the elements stacked against her. "Let's go," she told her horse. The animal made bold strides for the bank, just as ready as her to get free from the clutches of the river.

When Sybille dismounted, all that work climbed up on her shoulders. Her arms started cramping and her legs felt a hundred pounds each as she struggled heavy to her father lying on the edge of the creek. He was on his back, still wearing the rope. She stood over him, watching as he held his left arm.

"I would've been fine," he said, almost like nothing had happened.

She sat down in the wet sand next to him, afraid to say what needed saying. "I'm not stupid, Pa."

"Didn't want you getting pulled in," he said, rolling over to cough up the last bit of water lingering in his throat. "Don't be making more of it than that."

"I see. You were protecting me."

Fallstead offered no response, grabbing his arm once again and speaking something rapid under his breath.

"Don't you care enough to live? This ain't a good light you're in."

"I'd a made it to shore eventually. Calm down, Daughter."

Now that Sybille had her breath, she took a minute to ruminate over what he was saying. None of it felt right. He'd been acting like a spent cartridge, and Holt Fallstead didn't fall from his saddle, blundering horse or not. It all smacked of a man wanting to let the current take him away from his problems.

"Getting nature to carry you downstream," she said, finishing her thoughts out loud. A line of clouds with sooty undersides were threatening rain. They needed to quickly find enough wood to start a fire. Lingering on their feelings wasn't presently an option. "I'm content in letting you be yourself, all quiet, except you're not being yourself. That's all I'm gonna say at the moment."

"Keep your thoughts short, Sybille." He looked wild now, shaking from something more than cold. The water was vibrating from the ends of his red whiskers. "You don't want me going back into them ways. Stories and seeing it real—those got different colors."

She sighed and offered to help with his arm, but he waved her away. She stomped off and said, "Your welcome," just to remind him that she was a girl who'd just saved his old ass. There was no figuring it. Since she could remember, life had been pretty simple. She'd gone all over the country watching him earn a living by stopping people that thought they were tougher than the world and every bad thing in it. Sybille learned no philosophizing and no codes but learned to be content by the result of things.

Holt Fallstead did what he could because he could, regardless of purpose, even absent purpose. It was simple ability; that's what carried him along, and her in turn. She'd always thought so, anyway. Now that they actually had a clear path, when there was a real reason behind their destination, he looked drained.

Fallstead sat up and rubbed his shaking hands. As much as he wanted, the marshal couldn't practice what he'd preached. His thoughts were long and unwieldy. And Sybille could see the history in him, now more than ever. He'd raised a woman strong as any he'd ever encountered. Full of grit as any man that had crossed his path.

He wasn't acting like himself, plain enough. Before reaching Thunder Hill, there'd be parts of the story he'd have to fill in. Things he'd swallowed and kept down until they were stories and that's all.

But they weren't.

Maybe she was right about him wanting to let the river part him from the task. The past was darker and more complicated than she knew, and the future might prove to be just the same.

Or worse.

He got to his feet and slowly and made his way up the bank, feeling old and unsure of himself. Fallstead had grown used to picking his fights. That was the pattern he'd fallen into since... he bent things a certain way to keep himself and Sybille safe, but what was now ahead... it felt like many choices were removed. Fear. A feeling so foreign it took an episode like this to bring it out.

Enough chewing. He set himself to rounding up his horse and making sure the animal was uninjured. *Do what's next. Keep your thoughts short.* Sentinel Creek was to their backside. It had almost taken his life. Or had he almost given it? No matter. *Keep your thoughts short.*

Not long and they'd reach Thunder Hill. He'd take care of the fear one way or another.

CHAPTER 10:

A READER

"IS HE EVER GONNA BE DONE CATCHING WINKS?" THE QUES-
tion was raised by a thin girl named Stella Ann, aimed at an older girl
named Millie Dee. The pair were standing over Millie's bed, currently
occupied by Preacher Kip Laird. It struggled under the weight of his long,
hearty frame. He snored away, shirtless and lacking boots. Stella Ann was
forced to her toes peeking over Millie's bare freckled shoulder. She was
equally riveted by Kip's injuries and his physique. "How's a holy man get all
smooth and well-formed you think?" Stella Ann asked. "Is it the holy that
does that?"

Millie shrugged her roommate back. "He's young and handsome,"
she said.

"I can see *that*."

"This is what they look like, Stella Ann. You've just grown unaccus-
tomed to his aesthetic."

"I'm sure not following, Millie."

"Young and handsome don't need to come here too regular. When's
the last time a man didn't almost crush you with his extra layers?"

"The time's been drawn out since."

"See? There you go."

Looking at Kip made the thought of seeing her regulars later on all the more painful for young Stella Ann. "I mean, between all the fat. And the hair. Not to mention the smell."

Behind them, Jasper Bedford slipped in the room. It was one of three above the bar at the Thunder Hill Saloon. The rooms were notorious but rarely mentioned, something of an open secret in town. The product of some strange sort of muddled Victorian-American West hybrid morality, when looking the other way or looking to your own was the ultimate ethic.

Fortunately for Laird, only Jasper and the two ladies knew he'd spent the night. Not that he'd done anything besides sleep. Bedford had made full use of the girls' services while Kip hibernated; the Rapture itself might've come and he'd've missed it on account of exhaustion.

"What a night that was," Jasper said, lightly smacking Stella Ann on her flat backside. She giggled at the old lecherous writer and absorbed a look of admonishment from Millie Dee. They lived together in the room now, though Stella Ann was a fairly new arrival. Millie was a mainstay in Thunder Hill; she attended the church, watched Kip grow from a boy to a broad-shouldered man in just a few short years. She respected the Lairds. The family practiced nothing but kindness during her stint, a time long enough to see her go from comely to only handsome. God knows it would've been easier for them to cast her for Jezebel and leave it at that. What she did for pay was never condoned by the Lairds, but to Millie Dee the family rode a line of judgment and caring that very few ever seemed to nail down proper. Both parties tried their best at avoiding self-righteousness. It's not like she didn't get the contradiction. Being a Christian and a whore didn't make for an uncomplicated way to go through life. A girl from Georgia trying to make her part out west, pretty but maybe never pretty enough to land a man of means. Tough luck. God's plan. She knew not. Someday things would be different. That was her prayer when she could stand to face the Lord. A girl could only read Chapter Four from John's Gospel so many times.

"Preach! Wake up." Millie was kicking the bed's corner, near to slapping him. Outside the window she could hear rumblings of noontime Thunder Hill. Folks stomping in and out of the stores. Pretty soon a load of leathery men would be descending upon the saloon. That would be bad for Preacher Laird and the church. "Dammit boy, get your ass up!" she hollered, whacking him across the cheek with a heavy hand.

"Ouch," he grunted, attempting to roll away from dusty light streaming in through the bubbly window glass.

"Ouch nothing," she hollered again, shaking him by his neck. It wasn't doing the trick.

Jasper called out from the other side the room, making efforts toward Stella Ann's nethers. "Millie, my dear, if you're insisting the young man rise, squeeze on a part of his body blighted by discoloration."

"What the hell you mean? Oh, yeah," she said, shoving both hands flat down on Kip's bruised ribcage. He seethed and sprang up like a cat, knocking over a delicate lamp made in Paris according to one of Millie's lying customers.

"Holy Moses!" He struggled to the corner, engaging sodden senses to seize bearings. After a few foggy blinks and a quick check to see if he was wearing pants, he asked with whatever dignity was possible what he was doing there.

"Fear not, Mr. Laird," Jasper said, standing up from the bed across the oddly-shaped room. He was wearing blue union suit underwear with unfortunate little holes for anyone that might be spectating. "You were spirited away to this very location last night, unbeknownst to anyone besides we four in this room."

"Millie Dee," Kip whispered, looking like he was trying to force himself out through the wall. "Can you tell me who this fella is?"

"Hi," Stella interjected, voice full of flirt and flimsy southern affectation.

"Hey there, Stella Ann," Kip said, once again grabbing his pants around his privates. "Did I?"

"I can assure you that the status of your virtue remains as it was before last night's activities," Jasper said, motioning at Stella to fetch him a glass of brandy.

"Why's he keep speaking?" Kip asked, now looking down at the uneven floorboards to avoid the two sets of naked breasts in his vicinity. He hadn't noticed at first, taken as he was with the shock of the whole scenario.

Millie decided to unleash both barrels on the youngster. She'd dealt with countless men of every color type and creed over the years. A scared kid was no big thing, only until now she'd been cowed by the position he held in town, the respect she held for him, and the house of God his family looked after. No more. He was in her house, sinful and dirty as it was, and it was her turn to do the straightening out. "Listen, this dirty old drunk did you more than one kindness last night, far as I can tell. Be nice to turn up your eyes and thank him. Sit in judgment on anyone in this room, including yourself, just do it somewhere else and on your own time. We've got need to sneak you out the alley before the rags start piling in. If me and Stella don't get ourselves together and out on the floor, Joey's gonna be up here quicker'n Hermes."

The rebuke stung to purpose. Kip stood up straight and nodded apologetically at Millie Dee and the others. "I'll be off, then. Suppose I've handled myself like a proper jackass as of late, last night being no exception. Mister...?"

"Jasper Bedford, at your service, Mr. Laird. We actually had a brief meeting earlier last evening, but there again you were in a state of duress."

Kip rubbed his head. All things considered, it felt a dang sight better than the days before. "It's late, isn't it?" he asked.

"Why'd you think I'm so eager to get you out?" Millie returned. Her arms were crossed underneath her bare breasts; it was an interesting sight, and one which Kip had no ability to ignore.

"Of course. I'll get my things and be gone in a—wait. You said your name is *Jasper Bedford*?"

"I did indeed," the old man said, sitting back down on the bed and crossing his legs like they were joined for genteel teatime.

Kip was immediately grateful. He took a real look Jasper. His brain finally caught up to the hard miles he'd walked the last few days. *That's the guy. Kip, you idiot. He's the one you set out to find.* "This is strange, but I came looking for you last night. Guess I didn't get very far."

"Ah, now we're finally getting down to it. As much fun as I had with these lovely specimens during the wee hours, I have to admit that the anticipation for this conversation had me giddy on a whole different level. Tumescent to the point where I thought about calling in the doctor."

Kip saw his shirt hanging sadly on the end of the bed and reached or it. He was acres from knowing what a fitting response might be to Mr. Bedford's previous statement.

A knock on the door. Everyone stiffened at the sound of Joey the bartender's unmistakable rasp. "You girls need to get your parts cleaned and moving. We've got customers heading in."

Millie Dee and Stella Ann exchanged a nervous look, especially when Jasper spoke out. "Is that the fine man who runs the establishment?" Bedford was shockingly quick on his feet, moving from his pants on the nightstand to the door in a few breaths' time. He cracked the door. "Good sir. As far as payment, I think this should cover the time for the girls." He flashed a healthy stack of bills in Joey's fleshy face. "I'm heading off soon and yet they're simply too much fun to part with at the moment."

"That ain't how Mr. Trussel likes things run," Joey said, trying to get a better look inside. Jasper held the door firm with his foot. "Mr. Trussel likes the girls downstairs at first for classing up the place."

"And Mr. Trussel is the proprietor of this fine saloon?"

"He's the owner, if that's that you're saying."

"Strange he's not present, with so much going on in town. Leaves you with quite a workload, I'd imagine."

No answer.

"Exactly," Jasper continued. "No time for chatter. Let's get down to it. With no Mr. Trussel and me wanting the girls for another few hours, I think I can offer triple their rate and a promise to add a hundred percent to my very sizeable bar tab. You can go check it if you like. The total might even bring a smile."

"You got the money?"

Bedford gave Joey a sporting wink. "But it's in my hand, dear fellow."

"It'll be more than that." The bartender remained hunched, seemingly unimpressed with the amount of currency being thrust his way.

Bedford added three more bills to the stack and slapped it in Joey's hand. "Okay then," he grunted, lumbering back down the little landing. "Two more hours."

"Good man," Jasper said, looking spry and unaffected by the reduction in his funds. The door closed. "That's no problem. I've excellent standing with Thunder Hill Bank."

"What are you up to, you old coot?" Millie Dee asked, pulling back her curly blond hair. There was play in her voice—Jasper wasn't fresh and handsome but he wasn't a chore like some.

The writer clapped once, fully engaged with the day. He scooted back and took another small glass of brandy before hurriedly pulling on his standard brown suit pants. "That was about a few things, Millie. I didn't want Mr. Joey entering; the discovery of young Laird wouldn't have served any salutary purpose."

"Why would you care?" Kip said. The query was repeated by Millie, echoed by Stella Ann.

"Because it wasn't your choice to stay here. You shouldn't be saddled with labels undeserved. Poor as your judgment might've been yesterday, concupiscence won't be added to the balance."

Kip felt like God might be helping him. At the same time, guilt was riding up his spine. That was the way of it. Any proper assistance from the Divine was nice in the short term but humbling in the long. Here this old stranger was, defending his chaste nature, unawares of Kip's flagrant *concupiscence*. Worst of all, the deceptive kind. His affair with Lindy Samuels wasn't a simple, dirty transaction. It was the type that could ruin lives. It was already doing so. The young man put his head down in shame, wondering when Grace would run bone dry. Ma and Else would abandon him. The people of Thunder Hill, having no choice, would cast him to the darkness of Babylon, out from community's embrace, away from the caring hands of the Maker.

"Ladies," Jasper said, lighting up a thin cigar, "please leave us the room. I believe I heard the girls from next door heading down just now. You can take a load off in there while I converse with our pensive friend."

"I could use a little nap after last night," Stella Ann said, gathering up a robe from the corner.

"This whole situation is frightful odd," Millie said. "Why not just get him the hell out?"

"I paid for the privacy," Jasper said, now putting on his boots. They went on without so much as a tug. "And I've lost my extra socks. No matter," he said, grabbing for more brandy as smoke from the cigar filled the room. "Anyway, the privacy. And when our time is done, I'll still have the two of you under contract to create a distraction down there while I whisk the young reverend unobserved through the back."

The nature of Jasper's plan was clear enough now. Still, Kip needed more catching up. As the girls huffed and puffed to the adjacent room, Laird's complex of emotions must've found residence on his face.

"I think a few moments will help to clear things. Have a chair," Jasper said, moving from the edge of the bed to Stella's nightstand stool. Kip grabbed Millie's from the opposite side of the room and plopped down, trying to focus through the sun and cigar smoke.

"Apologies if I'm skeptical," said the younger man, pulling his dirty black shirt on. It smelled like a proper account of yesterday's proceedings. He laughed and felt the hot embarrassment in his cheeks. "My life's been turned for a loop, you see, and the more I go looking for answers the more questions pile up."

"Relatable, doing what I do. I'll try to cut to the heart of it with you, sir." Jasper struck another match and rotated his cigar into the flame. "Sorry. Damn things always go out on me. I get interested in something else. Anything else. It's almost a condition. Where were we?"

"You were talking about cutting to the heart of it."

"Ah, yes," he said. "Much as one can in this situation. Do you know a great deal about me?"

"I knew you wrote books about the Three-in-One Gang. I know that Loot Moreno is a pal of yours, because that's what they were singing about over at the jail. I didn't even have to snoop around to hear it. Am I the last one in on all the secrets?"

"I wrote the books," Jasper said, leaning back to grab them from Stella's nightstand. "Found copies on you last night. We observed you as you keeled over in the street. I knew who you were, but when I found the stories in your pocket, it seemed incumbent upon me to... well, here we are."

"Obligation, is it?"

"You're a man in search of answers, Mr. Laird. Larger scales, boundless quagmires. I used to search in a similar fashion. Now I'm a man in search of a good story and nothing more. Perhaps Providence is the headline when all's said and done, as your calling proclaims, but sin runs a close second. I'm still trying to put things together myself."

"None of this makes any sense," Kip said, rubbing his face with his hands. He was well-rested, but trying to fit Bedford's word puzzle together was tougher than bad Greek. "I don't know who I am. Would that bother you, sir?"

"I'll start answering. You start asking," Jasper said. "As they come to you, send them my way. Works best like that."

"I read those books when I was a kid. The Three-in-One Gang, Loot Moreno. They were vicious murderers and thieves. Pagan zealots, though I don't recall you going into much. I hit the dust before chance gave me time to give another perusal. One in particular, about a family he tried to save out on the prairie. A young boy."

"Sounds like you have a pretty sound memory of the tale."

"Is it true? What you wrote?"

"Let's bypass the nature of true versus accurate and get back to the heart, as I was talking about."

"That won't cut it." Kip wanted it straighter.

"All but one of those books was written before I'd ever met Loot Moreno or anyone else in the Three-in-One Gang. I was a frontier scribbler taking any job that came my way. Some of what's in there is true; some of it I made up to fill in the gaps."

"I don't understand," Kip said, tightening up his posture. "If *any* of those stories are accurate, why does every good man in town seem hellbent on helping Moreno? Why would Cox and Doc Rufus risk so much to break him out? What's your part in all this?"

"Far as my part, I'm an ancillary piece. I may feel a sense of responsibility, however, on two fronts."

"Go on."

"I told Moreno about your father's death. Suppose if I hadn't, there'd be no trouble. Loot's been holed up for years. He would've found out about Ben Laird eventually. Look, I didn't think he would jump on a horse and come riding into Thunder Hill. It never occurred to me. The man is smart." Bedford blew out a long and heavy cloud of cigar smoke. "Usually smart, anyhow."

"Still…"

"Okay, here's the deal. Loot Moreno brought you here."

"My father told me that much. I thought they were the crazy words of a dying man."

"Not crazy, young Laird. And though your father's reasons for the conveyance of information are mysterious, he seems to have told it correctly."

"Two fronts."

"What's that?"

"You said your responsibility was on two fronts."

"Yes. I care about Loot, like the rest of those men. They don't know me as they do each other, but they know what side I'm on. My duty is to help."

"This is bordering on fantastical," Kip said, scuffing a boot on the wooden crooked planks of the floor.

"It's only fantastical to the simple-minded. We both know you're not that. Keep the facts in front of you. Now here's another one. Loot Moreno saved my life, as he saved yours."

"Who is this guy?"

"He's what you might call a complicated man. Someone who walked a dark path and decided to walk another. It doesn't happen often in this world, but exceptions exist to every rule."

Kip let all the information go for a second and allowed the world back in. He heard the sound of the piano downstairs, men playing cards. He listened to the clutter of wagons and horses outside and people shouting howdy and good day to each other. Things were normal. He wondered how much longer that would last.

"One thing I've been thinking, probably more than anything else," he said, "I was thinking it since church the day of the funeral, somewhere in the back of my mind."

"I'm all ears."

"If Loot Moreno brought me here, saved my life, how'd that happen?"

"How'd you mean?" Bedford asked, tightening his wrinkled expression.

"Simple. Either he did or didn't come by my people. If he didn't, suppose Loot Moreno's part angel, plucking wayward infants at random from the cold world and certain death. If he did, what occasioned him to take me away? What in heck happened to my parents, Mr. Bedford?"

"I swear I don't know," the writer said immediately. Kip looked him up and down for signs of prevarication, but there was nothing. "All I know is he cared what happened to you. He'd come to check on you. Him and Cox, Ben and Doc Rufus. It was sort of a thing they had."

"A thing?"

"Yeah. Making sure you were okay."

"Seems strange. Motherly, even. We're not talking about the gentlest souls around these parts. Except Ben, maybe."

"I think there's something to what you're saying there, son. It was a chance to do something right. Like you mentioned, not the gentlest souls. Anyone who forged their own trail out here did it by a huge measure of sweat and probably just as much blood." Bedford paused, seeming to consider the subject anew. "Maybe you were penance for some, hope for others. You'd have to ask them each for their own. Might not get answers."

"On that we'd agree," Kip said, standing up and rolling his suspenders over his shoulders. "I've got my mind set on finding out everything. Spent enough time being protected."

"I'm not sure your father knew what he was doing when he told you about Moreno."

"Maybe not, but here we are."

Jasper scratched the top of his head and smiled. "Where we are is a prostitute's room, Mr. Laird."

"Yeah. Thinking it's time for a scene change."

"What'd you have in mind?"

"I've got to talk to Sheriff Cox. Make sure he knows that the word is out in the territories about Loot's hanging."

Bedford tilted his head in doubt. "You sure? I was told they were keeping the news quarantined."

"Heard it from my brother. The very person who sent the message out."

"You're kidding?"

"I'm not sure blame deserves to be leveled at Sydney. God bless my older brother, but he doesn't seem to be operating with all the pieces."

"Fair enough," Bedford said, scratching his overgrown gray eyebrows with both hands. They were long enough to fall down into his line of sight when he frowned in concern.

"There's more I want to know. Things I didn't get a chance to ask."

"I'll be around," Jasper said. "And there's always the others. They might be willing to offer some information, now that things are starting to get out."

Kip gathered the rest of his things. "You know, Mr. Bedford, I get the feeling that nobody's operating with the full set of facts."

"Perhaps we should all get together and compare notes," Jasper said. He smiled again, causing his cigar to pivot up.

"Perhaps we should. If everybody's alive in a few days, guessing you'll get the nomination for scribe."

"It would be my pleasure, Mr. Laird. Nice to finally meet you, by the way."

Kip offered his hand. "Thanks for pulling me out of the dirt."

"It's always fun to meet a reader."

CHAPTER 11:
HUNTERS

"FORGING OUT IN THE MIDDLE OF NOWHERE, MIDDLE *UH* night. This is flat dumb. I'm for thinking we turn around, Ford. Head ourselves back to Buckston. Loot Moreno? Loot Moreno?"

"I hoped maybe God would grant you the strength to shut your trap for a few minutes longer. Seems I'm a wishful type thinker."

The two riders steered their horses through darkness and an unseasonable fog, keeping the narrow rocky road by holding to an agonizingly slow pace.

"I just reckon nothing but bad can happen here. What are we after, Ford?"

"Are you getting more dumb as the years go by, Hyde? We're going after a bounty. The biggest one I've ever heard of. A body we can sell to the highest bidder. It'll make us legends."

"I get all that, but he's gettin' the noose. How the heck we stop courtly proceedings is past my thinking."

"What's your job, Hyde?"

"I'm a bounty hunter."

"Exactly," said Ford. "I thought hunting is what you did. I thought that's what we've been doing out here for the last two years. Two years of too cold or too hot, no women or ones that hardly resemble women. Prospects ain't getting any better, is what I'm saying."

"Okay."

The one named Ford took a swig of whisky and offered one to his disquieted companion, finding him through the moonless dark and fog with his flask. "We've been out here, picking up this mutt or that, getting by on common makers of mischief and card cheats. This one here puts us way up. Money, reputations to boot."

"But it's—"

"It's dangerous, Hyde. You've said it fifteen times since Buckston, and you're right."

"So, what are we doing?"

"When word went around back in town about the hanging coming in over the wire, remember how many people saddled up?"

"A few traveling types. We're the only two dumbasses of our ilk out here, far as I know."

"Not dumbasses, Hyde. Savvy men of business."

"A lot of people in Buckston know the stories, Ford. I'm one of them people. Can't read none but my older brother Kern used to rattle off those dime novels to me. Some grit in them yarns."

Ford pulled back the reigns as they made their way down a slope covered with rocks that could prove trouble for his horse. They'd have to be cautious; even slower than before. Still, he thought, pushing on through the night was better. He could think clear in the quiet dark. Currently he had several possible plans that were good enough in theory but lacking large portions of detail and consideration. They could shoot the sheriff and take the prisoner. They could cut a deal with the sheriff and take the prisoner.

Or they could just kill the sheriff and the prisoner in an attempted "jail-break." He was leaning toward the last.

Hyde was behind him now. He'd gone mute. As much as Ford hated his partner's constant prattling, he figured total silence would manifest worse down the line somewhere. *Just let him talk. Maybe it'll get out his system.* "Which stories you heard, Hyde?"

"You know the ones."

"Maybe. Or maybe we've heard different versions. Them's mythemological, half these yarns. Somebody telling a thing and passing it on with more ornaments attached that was true. Gets strange and full of fear-making by the time it makes its way to an otherwise brave soul like yourself." Ford couldn't help but condescend to his slower-witted associate.

"You think that honest?"

"Frontier's full of tales that'll make your hair stand at attention. My second cousin Billy heard tell of the damnedest."

"Dead Billy had the bad harelip?"

"Yes, Hyde. Dead Billy. Heard tell of this giant fella all covered in hair living up in the woods. Said the thing was like a bear, only it would go about like a man. Didn't say nothing, but it could think sharp, just like me and you."

At this, Hyde bent forward over his horse's neck and started to cackle into the night. "Whew, whew. Ugly Billy believed something that dumb?"

Ford sighed. "A lot of people believed it. Still do, I imagine. But you see my point?"

"Yeah, I see it. But Loot Moreno's scarier than some damn gorilla traipsing around the damn forest."

"Tell me."

"He's part Injun, part Mexican, part demon. It's in all the old books like I was saying."

"You heard those books being read?" Ford asked.

"I ain't saying it for sport."

"Okay. What else makes him scary? And don't be holding back. There ain't nothing but empty land between here and Thunder Hill."

Hyde was all too ready to justify his trepidations. "The man who churned up the Three-in-One Gang was named Titus the Exile. Was just a baby of some family of French trappers that came over here hundreds a damn years ago or something. Stories say he was abandoned by his people, left for dead on account of being sick. People weren't as sophisticated back then, suppose."

"Go on," Ford said, keeping his horse slow and on the trail, trying not to laugh at his nervous compatriot.

"So, Titus doesn't die, I guess. Gets found by some damn tribe out in the middle of nowhere. They practiced human sacrifice, all sorts of savage shit. It goes that they raised up Titus the Exile, taught him their ways. How to kill and not get killed better than all others practicing similar. How to survive and give up the people you deliver to the universe. The tribe believed that after a killing, you had to say some manner of crazy shit that went out like a telegraph to everything and everywhere. If you did it right, the universe would give you a glimpse of all three places, plus a helping of strength. Some sort of demon power or whatever."

"What's the three places?"

"Come on, Ford. You know damn well the three places. Ugly Billy told you. Everyone told you."

"Just making sure we're talking about the same thing."

Hyde pulled the scarf away from his chaffed face and let out a frustrated breath. "Heaven. Hell. Here. The three places." He spoke the words like forcing up a bad meal. "Something to do about being able to see everything at once. Never made a lick of sense to me nor anyone else I ever asked. Gives me the shakes though, sure enough."

"Yeah, it ain't a bedtime story for little ones," Ford said. "Finish it out for me so I feel caught up."

"Well, apparently our Titus lived with this band of damned savage lunatics until a plague swept through and killed every last one. Some say it was the Wrath of the Lord, or Jesus coming down with Holy Justice. Might be, or might be they all got sick and died like everyone else in this Godforsaken land."

"Killed every single one, huh?"

"Everyone except Titus the Exile. By then he was any man's better, strong as a bull and well-versed in all them rude ways. After that, he went out and started roaming the frontier lands. Mostly killing, I guess, saying those words, except when he'd pick up a recruit here or there."

"That part never made sense when I heard the telling. Why'd a guy like that want recruits?"

"What was that?" said Hyde, distracted by something in the wind.

"I was just saying that it's strange the bloodthirsty monster you've described would want much company around."

"You asked for the story, Ford. I'm telling it like I know."

"All right. Apologies."

"Anyway, supposing he wanted recruits for the same reason anyone would. It gets lonely out here. Type of lonely that'll make a man crazy." Hyde was shivering as he spoke, all the way down to his saddle. The telling was helping Ford with a needed distraction but for Hyde it was bringing up fears he'd just as well not face.

"Huh," Ford grunted. "So he needed partners, however you look at it."

"That's what I'm saying." Hyde said, trying to sound full of resolution. He suspected his companion was making him tell the story to trip him up, but he'd gotten through right enough. "You tell the rest—like you know it," Hyde said, renewed with confidence he'd turned the tables.

"Fine," Ford said, clearing the cold from his throat. "Titus the Exile roams the land with the Three-in-One Gang for untold years, murdering and raping, taking anything they felt inclined to take. They were a band of outcasts and half-breeds, people that no one wanted around in the first place. Then one day, Titus's best man challenged him. They say the man wanted to leave the gang, only, there was no leaving. They fought. Titus died brutal."

"And who killed him?" Now Hyde was doing the spurring.

"Loot Moreno. The *stories* say that Loot Moreno sawed Titus's head clean off with a hunting knife. When the rest of the gang came to exact revenge for their leader, Moreno killed them too, down to the last one. Innocents got killed in the process. More than a few sodbusters slain, caught between."

"And *this* is the man we're going to try to collect," Hyde said, like finishing a closing argument in court. He waited for some sort of clever reply from his partner, but nothing came. Ford rose up in his saddle as they began to crest the hill. "You see something?" Hyde asked.

"Don't get all frazzled, but yeah. There's a fire up ahead."

"Bandits, you thinkin'? Injuns?"

"Looks measly. I doubt a bunch of banditos or redskins would make a fire that small. Guessing it's weary travelers, like us."

"So, should we go around?"

Ford looked behind at his companion. The fog had just about lifted and the full moon was casting a decent portion of light on their surroundings. "No, I imagine they've already seen us. Don't want to go tearing into night off trail needless. Probably get killed tumbling down some dry creek bed."

"What then?"

"Keep a hand on that old Colt and stay sharp," Ford said. The trail widened at the bottom of the hill and the fire grew larger in their vision until they could see one solitary figure sitting calmly by the light of the flames.

"Thought I heard a rustling out there." The voice took them by surprise. A woman underneath the hat of a cowpoke. Not much accent, smooth and pleasant. A young woman.

"Howdy there," Ford said, gently removing his heavy grip from his gun and pulling the horse to a stop. He held a hand out for Hyde to do the same. They were close to the fire. Any closer, the heat or playing flames might frighten the horses. Ford held onto the reigns but put both hands atop his saddle horn in a very deliberate fashion. Hyde mimicked his every move. "Cold night out here," said Ford with a flat but friendly tone. Something a fellow weary traveler might say to another, but nothing fancy and nothing that could start a dust-up. He was curious about the woman right off. It wasn't a typical situation. She was alone, not wearing a skirt or dress. Man's clothes, or at least practical, like man's clothes. He looked for her horse to see if it was tied off by its lonesome, but the light from the fire didn't travel far enough to eye much of anything.

"You betcha that air's got bite," she said, nodding at them and taking a puff from a long pipe. "You boys are welcome to the fire if your hurry isn't too hard. Guess riding at this hour, you just might be."

Hyde shot a solicitous look at his fellow bounty hunter, sure to shiver audibly while doing it.

Ford let out a sigh of surrender and said, "That'd be awful nice of you, ma'am. I'm called Ford Wicker. That there's Hyde. Just riding for Thunder Hill, but looks like we could do with a quick sit and some warming up."

"Great," she said, casually taking in another rush of pipe smoke. "My name's Sybille. About thirty paces back behind me there's a tree where y'all can tie your horses. It's just out a view of the fire, halfway yonder between here and the creek."

Hyde took both sets of reigns and rounded the fire, pulling the spent horses through the quiet dark until he came upon the tree. Not one but two animals were tied off to the lowest thick branch of a solitary evergreen. Hyde grabbed at his gun in his normal fashion and thought to call out, but figured that'd just get him a telling off. Ford would brand him sissified or needing short pants. *I'm not for* that.

He secured their horses to the same branch, talking to himself all the while. The mangy bounty hunter, slow-witted as he might be, was having a disputation in his mind that would've plagued a man much more intelligent. Yelling out there was another horse might set Ford and the lady on edge, maybe even to the point of drawing down. Could be she wanted such a dustup, but Hyde had a hard time making sense of that thought. Why tell him the location of the two horses if it was something to keep secret? *Dammit,* he said, trudging back to the camp heavily through dirt and sage. Rattled as his cage might be, the scene he returned to was calm as a cup of water. His partner sat against a log on the side of the fire they'd come from. The lady looked like she hadn't moved, one leg out, one leg tucked close to her chest, still smoking on that pipe. They were jawing like two old friends at the end of a long day's drive.

"There he is," Ford said, doing his best to roll a cigarette in the intermittent light. "Come and take yourself a load off, Hyde."

Sybille watched the returning bounty hunter steer his body around the flames before nervously finding space next to his companion. She could see holes in the bottom of his boots and hear whatever teeth he had left chattering. Hyde was a scraggly specimen, too fidgety a disposition for a tracker of men. "Mr. Hyde," Sybille said, "hope there was no trouble finding that tree."

After stealing a fruitless look at Ford, he offered a stunted *no* and adjusted his hat so the tattered brim covered his eyes.

"Anyhow," Wicker said, "we're just passing through, on our way out to the coast."

"That far, huh?" Sybille asked, still as a rock.

"Why not. Right, Hyde?"

"Right."

Sybille leaned forward and blew her pipe smoke so it mingled with the fire's. "You okay, Mr. Hyde? You seem a little skittish."

All he could think about was that other horse. It merited telling Ford. He was sure of it. But he stayed off it, under the spell of the rare beauty across the fire. "I'm fine."

"Sorry for the questions. Breeches good etiquette, surely, but I wasn't raised with the gentility of a proper lady. Rough round the edges," she said, smiling icily in the subtlest of ways. The expression came off as strangely playful to Ford and wholly unnerving to Hyde.

"We're not bothered," Wicker said, keeping his eyes trained on Sybille and holding his hands out to the fire.

"Oh, I don't know," she said, smacking her pipe empty against a rock. "He's probably bothered—wondering after the other horse."

"What horse is that?" Ford asked, pulling his hands back, tense with sudden suspicion.

Sybille put her head down and looked into the dark empty of the cleared pipe. Behind the bounty hunters, the answer came. "My horse."

Before either man could turn, Holt Fallstead had an arm around Hyde's head. He sank his hunting knife deep into the side of the man's neck. As he yanked out the blade, blood sprayed forward onto the fire. The body fell forward, convulsing against the ground. By the time Ford's mind caught up enough for him to make a move, Sybille had already drawn her pistol and fired a round at his feet. "Wouldn't go for that piece," she said, eyes quickly darting from the fresh corpse to her father and finally back to the bounty hunter. He'd already abandoned fighting notions and was making a feeble attempt to belly-crawl away, filled with dread and an animal's instinct for survival.

Fallstead moved quickly, driving his bloody blade into the back of the desperate man's right leg. It went straight through the other side and into the ground. Ford let out a scream loud enough to wake every critter in the valley. "Had enough noise from you," the lawman said, wrestling the knife free and moving around to the head. Fallstead twisted the wounded man's face upward and inserted the blade into his mouth, sawing off his tongue with practiced efficiency.

Sybille stood up to survey her father's work. She walked over and moved Hyde; his head fell clear off. Fallstead was sitting next to Ford, trying in vain to scream with only a stump and broken teeth in his mouth.

"You weren't too partial to these boys I guess," she said, moving with more caution. She'd dealt with violence and been witness to all kinds—even so, the unvarnished brutality had her spooked.

Ford's muted ululations were taking on a miserable form. He was pounding the ground with spasmic hands and sputtering up blood and little chunks of whatever remained of his tongue, trying without result to drag himself and his gushing leg away from Fallstead. The marshal positioned himself calmly by Wicker's side and wiped his bloody steel on the dying man's fringed suede jacket. "We heard y'all jabbering from over a mile off," Fallstead said, "so I went out on foot to follow you alongside the trail." He talked flat and hard and devoid of emotion, like ordering at a restaurant with no time for idleness. "Lot of rocky terrain around here. Sound travels. Should learn to ride quieter."

Ford continued to gag. He tried turning on his side but Fallstead wouldn't let him move. "Your friend was scared. You overestimated your worth. Seems he was the more appropriate party now, don't it?"

The question was met with the sorriest series of groans Sybille had ever occasioned to hear. The man was desperate for the other side. "Pa?" she said.

Ignoring his daughter, the marshal went on. "While y'all were talking, I was listening. Most of the story was right, though you could never understand. I say this because your life is going, and only because your life is going." Fallstead took the blade and slid it into Ford's ribcage, twisting it as he continued. "And I'll make you and your friend my offerings."

"Pa?"

"The major part you and your partner left out. After Moreno butchered our leader, he killed everyone. Except me. They called me Dan Clayton back then. Sought vengeance until I was sure he was dead, and my old ways withered away." Once again, he pulled the knife out, bringing it back down under Ford's shoulder and yanking it diagonally across his torso. Sybille made a brave effort to keep watching but her stomach knotted and she had to avert her eyes.

Fallstead knelt over the corpse, breathing heavily. The last cut took a huge amount of physical strength. Ford was opened up like a fish; all manner of organs exposed. The marshal's hands and face were painted with a thick coat of the bounty hunter's gory remains.

"Pa?" Sybille said once more, standing flat-footed and motionless between the two dead bodies.

"Made a mistake," Fallstead mumbled. "Made a mistake. Made a mistake. Moreno's still alive."

"Didn't we already know that?" Sybille asked, rocking back on her heels. Her father's behavior was fitful now, almost rabid. It didn't line up at all with the stoicism she'd come to know through the course of her life or the calm displayed during the killing. She chose her next words cautiously, trying to find a crack in his trancelike state of darkened reverie. "You okay, there?"

Marshal Fallstead, formerly Dan Clayton, stood up and turned toward the fire, staring into the flames. "Since you could hold a gun you've wanted to know about the old ways. Every kill, I see you make the symbol. You try to hide it, but it doesn't get by."

"Just curious. The little you've told me, plus the things I've heard. And, I think there's something to it. Something useful."

"There is. Something useful."

"So, what about these fellas? They seemed harmless..." Sybille stopped short of making a full-throated inquiry. Considering what she'd just witnessed, it seemed the only reasonable option.

"They were going to get in my way." It was Dan Clayton looking into the flames now. The years of being Holt Fallstead had melted into ash and blown away. "You said you wanted Moreno for what he did to me. The death of my brothers."

"Of course," Sybille said.

"You'll watch then. What you want takes more than drawing a circle in the sand."

The next hour was the most jarring Sybille had ever taken in. She looked on as her father removed the larger organs of the dead men, scattering them around two circles, each large enough to encompass a wagon. She sat in one while her father centered himself in the other, repeating strange words that he recited to the endless sky. Close your eyes, he told her. You may not see this time, he told her. But soon enough this will give you vision and strength greater than a normal soul, he said.

When they were done, he ordered her to take anything of use or value from Hyde and Ford's horses. Dawn was an hour away when they resumed their journey toward Thunder Hill and Loot Moreno. Her father seemed steady and sharp-eyed after the circle. Sybille herself felt changed, though not in any particular way. She felt tougher, perhaps. Lonely, even though she now knew her father like she'd always asked to. *Maybe Pa was right about the strength and sight. Maybe. I don't know, dammit.*

After rolling it around, she looked back up into the sky and made a sort of peace with it for the time being. Sybille had pined to witness the full extent of the Three-in-One Gang's mysterious practices for most of her life. Like her father said, since she could hold a gun.

Loot Moreno had pushed her pa back to a former state. This wasn't the marshal or the man at the creek.

Sybille showed her horse a kick, reckoning the merits of what had just taken place were about to be tested and tried, one way or another.

CHAPTER 12:

AN EARLY STROLL

KIP DIDN'T NEED LIGHT TO FIND THE LAIRD FAMILY HOME. Nor did his eager dog. They were moving quick down main street toward the end of town. His plate was full like it'd never been. Despite all to come, Elsie was taking up most of his head and heart. There was no time for apologies or attempts at setting things right, not with logic. He cleared his throat. Logic would have to wait. "Steady Ambrose. Sit still now, or I'll leave you tied up friendless." Kip gave the front door a determined series of knocks, hoping someone would answer before his dog scratched a hole through to the other side. It was cold and the fog had lifted for clean air; a decent time interval before the sun started its ascent over the high ground east of the valley.

The door opened with a creak that matched his nerves. Elsie's face appeared strained as she rubbed her golden hair. One of her full cheeks was red and the other pale; he'd obviously roused her from solid sleep. "Sorry, Else. Didn't want to have to wake you or Mama up."

"Your actions speak opposite." Her address was quick and coarse. His enthusiasm was well matched by her standoffishness.

"Yeah," he said, taking off his old hat as Ambrose tried to nose a way into the Laird house. "He's crazy, this one."

Elsie's eyes grew big and soft as she looked down and smiled at the golden retriever's unfettered ambition. "He's a good boy," she said. Kip was grateful for the cheer back in her voice. Her scent almost overtook him. It was two types inviting. She smelled fresh and warm and slightly perfumed like a woman and she smelled enough like home to make him weak standing there.

"I need you to take him," Kip blurted.

Her face tightened. "Off leaving things like you did. How'd I know you were *still* going to ask for something?" She was whispering for the sake of their mother, but it was obvious now she'd have preferred a hotter tone.

"I've been neglecting a lot of things. Been stupid, and you don't even know the whole of it." His head was humbled and his hair had fallen over his eyes and chin.

Elsie was waking up quick. "Do you even know yet what you want to apologize for? Maybe next time I come up to your place her scent will be on you again."

"You knew? The other morning?" So much for working up to a confession. Kip considered maybe it was a gift. A reprieve. He hated the little coward hiding inside, the one making her figure things out for herself.

Elsie scratched the little dimple on her chin and yawned away the last of the night. She shook her head. Kip knew before she spoke that the condescension was about to let loose. "The woman wears enough of that cheap perfume to make a lasting impression. Enough even to cut through the stink of booze you had from the night before and pretty much ever since."

"Well shoot, Else." Kip smiled weakly in self-defense and went back through the last few days and his conversations with Elsie. All the clever ways he'd imagined amends. It was all a waste. He should've guessed Else had him figured and then some.

"You're a good preacher, Kip. Good at chopping wood, pistol shooting. More than decent on a horse. But I wouldn't put subterfuge high on the list of your qualities. She'll get you killed crying on you in the street like she did."

"Else."

She held up a hand. "I didn't have the stomach for a showdown, even knowing you were carrying on. So we're both liars and yellow, though I won't argue you're much worse."

"We're breaking Loot Moreno out of jail." The words shot out of his mouth before he could weigh the soundness of letting them go.

"What?" she asked, laughing a little, lifting his chin to gather what she could from his avoiding eyes.

He stepped to her bare toes, propelled by her touch. She didn't back away. The cold high-country air sent a chill down his neck. "I was fixing to sell a story about me and Doc Rufus going over to the Bristols all day, but I'm not lying to you anymore."

She wasn't laughing now. The firmness in his voice and the agitation of his chest moving in and out convinced her the moment had weight. "The man's set to hang today," she said.

"That isn't happening."

"Because he brought you here as a baby? I can't remember. Are you Moses or Romulus?"

"Because I need more answers. I've only got some of the story, and I want to understand. He's the reason I'm alive. The reason I'm here. That there should be enough to merit walking out the path."

"The reason you're alive. Says the fine men who've been lying to you your life long."

"You'd have to put Pa in that grouping of liars."

She slapped him hard. The snap carried through the thin air. "What are you going to do? Go in there and bust him out yourself?" Elsie's light

skin was turning hot as she contemplated and calculated the worst out-
comes. There was no restraining her practical side. "You're going to get
yourself thrown in a cell. Or killed. Tell me this plan."

Kip put his hat back on. "No. I'm not saying anymore. Less you know,
the better. In case there's trouble."

"What happened to not lying?"

"Not telling you specifics isn't exactly lying." He kissed her on the
cheek before she had a chance to reel back her face. "Sorry Else, but I've
got to be bold. No one comes close to you and I love you for it. There it is.
Hopefully you'll be able to forgive me." He went to kiss her other cheek but
found her lips instead. They lingered and breathed on it. Kip had both big
arms around her while she moved in powerful little womanly ways inside
his embrace.

Elsie pulled away not wanting to. "You don't have claim or right, the
way you've been." Now she was being less than straight. No doubting she'd
forgive him his running around—the kiss only served to speed up the process. It still hurt, but she loved him clear. Faith they could bury the hatchet,
somehow, through everything. "But come back here after your adventures
and see to me. Be careful."

He tipped his hat and nodded down at her. "Stay inside today and
watch over Mama. I can't force you, but I'm asking you not to tell a soul."

"Kip, don't get killed helping out your savior. It's unproductive. And
I'll be needing you around."

"I've got to go. I wish I didn't."

"Then go." She pulled Ambrose in and shut the door in his face.

He turned abruptly feeling better and worse about the day. Walking
toward the heart of town, he told himself Elsie and that kiss was all that
mattered then told himself to put all that on hold.

It was set up to be the busiest of mornings. He nodded and gave a
flick of a wave as he passed by the livery. Speeding by the butcher shop,

he came to Mr. Weaver's freshly-painted telegraph office. It was still too early for anyone to be up and about, dark enough to prevent folks from recognizing the particulars of a face from any distance. Kip gave the street one more up and down glance and went around to the back of the simple one-story building. Before he could knock, Jasper Bedford was at the door, lantern swaying in hand. "Greetings, Mr. Laird," he whispered. "We're cutting it close."

"I know. Any problems?"

"Come on in. No problems. The girls purloined Mr. Weaver's keys without a hitch. He's naked as a jaybird, sleeping off a long one. I had to talk all night to that man before he decided upon taking up with the ladies. Hard to say if I've ever heard someone speak longer with absolutely nothing interesting to say. Loot can consider my account squared after today."

"Did you disable it?"

"I did indeed," Jasper said, pulling out a flask from his trademark brown suit jacket. "This device will not be functional for at least two weeks. I rounded up the spare parts as well. He'll have to order new."

"But no permanent damage?"

"None. You needn't worry your Christian soul about depriving the banal Mr. Weaver his livelihood."

"Are you still drunk from last night, Mr. Bedford?"

Jasper rubbed the heavy bags under his eyes. "I am. But only just. I'd like to think that it's still last night. And as I said, it takes a river of spirits to endure that insufferable stooge."

"You better get on."

"I'd better. And don't worry. Our sirens will slip the key back and he'll be none the wiser. Until he gets here, of course."

"Okay," Kip said, realizing he was breathing rather heavily. "You didn't let *slip* the specifics of the plan to 'our sirens' by any chance, did you?"

"Never. Maintaining confidences goes part and parcel with my life's calling. I'm sure you bear a similar cross, being a man of the cloth." Jasper was moving his hands like a conductor. It seemed to Kip that the writer's drinking had him buying into the eloquence of his own speech with too full a heart. Somehow, though, it was endearing.

"Well, I appreciate you doing it," Kip said, catching and shaking the old man's hand. "Hopefully the crime will never get back to us."

"Crime?" he scoffed, teetering forward a bit. "No utility in self-flagellation, young man. Forward we must march."

"I guess that's right."

"Chin up." Jasper patted his co-conspirator on the shoulder. "Go on now. There's still a lot to do."

"You headin' back?" Kip asked, having no choice but to trust that Jasper was equal to his tasks.

"I am. Hoping for another go with Stella Ann before the sun's up in earnest."

Through grinding teeth, Kip said, "Just get him back the key."

"Don't worry, Preacher Laird. Can I call you Kip?"

"Of course."

"Call me Jasper. Now that we're getting to be friends, only seems right."

"Yeah. Seems right."

"Oh, come now," Bedford said, sensing Kip's stubborn trepidation. "We all get dirty hands eventually."

CHAPTER 13:

THE PRISONER AND

THE PREACHER

"JEE-SUS!" SYDNEY LAIRD JUMPED AS LIGHT FROM AN OLD kerosene lamp filled the little jail. It had been dark and quiet coming in; he'd just hung his hat and locked the door behind. It was rote practice, easy to do, even absent illumination. Now he was turned around, eyes made wide by the massive figure of the man he was still calling Brandon Calhoun. The prisoner had the sheriff's revolver aimed steady at his head. Cox was lying unconscious on the bed in the back corner of the cell. It looked like blood on the floor. Syd was there on the sheriff's orders to come in early for the sake of preparedness, seeing that the hanging was to take place at the height of day.

So far, things were off to a rough start. "Easy, Calhoun," Sydney trembled. His normally languid senses were sharp. He could smell the gun oil. The pool of blood. The sweat of the unwashed prisoner. "Let's just talk about this. No need for craziness, if you get me."

"Calhoun" wasn't for talking. He closed the distance to Syd before the deputy could put a hand to his own sidearm. Sydney found himself disarmed in the jail cell a few seconds later, checking to see if the sheriff was still alive. "What'd you do, you son of a bitch? Did you kill him!?"

"Not sure. Do me a favor and take a look." Deputy Laird watched the giant who'd been planted behind bars thumping back and forth free and wild through the little jailhouse, gathering the items they'd confiscated when he was arrested. He overcrowded the space with his size and frenzied purpose. Sydney looked away from the brute to examine the wound on Cox's head best he could. It didn't appear to be a bullet hole. He tore off a yellowed piece of the cheap jailhouse bedding and used it to dab the cut. It was hard to see through the sheriff's dense salt and pepper hair. "He'll be fine," Loot said.

"Shut the hell up," Syd said, near to tears. "I don't aim to believe a murderer."

"I don't expect belief," the criminal said, stomping into the cell, now with his own dark pistol drawn and cocked. "Get back against the wall."

Two minutes later, Sydney found his hands shackled behind his back. The restraints ran through one of the vertical bars keeping the bed up. He was trapped, and there was no complaining about it. Half the pillowcase was stuffed in his mouth and layers of cloth were wrapped around the lower part of his head so he couldn't spit the gag out. He bucked and moaned and tried to rouse his boss, watching with strained red eyes as the condemned man turned official fugitive, slipping out in full livery into the predawn dark.

After wrestling the restraints a few more frustrating minutes, he finally took a rest. His thick wrists were bleeding and his eyes were stinging with sweat from the strain of trying to break free. He looked around and tried to figure out what happened. Food on the floor. *That's it.* Sheriff Cox out of fairness was likely trying to give the lunatic a decent last breakfast, only to get brained in the process.

Syd moaned and whimpered as loud as the gag would allow, but it was ineffectual. Kicking at the floor with the heels of his boots, it was clear.

He wasn't doing a thing until Cox woke up or Elbert Rooker made his way into work. No telling when that would be. ER wasn't the kind you could set your watch to. "Eehhhd," Sydney said, coughing on fabric. He was trying to say *shit*.

* * *

Three light raps on the barn door. Doc Rufus cracked it open and nodded sharply at the new arrival. "Everything go okay?"

"Good enough," said Moreno, entering quick and breathing hard. "But maybe you need to get over to the jail and tend to Amos. I hit him damn good on the head. Twice." Though the outlaw was speaking to Rufus, he was looking at Kip and remembering. They'd all been there together before, that very spot, keeping secrets. He pushed the memories down a useful amount, enough to give him a sense of obligation but not too much to weigh him useless.

Kip was holding the reins of two horses in the center of the little barn as he set eyes on Loot. He was even more imposing now in his long pale sheepskin coat, holding a heavy scatter gun in one hand and a rifle in the other. "Hey, Pecos." Loot walked up slow and rested his head against the nose of the sturdy animal, aware he was avoiding Kip's eagerness. "Hey there, amigo. Sorry to leave you locked up in that livery so long." He rubbed the dark brown hair between the horse's ears. "Any consolation, I know just how you feel."

"Twice you hit him?" Rufus said, interrupting the reunion between man and beast. "I hope you didn't do anything permanent. Damn, Loot."

"He made it clear, Doc. I told him a bad knock to the head was nothing to take light, but the man's mule stubborn. He wants this ruse smacking authentic."

The doctor kicked weakly at some loose hay and checked his gold pocket watch. "But you know the plan. I can't just go busting in there before the sun's up." Elias was whispering fast and taut. For Kip it was off-putting; Doc liked the sound of himself and was normally given to stretching words. "Talk about suspicious. It would cast attention on our designs. Heading over there now? Heading over to check and see if Cox *happens* to be unconscious?"

"You're right, Doc. Getting back to your place is the ticket," Kip set himself into the proceedings for some calm. "Stick to the plan. When Rooker shows up to that jail and sees trouble, you'll be the first person he runs to. Best it looks like you've been cozy in bed all night."

"That was my original idea."

"Just saying it back to you," Kip answered with a lowered head and humble tone. With time pressing he wasn't for arguing. "Is my brother okay?"

Moreno almost flinched at the question. It was the first time the boy had ever talked to him. "Your brother's fine," he said with a cough. "Being made to look a fool will have him bucking to find me."

"We'll take care of that," Kip said, handing the reins of both horses to Loot. "Besides, there's not an able tracker in town besides Cox, and he's not going to be shoving his best foot forward."

"You're a good tracker," Doc Rufus said, peeking out the barn door. "So, you'll probably be called upon if they cobble a posse together. Need you back here fast. You're cutting this thing real close."

"We've got moving parts, sure enough. Best I make tracks and get back before anyone gets wise."

"Deception," Rufus said, holding Kip by the shoulders like sizing him up. "I've known you all your life. This worries me. You've never been able to lie about a goddamn thing."

"I'm better than you think when pressed," Laird answered, giving Moreno a steady look through the dim of the barn. "I'll hold up my end, seeing as I owe. Hope there's a talk and some answers at the end of it."

Moreno stayed silent and offered Rufus a loaded expression that he tried to hide from the boy. The fugitive's insides were tangled in knots. He didn't like Kip involved, didn't like binding and gagging Ben Laird's oldest. None of this would've happened if he'd just stayed clear of Thunder Hill. None of this would've happened if he'd been made normal and lived a normal life. "We need to set out," he said gruffly, filling the other horse's saddlebags with gear. It was a spirited gray colt previously owned by a church parishioner traveling for his trade. The Lairds were tending to it in the man's absence and most likely nobody would think to come asking after it. It was a chance they'd have to take. If all went well, the horse would be back soon enough to placate any inquiring minds.

The Laird's barn was behind the church; the last manmade structure in town before six miles of uninterrupted prairie. Rufus opened the backdoor and tipped his hat to Moreno. Before he could convey parting worries, Kip was tearing off into start of dawn on Pecos, striding proud toward the bottom of the foothills. It was an exuberant ride, and done for a reason. The tracks needed to be spread in a way that had the look of a man and horse making a wild run for it. That, and Kip needed to be back in town when news of the escape hit.

"Hope he knows what he's into," Loot said, trying to control the colt he was on. "Though I suppose that's impossible, considering what we've told."

"He's a good kid," Rufus whispered, tipping his hat again as if to say *get going*. "When things settle, you'll learn him the rest."

"Yeah," Moreno said, "I was thinking about that. Must be even in his dying sickness Ben thought it was time for the boy to know. Anyhow." The big outlaw tightened his massive legs around the body of the unfamiliar horse and urged him along, pulling the frisky animal around in the opposite direction of Laird and Pecos, back to his hideout in the mountains.

CHAPTER 14:
DIFFERENT IDEAS

THE SUN WAS RISING QUICKLY ABOVE THUNDER HILL, LESS than two hours from high noon. After their encounter with the bounty hunters, they'd put in a hard ride to get there before the hanging. They hadn't heard of the escape and were still planning on taking their own look at the prisoner.

"Place is a regular hive of activity," Sybille said, riding close to her father. She had her bandana up and hat pulled down to her brow. There wasn't but a little room to negotiate up the main thoroughfare and thickening dust made it hard to stick to a fixed line. Regular folk were coming in on wagons from local homesteads; dodgier types were trotting eager on horses from parts unknown. Many had descended for the entertainment of a hanging, the surrounding atmosphere of activity and excitement, or maybe to see (like them) if the person destined for the noose was really Loot Moreno. Clearly, the telegraph she heard mentioned in Boyd City had made the rounds. Judging by the turnout, Sybille guessed those little dots and dashes had spread to every corner of the territory.

They dodged a rusty wagon of farmers and passed by groups of drunks talking loud by the gallows. Sybille whiffed the fresh lumber, even with all the shit and stink associated with a crowded little town like Thunder Hill. Based on the number of buildings lining the street, she guessed that maybe three hundred people lived there regular. Maybe another hundred on the surrounding farms and ranches. Today the place was glutted with twice that.

"I'm going to get a drink," her father said, barely loud enough to hear. "Find somewhere to hitch the horses and meet me over at the saloon."

He dismounted and handed her his reins without a look. They hadn't exchanged words since the "ceremony" out on the trail. She'd say something and he'd look ahead and keep riding, or he'd bark a few syllables and want it left there. Sybille watched him walking through the bustle of the road to the saloon, making everything and everyone deviate from his path. He hadn't had a drink in years; she didn't know how to feel about it. They had business to take care of. He was surely different. Maybe forever different. She reminded herself once again that this was her desire: the chance to see her father as he was in the days of his prime, to be part of the legend. She shook her head and brought the horses to a hitching post with some spare space just ahead, trying not to think so much. It'd been a long, turbulent night. *I just need a wash and a drink. Need to kill Moreno. Might be, that sorts Pa right out. He'll be Dan Clayton again, old skins shed.*

After hitching the horses, Sybille noticed a figure trudging up through the alley toward the street. She patted her horse and sharpened her eyes for a better look. He was young, maybe a hair older than her, but it seemed like he'd been through the ringer. He wasn't heeled and didn't carry himself like the sort that would be. Indeed, he was the opposite of menacing. Still, something was off. She couldn't quite figure it. He was coming right for her with his head down, sweat dripping from shaggy brown hair.

"You okay there?" she asked, but he didn't catch it. The clamor of the town conspired against his hearing. She started to ask again as he pulled himself up onto the boardwalk, but the chance was averted by a girl tarted up whore-like with crimson lips and red hair who seemed to appear out of nowhere. The look on his handsome face was apprehensive at best. They were having it out smack dab in front of the general store. An aproned oily fat man came charging on the scene and stuck his finger in the face of the sweaty one. Sybille looked up. Grimes General Store. *Bet that's Mr. Grimes. Probably not too happy having a love quarrel on the precipice. Hanging days were good for business.*

Sybille knew she was staring and didn't exactly know what had her captured. She thought the stranger was pleasant to the sight and strong-jawed, but she'd seen plenty of those types on her travels. Something else. Like he wasn't going through the motions. He had some tough meat on his plate.

Maybe she was just watching normal life, and normal was suddenly all the more fascinating set against what she'd recently experienced. The night had taken and added things to who she was before. It was still for sorting out. *I need a drink worse than I thought.*

* * *

"I'm sorry, Mr. Grimes." Kip couldn't afford this hitch. The day was far from done and Grimes and Lindy weren't giving him time enough to pray for patience.

"Customers, Kip. This is a big day. Now with no hanging, nothing going but the festivities, you might as well put the noose around my neck, interrupting traffic. You know how Mrs. Grimes gets."

"You're right. We're moving. I sincerely apologize, Mr. Grimes."

Only mumbles as his landlord scuffled back inside. Kip pulled out his shirt from the waist of his pants and used the lower portion to wipe his face. He was looking over Lindy's hatted head at the trough just below the boardwalk, wondering if the pretty cowgirl standing next to it would take offense if he dunked his head in.

"You gonna answer me?" Lindy asked, snapping her little fingers relentlessly. "What is going on with you?"

"Nothing. Chopping wood out back."

"Did you cut down a forest? Something's not right. You're not being all the way honest."

Nope. And she couldn't imagine the secrets. The hard ride on Pecos through the fledgling light, six miles at close to full tilt. He knew the terrain, but that didn't mean it wasn't a dangerous sprint, uneven most of the time. Hitching Pecos up secure behind Miller's abandoned cabin in the lower foothills. Dragging Miller's old canoe into the river and getting downstream without being tossed by the whitewater or dashed into a rock. Hiding the canoe where it would take a miracle to find. The dang thing weighed a ton, even for Kip's strong back. And then, running the soles off his father's cavalry boots back to town. Blisters on his feet or maybe just skin rubbed all the way to the bone. He was afraid to check. Not your average five or six hours, *Lindy*.

"I've been chopping wood," he said again, slowing his breath to confront life at normal speed. "And you can't come doing this in the middle of the day." He knew he had to be delicate; he couldn't say the truth whole, that their little sinful adventure was over. That'd only do to set her off, make a spectacle, and confirm beyond all doubt whatever suspicions Lindy's fiancé might've been harboring since her and Kip started carrying on. "I was chopping wood as a way to relax."

"What's that supposed to mean? Relax?"

He looked softly into her sharpened eyes and tried to forget that he was lying, imagining that was the way of top liars. "Doc Rufus recommended it. Ever since my father passed, I've been all out of sorts. That's pretty obvious."

She nodded but didn't speak. Okay. Progress.

"So, Doc told me that serious physical exertion could conquer this rotten feeling I've been having. I'm not sure if it's the melancholia or just part of normal grieving, but it seems like it's working."

"Make yourself so tired you don't have time to be sad. That kinda thing?"

"Nothing gets by you."

She was all smiles now. He could see almost every tooth while she turned her shoulders back and forth. "I know something else like that. Physical exertions to your heart's desire. All the sweating you can handle, beautiful."

"I promise we can talk about it later. Got a few things today."

"Always walking away."

"Okay. You have a good one, Lindy."

What is she doing, out here in the open? If I don't get killed for this prison break, I'm gonna wind up with a bullet in the head from Lindy's betrothed. Seems she's determined to witness my demise.

Now with a little separation, he was relatively confident that he'd talked himself gone. "Can you believe it?" Lindy called, causing him to wheel around.

"Believe what?"

"Brandon Calhoun."

"Who?"

"The prisoner. Escaping and all?"

"Oh yeah," Kip said, hands nervous in his pockets. "Quite a situation."

"*Quite a situation*, he says." A flutter of eyelashes. "You're too much."

As Lindy finally shuffled off, he exhaled a measure of tension and shook out his hands. Walking the other way, he tipped his hat and showed a little smile and light look of relief to the cowgirl.

"Busy day," Sybille said.

Kip took more notice of her winning appearance, noting her figure and the gun belt that she wore low. Not the look of a prop; it was suited for her size and the leather holster had seen a run of days. Their green eyes met as he held out his sweat-stained shirt, highlighting his ragged state as confirmation of her observation. "Busy day. You hit it on the head, ma'am."

He thought nothing more of it. Sybille didn't know what to think.

* * *

"You're with the U.S. Marshals, I guess," Bart Trussel said. He was a thin man with a pocked face and a head too bald and wrinkled for his age. Trussel wasn't much more than thirty; the saloon had come into his possession after the early death of his father. He spent as little time as possible in Thunder Hill, but here he was, in town for a hanging that wasn't going to happen. Just his luck. "Marshal's a mighty big deal around these parts," Trussel added. He was behind the bar helping Joey with the overflow, mostly drinking, trying to get through the banality of another day wasted in the middle of nowhere. "You don't say much, do you? Wish the rest of this bunch were so well-mannered. Group of no-goods and profligates, I reckon. The rest, dumber than rocks. A few of these here already went out looking for Calhoun. They couldn't track a damn elephant through snow. They're already back, begging for drinks and free turns with the girls like they've forged out in the name of duty. You believe that? A pathetic gaggle, I'd say. Drunks, obviously. Guess I shouldn't complain about that part." Trussel pulled a dusty bottle from underneath the bar and poured himself a day's dose of murky whisky. "Well, best I keep watch on Joey here. He's studying to be a half-wit and ain't making much progress."

While the saloon owner was talking, Dan Clayton had been thinking. He didn't want the last two decades of being Holt Fallstead getting in the way of his original self. The false skin was shedding but he needed to save a little for what was to follow.

Clayton wasn't surprised to hear about the escaped prisoner. If it was Moreno, not surprised at all. *Remember. Be everywhere. See everything.* "I'm *Deputy* U.S. Marshal Holt Fallstead," he said, pointing down to his empty shot glass before Trussel could walk away. "Not a U.S. Marshal."

Trussel pulled up an eyebrow while he poured his customer a drink that spilled over the sides. "Sorry about that."

"Never mind it."

"So, when I think of a marshal—"

"Likely you're thinking of someone like me. Deputy Marshals."

"How'd you come by that type work?" Trussel asked. He was close to yelling over the soused shopkeepers and sodbusters talking themselves up in the idling day.

"My gun to this or that cattleman or railroad tycoon till I got to where I had the measure of most. Working for the law's not much change. Steadier for my daughter."

"Oh. You've got a family."

"I've got a daughter."

"Huh," Trussel said, having one more shot.

Clayton was already thinking slower and talking faster. It'd been years since the bottle. The insecurity riled him. "Keep my business to yourself," he said, squeezing Trussel's arm and trying to blink away some of the haze starting to form over his eyes. "Me being a lawman, I don't like people knowing too much. Probably shouldn't have said anything."

"Sure," Trussel said, wresting free from the grasp to see a fresh group coming through the swinging doors. The crowd was growing by the second, men pushing into Clayton's back trying to get an order in. They were talking over each other and about the same thing. Clayton couldn't make out more than *he's coming* and *Cox* and *I need a drink*.

The whole room seemed to swing around at once. Clayton finished his shot and slapped a thick coin on the bar, not knowing the price of five whiskies and not caring all that much about collecting change. He was angry at everything. Not knowing how to drink anymore. The useless men cluttering up the saloon, pretending their lives weren't absent meaning. He wanted to kill one of them or all of them on the chance he'd feel better. So he could get back to seeing everything and being everywhere.

"Gentleman." The newly arrived speaker had a reserved voice and he wasn't attempting to overpower the din of the saloon. Eventually all was quiet and he proceeded evenly: "I don't need to tell you that in the wee hours I made an ass of myself. Got too close to a snake and took a few bites for my trouble. Had this fella pegged for one of them pining for the after-life. He lulled me careless, and I made a ridiculous mistake. I know some of you have already been out looking for this man, and I'm going to strongly advise against it. He's dangerous and he won't be trading words but bullets. I've picked some men and we're heading after him now. His horse has a dis-tinct shoe and we found a trail leading away from the edge of town toward the foothills. Figure he'll try to lose us up there, but he can't have much in the way of food. Between that and the bum of his leg, we'll catch him."

"Sheriff," Trussel said, waving at Cox as he stood on a little stool behind the bar. "When you get a second."

Cox nodded at the barman and clapped his hands together. "All right then, boys. Do like I said and leave this one to me. Be about your business."

After the sheriff pushed through to the bar, Trussel had a bright idea hanging off his lips. "You should add another to your group," he whispered. "This here's a marsh—deputy marshal. Deputy Marshal Fallstead."

Whatever the topic, Cox wasn't much for expanding on it surrounded by a hundred drunks with fretting trigger fingers and delusions of catching outlaws. He looked at the barman as something to tolerate and then nod-ded for the marshal to follow him outside, across to the jailhouse porch.

"You any good?" Sheriff Cox asked, wincing from the sunlight and the lingering headache. He took visual inventory of the marshal after his eyes adjusted. A humorless face, heeled with a heavy rig that seemed a fit for his thick arms and shoulders. He appeared to be well-traveled. Lined skin and a red-gray beard, weeks from a trim. "Your name's Fallstead?"

"That's right."

Heads were turning toward their way from the street, wondering who was important enough to occupy Cox's attention *now*. It was starting to wear on Clayton. "I was passing through, but I'll offer a hand."

"Do much tracking?"

"That's the job," Clayton said, trying not to sound irritated. "What's his name? Brandon Calhoun?"

The sheriff didn't know if he heard doubt in Fallstead's voice or if the man was simply ill-mannered. He wouldn't react either way. "That's right. Calhoun. Saddle up and meet us down by the livery. The town will compensate time and provisions. Be outfitted in a half hour, ready to ride for it."

"Seems strange you waited this long."

"I don't have a big mouth so maybe you didn't hear. I got cracked good and hard. It shouldn't matter. Nobody knows these parts better than me and another man we'll have with us."

"Okay, Sheriff."

Clayton tipped his hat to Cox and strained his gray eyes at a young man who looked to be meeting them on the jailhouse steps, hungry about some business. "Amos," the young man said, "how are we doi—"

"Kip Laird," Sheriff Cox interjected. "Marshal Fallstead, this is the fella who runs the church down there end of the way."

"Howdy," Kip said, stumbling a bit as he slowed his bearing. He extended a dirty, sweaty hand toward the new arrival. "I'm very pleased to meet you."

"The town holy man, then?"

"Far from it. All fall short of the Glory, but I don't know need to tell you that."

"Not sure I take your meaning."

"I just meant, facing criminals and all … I didn't mean any offense." Kip was fumbling. The marshal didn't seem to have any give. Social awkwardness was something he seemed fine sitting in.

Cox didn't like the tone or where the exchange might lead, so he decided to nip it. "Point is, Fallstead, this here's my other good tracker. Let's get squared away and hitting the trail before losing the day."

"Reverend," the deputy marshal said, walking away into the road like he'd been waiting his whole life to get free of the conversation.

"Kip's fine," the preacher rejoined, not sure if he was heard.

Cox slapped Laird on the shoulder and immediately wiped his hand on his pants. "Damn, kid. You're sweating bullets. Everything okay?"

"Good as it can be, I reckon. What's with this marshal?"

Cox waited for a group of local wives to pass by before answering. "It's a complication not welcome. That man smells bloody. Refusing his services, though," Cox stopped and rubbed the sunken bridge of his nose. It seemed he'd be content in never speaking again. "Refusing, that might've been taken for strange in front of all the men back there. Damned Trussel. Never had a word with him didn't end in aggravation."

"We'll work around it."

"Try to keep shut on the trail, especially until we know what sort we're dealing with."

"Fella seems sorta brusque," Kip said, putting his hands on his hips. He realized he was still breathing hard from the morning's activities. The sheriff and preacher watched the marshal walk down the busy street with a sort of mechanical indifference until he stopped and fixed his attention toward the useless gallows.

"Yeah. You won't let that bother *you*, though, being about second chances and forgiveness."

"I try to be, Sheriff."

"I guess." Cox spit a stream of tobacco juice ahead of their steps and lightly touched his pounding head.

"Doc get that mended up?" Kip asked. He was using his height to inspect the wound.

"I'll be fine. Get yourself cleaned a little and sorted. Looking like stepped on shit. Smell like it too."

"It was a long morning."

Cox wasn't for more back and forth. "The path we've chosen," he said, scratching near the missing portion of his ear. "Let's play out the charade, hope we don't get found out for the pack of lying coyotes we are."

CHAPTER 15:

OBLIGATIONS

LOOT TUGGED THE REIGNS AND PULLED A SPYGLASS FROM his saddlebag. He'd won the instrument playing cards with a merchant seaman a few decades back. It didn't open and close so well, but the parts that mattered still worked. *Sorta like me.*

Nobody seemed to be coming up after him in Durington Valley. A group of three riders looked to be down in the rock creek five or six miles back, but they were chasing their own tails. Moreno had taken his horse through enough water and over enough crags to make picking up a trail difficult for anyone without the Eye. He let out a hefty sigh of relief and closed the stiff spyglass with some cajoling. Feeling his leg he grunted, still in pain from the bullet wound. The gray colt was proving a fine horse, but he was a harder ride than Pecos. Something difficult putting words to. Their rhythm was off and would be until one day it would click. Loot figured by then, he'd have old Pecos back. Hoped, anyway.

"Let's go, Rocco." Loot had taken to calling the colt Rocco on account of his color, similar to the granite rocks that stuck out of his mountain back home. At their present pace they'd reach the hideout sometime after midnight.

Dodging the hangman and a fast horse could prompt a man to a good clip.

Loot clicked to speed the horse and flipped the reins, clenching his massive legs against Rocco's heaving sides. "Let's get moving, little brother."

The hill trails got rougher as they ascended, the woods thicker. Extra cover from the trees was a tradeoff that sat well with Moreno. For an added layer of careful, every so often he'd circle back and ride off the trail, just in case anyone was lucky enough to pick up his tracks. It wasn't wise to be optimistic, but after a few checks he couldn't help it. He'd been a bad man for a long time, dodged jams that would make most men fold. Having help made being on the run pretty simple: they go one way, I go the other.

After another steady half hour of trotting over uneven ground, he gave the reins a pull. "Little stream up ahead, Rocco. We'll get you a drink and then push on." Loot knew the horse needed a break from carrying his big body. He'd hazard a stop. Respite would prove a wise investment for the colt down the road, even it was just a few minutes. A look at the sun told him it was getting to be about five in the afternoon. He hadn't slept decent in days, and the years sat awful heavy on his shoulders. *No.* Sitting down might tend you toward sleep. *Don't you think about it.*

"Here we go, Rocco," he said, coming to a sunken piece of ground running along the stream. Felled trees made it a spot with decent cover. Loot tied off the colt and gave him enough slack to slurp up the cool runoff until he had his fill. After dunking his own canteen in the brook, Moreno had a long drink and fell back into the soft high grass near the water. "Get it while you can, boy," he told the horse, washing his face to keep his eyes from slouching. Fatigue was crashing over him. He didn't know it, but the wound under his chaps had opened slightly, causing a slow and steady bleed. Combined with the perpetual motion of the escape and the exhaustive nature of the preceding days, even the robust Loot Moreno was struggling against the inevitabilities of human weakness. He looked up at the sun again. *Oh yeah. Five. Five. Maybe just five minutes. Five minutes sleep and then home free.* His calloused thumb traced the circle on the back of his other hand, over and over through his glove. Between each circle he'd run his thumb straight across the two straight lines. Old habits. *Five* minutes. The usual memory cloud of gunfights and blood, powerful sins and powerful penances didn't stall him from drifting off; the cloud would still be there, waiting on the other side of consciousness.

* * *

"Does this make any sense to you?" asked Thunder Hill Deputy Elbert Rooker. He was patting idle Pecos roughly between the ears. The quarter horse was tied to a porch support of Lem Miller's old cabin, trough right under him for the reaching. "I got it," Rooker said, snapping his fingers so the others might enjoy every aspect of his process. "Calhoun's close. Just went out to kill him some rats and squirrels over there in them woods. That's what those Indian savage sons of bitches do. Rodents like rodents."

They'd already surrounded the cabin and investigated enough to conclude it was empty. The messy trail left by Kip led straight to it. They fiddled around, Cox and Kip, acting like it was work but not too much work to find Pecos's tracks. Fallstead's presence made the game more difficult than either of them liked. Playing an unfamiliar opponent was frustrating at best and impossible at worst. Sort of a shot in the dark. There were six in the party. Fallstead, Cox, Rooker, Kip, and two other reliable men from Thunder Hill with military experience and a fair amount of time spent with weapons in their hands.

"What do you think, Kip?" Elbert asked. "What might your daddy contemplate after seeing this situation?"

Rooker was throwing an insult at him, insinuating that his skills at tracking were only what they were because of his managed upbringing. Kip wasn't insulted. He felt sorry for ER, always a step or two behind, but especially now. They were following a trail of breadcrumbs he'd left himself, after all. Rooker was patting a horse Kip had been atop earlier that day. And even with all his present handicaps, parceling out grace to the deputy made for hard duty; Rooker was incompetent and had a streak of mean born from insecurity that did him no credit at all.

"Do you really think that?" the preacher asked the deputy with uncharacteristic bite in his tone. They were out in front of the cabin and had a little bit of privacy. The others were holding position around the sides and back of Miller's derelict little structure.

Rooker was honestly confused. He'd said a lot. Kip would need to work on being more specific. "Think what?"

"That Indians are rodents."

"Sure," Rooker said, scratching some dirt from his fancy pinstriped suit. Dapper and wanting to show it, even in the middle of nowhere, surrounded by a cast of men. "You've seen what they do. How many people you know been killed by them? They don't go for things righteous. Demons, them."

"What are you talking about?" Kip asked, now fully confused. Cox was walking over with something to say, but he was still intent on trying to nail down some kind of answer from Elbert.

"You being a junior cloth man, I guess you don't ponder the darker side of things so much."

"You might be surprised."

Rooker stood up as proud as he could next to Kip's size. "When you're facing down the business end of a gun and a bad man wielding with designs, your mind goes places."

Elbert was maybe a year or two older than Kip. Laird knew for a fact that he was repeating something he overheard or read. Rooker had never seen a scrap where iron played in. "Never mind the darkness, ER. You didn't answer the question about rodents." Kip was ready to settle for a modicum of honesty and move on.

"I don't know, Preach. No, they ain't rodents, technically. Though there's a bit of something nasty and unwanted like that in every person, I reckon."

"You're touching it with a needle there," Kip said, giving Rooker a light jab on the shoulder as the sheriff arrived. It was a moment that he'd try to remember: witnessing a spark of open reflection from a person full of prejudice and undeserved self-regard. A moment to add to his limited experience as a "junior cloth man."

"There's drag marks going down to the river," Fallstead said, appearing suddenly with short, angry steps. "Did this Miller have some sort of boat?"

"Oh yeah," Rooker interjected. "Pretty sure it was in cobwebs, but it might've still floated."

"That's most likely what he did then," Cox said, trying to behave like he would in any other search party. "Took to the river. Damn."

"Where's it go?" Fallstead asked.

"It links up with another tributary about two miles down, and then it'll take you all the way into Big Rapids, edge of the territory," Kip said. It made him feel better to offer actual facts, even if they were meant for deception.

"There's a train station there," Cox said. "Pretty busy one. Guess we should hightail it thata way."

"He's not using trains," the marshal said, walking away. He mounted his horse looking ready and raring. "This one doesn't use trains." Fallstead seemed raw not to have found a fight.

"You sure?" Cox asked, having to call out pretty loud with the marshal moving so quick. "Almost sounds like you know this Calhoun."

"I'm heading back to town, Sheriff Cox. Meet up with my daughter. And we both know this chase ain't for Brandon Calhoun."

Deputy Marshal Holt Fallstead kicked his horse, leaving a thick cloud of dust in the faces of Kip and Cox. It was the perfect indignity to compliment the feeling the lawman had left them with. Fallstead carried himself curt throughout the search, but it wasn't churlishness or pettiness without purpose. There seemed to be a weight to his sideways reactions and stony eyes. Kip and Cox were wobbling as he rode off, beset by the complication to their plans.

"Can you believe that dude?" Rooker chimed. "Who in the devil's damned does he think we're chasing?"

* * *

Loot was bleeding and tired down to his bones. The few stops afforded were on account of his passenger. The little one didn't cry all that much, except when it stormed. Moreno would hunch over as they rode along, shielding the boy's face with the wide brim of his hat. In good weather, Kip kept hushed. That's what Loot was calling him. Seemed as decent a name as any, and whatever the boy was trying to say, it sounded like *Kip*. He'd been reluctant to name him at all, figuring the child wasn't long for the world. Day after day, though, little Kip endured the haphazard care of a brute that most men would run away from on sight.

It was luck, more than anything. A whole lot younger and the boy would've died from a lack of mother's milk. Luckily, he drank whatever Moreno gave him. Even ate mushed beans. It was one less thing to worry about, and Loot needed any break that happened his way. Dan Clayton and his gang didn't have a quitting streak; they'd ride him down until he either faced them square or figured out something clever. Whatever the play, the kid couldn't be part of it.

Moreno reckoned he was at least three hundred miles from the farm where he'd taken the boy. Rescued, saved, stole. Anyone with a mind to have an opinion might find something different to say on the subject, but it wasn't of consequence. Not now. Not when they were just trying to survive.

Early in the day he came to a clearing on a hill that offered a decent view of a valley. It looked like the sort of place he'd want to end up. The kind of place where a baby could get a fresh shot at things. The sun threw its light upon a little town six or seven miles down in the flats; Moreno bobbed the little boy in his aching arm and said, "There you go, fella. See that burg yonder way? I'm betting they'd love to have a gent such as yourself."

Kip.

"Yeah? No. Not me. Me, they'd shoot down quick as a blinking."

Kip was chubby and had green eyes that barely wandered, always wide with wonder. Loot didn't plan on forming an attachment with a babbling kid, but the prospect of leaving him behind made him soft as he'd felt since forever. "We'll head on in after dark. You'll get some proper help and seeing to."

Moreno made good on his promise. After midnight, he carried the boy up the steps of the church at the edge of town. It looked well-built and new. The smell of fresh paint still lingered on the air. Loot reckoned it was a recently-formed town. They were pretty far north in the territory. About as far west as civilization had dared planting roots.

"Who are you?" The question was whispered and came out of the dark to Loot's left. He suddenly realized he'd been standing there holding Kip for more than a few minutes. *Do I run? I'm nursing a bullet wound and a gash thanks to a Bowie knife. Ain't running anywhere. How'd that go? I set the kid down and just take off?*

His first instinct had been to draw his weapon and fire in the direction of the voice, but that softness was working on his harder edges. It was a good thing too, now that he was seeing the situation play in his head; a gunshot ringing through the dead of night would have the whole town quick up his ass. He didn't feel like answering the questions of an entire population of pioneer heads and hands. He'd try to keep it one-on-one.

"Who the hell are you?" Loot asked, clutching the sleeping boy tighter to his chest, underneath the sheepskin of his long coat.

"My name's Ben Laird. That's my house right behind me, and those steps you're standing on are attached to my church."

"This is your church?"

"That's right."

"You don't look like a preacher," Loot said, saying exactly what was on his mind, trying to figure out how many lies he needed to tell and how they needed telling.

"What's a preacher look like?" Ben Laird was about ten feet from Moreno, holding a lantern out in the dark and squinting to get a better view of Loot and his young charge.

"Not sure. Figure preachers on being old. Scrawny types."

"Some are. But old scrawny types don't pass for fit in this part of the country."

"Guess there's some sense in that, Preacher Laird. You got a gun down the back of your trousers?"

"No gun. No weapons. What's his name?" Ben asked.

"He seems to like Kip. But I'm not sure what his parents stamped him."

"You were just going to leave him?"

"Figured as much."

"Usually it's babies."

"What?"

"People leave babies. They say, anyhow. That fella looks a little old for the practice."

"Well, I can set him anywhere. He sleeps like a rock. Thunder makes him fretful as a nightmare, but other than that, he's a good boy. Made sense, a nice town, nice church, someone would take the reins."

"You've got a lot of faith."

"No. Made sense is what I said. Faith don't figure in. Done with that." He thought of the mark on his hand, wanting to scrape it off and erase his memory of anything mystical.

Ben Laird didn't know what needed saying. He'd never come across a bloody giant holding a tiny child he wanted rid of.

"You're hurt."

"Yep. I've been in better ways."

Ben didn't want to stand out in the open for the whole town's notice. He had to make some judgments on the quick and pray they'd be wise. The stranger looked menacing, but he didn't *seem* it. The way he was holding the boy, probably, but something else. A sadness behind those dark eyes. Ben wasn't afraid, but he figured not to take it all on faith. Like the man said, sense needed to have its day. "How about I put you up in the barn back behind my place there?"

"Put me up how?"

"It ain't gonna be fancy. But there's hay enough to fashion you something to lay on. Looks like you need attending."

"You got a doctor?"

"That's what I'm driving at. He's my closest friend. Your luck, a surgeon in the War. Lives three minutes' walk down there. Looking at it I can see you ain't dying quick from those wounds, but they'll kill you eventually."

"You an army man too, Preacher Laird?"

"I was. Same outfit as the doctor. And we won't tell anybody."

Loot didn't think to answer the last part. He wasn't for trusting. Not yet, anyway. "Kid stays with me. Show me the barn."

Ten minutes later Doc Rufus and Ben returned to the Laird's barn. Loot was nodding off on a barrel of straw, Kip curled up against his left side. As the door creaked open, Moreno snapped up and drew his pistol in the direction of the sound. His vision was cloudy. He'd let the preacher's cordiality get the better of him. "Stay still," he said, waiting for his view to clear.

"We're not moving. No trouble, mister. Just brought the doc, sure as I promised."

"Name's Rufus. Doctor Elias Rufus. You'll find my treatments more efficacious if you refrain from pulling that goddamn trigger."

Loot slowly lowered his revolver and checked on Kip. The boy had barely moved an inch. "Best you get on with it, then."

The doctor and the preacher walked across the barn and over to the stack of hay where Moreno had positioned himself. It was fairly well lit, three lanterns in a small space. Loot remained seated casting judgments at the two young men standing over him; they seemed like brothers, except for the doctor's bushy mustache. It made him look older than the preacher, but Loot suspected that was mostly illusion. They were tall and straight, thick enough to survive a war and drag their asses out to the middle of nowhere as a reward for time served. They probably believed themselves hard men. According to the normal ways of the world, could be they were. His world would've chewed them up in two shakes, though, and there was no way to make that clear short of shooting them down and letting them die slow and painful. He issued a sad laugh, recalling the men he'd run with. The kind that would take help and good nature and offer suffering and horror as payment. Monsters. These boys didn't know shit-all about monsters and the darkness that drove them. *I was the worst one of the bunch. What? And now I'm different? Rescue one little runt and all is well?*

"I'm thinking we come to a resolution," the doctor said, setting down a hefty leather bag and crossing his rugged arms. He peered at the gun and the mark on the hand holding it. "I've seen that symbol."

"Elias," Ben interrupted. Earlier he'd seen the mark on the stranger's hand and formed a few conclusions behind it. All the more reason to go easy.

"Look," Rufus continued, "I'm inclined to patch you up, under the auspices of Hippocrates and all."

"Talk simple," Loot grunted. "Haven't spent my years around fancy folks."

The young doctor made an assessment of Moreno's clothes. Everything but his shirt and boots appeared handmade. "I imagine you haven't, which is why we're pressing to disarm. Call it a trade, weapons for healing. I don't see a better offer coming your way, rube."

Ben took a step back and measured the faces of his friend and the wanderer. The request was reasonable, but they didn't know the sort they were dealing with. Didn't even know his name or how he'd come to this unlikely pass. Though with that mark, one could *suspect*.

Moreno looked up at the doctor and then at the gun in his hand. He was starting to drift again. The journey and the wounds were catching up. Maybe it was the roof over his head, the best shelter he'd seen since breaking from the Three-in-One. The man he'd always been wasn't the sort to give over to propositions, but he was running from that man, maybe even more than Dan Clayton and the remnants of his gang. He set down the revolver in the hay by his feet and pulled the blade from his belt, placing it deliberately next to the gun. "I want the boy looked after. If I die, I want the boy looked after. There's men could be coming out there. Coming. They're coming. If I die... obligations..."

It was all he'd manage before losing consciousness. Laird the nurturer and Rufus the dictator tended to him that night and kept him convalescing and secreted for the next few days. The preacher vowed to take Kip into his home and the doctor promised to store the secret, save one young deputy in town. The night before Loot was set to leave, Amos Cox came into the barn alongside Elias and Ben. "I'm the best in these parts with a gun," he told Moreno. "Sheriff Taylor's used up, put to pasture after the end of the month. Job's gonna fall to me."

"Good with a gun ain't enough. Not if Dan Clayton comes around here and catches any scent I passed through."

"I'm good enough to know that," Cox said. He didn't have a big personality one way or another like Rufus or Laird, far as Loot could tell. Typical lawman, siding on keeping things under his hat.

"You don't know what good enough is. None of you do."

Cox didn't blink. Didn't move a muscle. "Why I want you gone a distance. Your trouble goes with you."

The answer seemed thoughtful, enough to settle Moreno. "Fair enough."

"Will you go after him, now the boy is safe?" Cox asked.

"I'm not sure I'd win. Clayton's fast as they come, and he loved our leader like god and a father wrapped in one."

"That's not what I asked," Cox said, squinting and careful in his expression and posture.

"No," Loot said. "Figure this far out in the hills, a man not looking for trouble might actually find some peace. I'm done fighting. Unless I'm backed in, I'm done. Got me nightmares enough to last a million lifetimes."

Ben approached and shook the recovering outlaw's massive hand, doing his best to match the squeeze. "I hope you find your peace, Loot. Maybe it's a long way up out of the dark, but you can do it. All of us are reaching up for the light one way or another."

"Pretty thick, Laird. You're talking to a killer. Killed most of my gang bloody with a blade." He wouldn't go into more details. It was half a fog already. Loot didn't want to think deeply about cutting down his former riding companions, much as they deserved it.

"We've all killed," said the preacher, nodding at each man in the barn. "So don't think you've got the patent on regrets."

It was getting late. Amos signaled simple farewells to Moreno. The dapper doc offered a fancy grin and a *so long, rube.*

Moreno set himself to sleeping that last night feeling stronger in body but fitful all the same. He worried about the boy, worried that these young men couldn't hold down his secret.

Ben returned a little later and prayed over Loot, believing the outlaw unconscious. It must've lasted thirty minutes. Repeating the same thing over and over. Moreno didn't move. He didn't know if the churchman's words would have any effect, but he let them be said. Maybe to make the preacher feel better. Maybe to make himself feel better. He couldn't say.

Ben's prayer: *God, watch over this man. Whatever his past transgressions, you led him here to us. Let his spirit find peace and forgive him his evil deeds. We that keep this secret have killed and wronged our fellow man. We have all transgressed. Deliver us from our sinful ways and make us upright, that we may watch over this child and allow him to become a good and righteous servant. We thank you Lord. Inscrutable as You might be to us, You continue to bless us. We are humbled by the gift of this innocent. Let us know the time for bravery, the time to act, and the time to hold fast our spirits and our tongues. God, watch over this man. Whatever his past transgressions...*

* * *

"Wake up, mister. Wake up."

Loot smacked his dry lips and opened his eyes. A flaxen-haired little girl in a tan calico dress was standing over him. She wasn't much taller than the grass he'd been sleeping in. *How long have I been down?* He looked at the sky while she tugged on his sleeve. Near seven. The sun was beginning to hide behind the mountains in the west, coloring the sky a soft orange.

"What are you about, girl?" he grumbled, sitting up now and looking over his shoulder. He couldn't see anything in the trees. Nothing in front but the girl and the brook. "Where'd you come from?"

She started jumping from foot to foot, pointing back through the trees to the trail. "My mama and papa are over there. We've got two mules. *Two* mules. I named them Charlie and Gravy. A wagon too."

He pulled his hair back and tied it off. "Y'all come up here with a wagon? This trail's hardly good for that." Moreno was talking to himself more than the girl. He stood up and squinted in the failing light. "Don't see a damn thing. Where are your people? What the hell you doing straying this far off the trail by yourself?"

"Isabel! Where are you! Isabel!" A woman emerged from the trees. She had yellow hair like the little one. Pretty and pale with splotches of red in her cheeks. They were the same person, twenty years apart. Moreno had the ridiculous thought to hide, but he was beat to the punch by Isabel. The girl shuffled behind his legs in a playful attempt at cover. "That's my momma," she whispered. "She's hot mad I think."

"She ain't the only one, kid." Loot gave her little head a slight pat. Not her fault. His old ass, falling asleep during a damn escape. Damned ridiculous.

The woman stopped cold at the sight of Moreno, eyes like she'd stumbled over a grizzly. She was trying to speak but failing. The power to make sound had been ripped from her body right then and there by one of nature's menacing creations.

"Where's the fool?" Loot asked, smacking his hands together in an effort to release the woman from her stupor.

"Sorry?" she said, tilting her head to see her daughter still clinging to the back of Moreno's legs.

"The fool. The idiot. The stupid son of a bitch that brought a young woman and a sprout up this trail. It ain't made for slow moving wagons. Can't believe you even made it this far."

"Izzy! Laura! Where y'all at now! We got to set camp before it gets too dark!"

"Here he comes," Loot said. He looked down and whispered to the girl, "What's your pa's name?"

"Day-yule."

Dale came out of the trees holding a single-shot rifle giving over to rust. He was scrawny and too long in the limbs for his clothes. Looked like he'd seen maybe a score of summers plus five. "W-who are you?"

Loot didn't acknowledge the young father's question. He turned around once more. "Isabel, go over there to your ma. She ain't gonna be mad."

"Promise?"

"I promise, kid. Now go on."

"We're not looking for trouble," Dale said, trembling as he sidled up to his wife and daughter.

"No talking," Loot commanded, wiping his eyes. "Not yet. And don't none of you move, either."

"But. Sir."

"Dale, do as your told. I've got thinking to do. First, I'm going to splash some of this brook water on my face. Stay right there."

Loot moved casually and did like he said, turning his muscled back to the young family. He dropped to his knees and had a drink before waking himself up with a few scoops to the cheeks and eyes. Wiping the wet through his hair, he returned to his original spot. "Come here, Dale," Loot said, setting his hands on his hips.

"But—"

"You're not to be talking yet, Dale. I was clear as day on that."

Dale took in the sight of his pretty wife and daughter and swallowed audibly, like the twenty feet over to Loot was akin to walking the plank.

"Come on. As you said to your family, we're losing the light."

The family man shivered as he came over. Loot wrapped a heavy arm around his slight, shaking shoulders. "Y'all can stay or go, makes no matter," Moreno said to Laura and Isabel.

"Oh God," Dale cried, shrinking against Loot's body.

Loot rolled his eyes. "You ain't—damn jackass. Know what Laura," he said, looking up, "probably better you just give us a second to settle on a few things."

Laura snapped up the child and rushed out of sight, back in the direction of the trail.

Loot kept his arm clenched around Dale and led him down the easy bank of the stream. "Is this where you were thinking about camping for the night?"

Nothing.

"You can talk now, Dale. And stand up straight. Come on, kid."

"We heard the water. It's been a hard few days on the road, so I figured it was worth coming over for a look."

"A good idea, but ironic."

"Ironic?"

"I'm not a man that uses sideways words, but I've got this old friend; he's a writer. Ten-dollar words when five cents works the same. He gives me books sometimes when he visits. Big books. Words like *ironic*."

"I don't understand."

"I'm trying to make it so you do," Loot said, pushing the hunched-over body of Dale away to a decent remove. "Look me square, son."

"Just don't hurt them. We don't have anything."

Loot shook his head. "You got a leather strap around my nuts. That's what you have."

"What do you mean?" Dale could add confusion to his terror.

"Betting you're heading out to settle near one of the northwest towns."

"Yes sir. We're on our way to a place called Thunder Hill. It's a burg on the rise, they say. Apprenticing. My dad's brother is a blacksmith there."

"Big plans."

"Yes sir. Set out from Missouri a few months ago and back near Red Oaks a fella said there'd be some hill trails that would take us that way a lot quicker."

"A fella near Red Oaks. That sounds about right," Loot said.

"Is that what you meant by ironic?" Dale asked, looking at the stream. He was parched all the way through. Dead skin was hanging off his lips and the tip of his pointy nose.

"Not really, Dale. Go ahead and dunk your head in that brook. Water's fresh as it gets."

Loot looked back to the trees. The young wife was clutching her kid, watching to see what the Fates might have for Dale.

"Thank you," he said, wet halfway down his weathered shirt and water dripping from his scraggly hair.

The day's light had just about run its course. Fireflies lit up the clearing. Fish were jumping in the creek as the bugs hovered low over the water. It was a pretty scene. A nice place for Dale and his nice little family to settle in for the night.

"The fella near Red Oaks."

"What?"

"Dale, whenever some greenhorn or tinhorn gives you advice about a shortcut, try not to be so stupid. Stupid decisions will get you and your family killed. Ain't nobody here to save you when things go bad in this country. Looking at you I can tell y'all are about run out."

Dale wiped some of the water from his face. "Yes sir."

"And I don't care if you have to tie that kid to your waist. Never let her off to go running away. She'll be supper for a mountain lion, or worse, she'll run into a man like me."

"Okay."

Loot rubbed his leathery forehead and blew out a breath loaded with frustration. "Y'all plant yourselves here for the night. I'm pushing on. That stream's got trout. Can you fish?"

"Not bad."

"Catch some food and feed them ladies. Luck and you'll make it where you're going in three days."

Loot slapped Dale on his frail shoulder and started kicking through the high grass to collect his hat and horse. He needed to move faster now, dark or not, rough terrain or no.

"Who are you, mister?" Dale asked.

"You'll find out soon enough," Moreno said, passing by Laura and Isabel. He gave the little one a wink that made her smile.

There was nothing else to do. A life of running made the decision an easy one to come to. As soon as he set waking eyes on the girl, Loot knew all the ways it could play out. Maybe the family would go to Thunder Hill and talk about the man they saw on the road. It would be hard not to, people still yapping about the dark rogue that stole himself away from a hanging. Or maybe they'd keep their mouths shut if he begged or paid them enough. That'd be worse. Some hard-type bounty hunter assholes would eventually come around asking about the new family that just came to town and what they'd seen on the trail. Assholes would go to Dale and put the boots to him until he talked. The real tough manhunters might even threaten or hurt little Isabel or Laura. That would put Kip and Doc and Cox in the shit. Jasper too. Dale had seen the gray colt that was being kept in the Laird's barn. Ben's widow might come under fire. His daughter. The whole plan had been blown to smithereens by a little girl named Isabel. *No. Not her fault*, he said to himself, guiding Rocco through the evergreens. *What happened to your five-minute nap? What happened to staying out of trouble? You have to make this right.*

Riding off, he realized that he never explained irony to Dale. The kid and his family had done nothing but make fool decisions, but they were still kicking. The choice to come up on that creek was smart enough, but it was the one that put their lives in danger. A younger version of himself would have killed the whole family and offered them up as he'd been taught by his mud-born teacher, using them for the power he once believed pushed him on. They'd give him not a second of worry. Just food to satisfy the wicked universe and the wicked beast living in his soul.

The old days.

Loot needed to find a place to stir up his resolve and let his leg recover. After that, it was back into the lion's den. Moreno wasn't done with Thunder Hill.

He had obligations.

CHAPTER 16:
THE LADY WITH THE PIPE

NIGHTTIME. THE SALOON IN THUNDER HILL WAS STARTING to fire up, though it'd already been buzzing with activity more than most days. Jasper Bedford stood outside and adopted a noble pose, taking in the cool air with a full pipe and a tall glass of beer for company. The beer was a break from a long run of hard liquor and listening to tall tales from locals and passers-through. He had a notebook full of anecdotes to fill his paper, maybe even enough to write a book. The trip to Thunder Hill had awoken in Bedford a fresh enthusiasm to describe the kinetic nature of life on the border of civilization. The will of the wild and the will of man met and heightened on the edge of things; there were so many ripples to explore. He was starting to feel like the great western bard he'd set out to become before necessity forced his artistic predilections to the back of the railcar.

He smiled at every yokel stumbling in and out of the place, touching a bony forefinger lightly to his head as a sign of respect, as was his custom. He'd worn a hat in his younger years, but experience had taught him that people tended to be more open to a stranger lacking the luxury of hiding their eyes or thoughts underneath a brim. He was more than happy to let the remnants of his unkempt hair go unfettered. Seeing a painting of Ben Franklin figured into the look as well, though he'd never told a soul.

"Howdy," he said, touching his head twice to a couple of dusty, wobbling strangers. Bedford liked saloons as much as any man walking the earth. A weary soul's refuge for pleasure, sure, but there was method that ran parallel to his hedonistic needs for booze and women. Saloons were more often than not near the center of town, providing a good view to whatever might be transpiring at any given moment. It was how he came upon young Kip Laird the night of his fight, and how he'd seen the young man collapsing from a day's worth of all he could handle.

Now he had his eyes set on the telegraph office. An attractive young woman with tumbling brown hair dressed in cowboy garb was exiting the office and making tracks in his direction. There was a swagger in her walk, hands on her gun belt, thumbs tucked down the front of her tanned leather pants.

Jasper took down a quarter of his beer and sucked thoughtfully on his pipe, coming to sit in one of two rickety wooden chairs on the saloon porch. As the girl hopped the steps, she looked over the swinging doors inside and then turned her head left toward Jasper. The light from the interior gave him a better glimpse of her; there was a serious beauty underneath all the posturing and resolve. He touched his forehead and smiled. "Howdy," he said, going back to his pipe.

"I like a good pipe smoke, too," she said, moving a few steps in his direction. "Mind if I sit and take the town with you?"

"I'd be the dimmest man in the territory to refuse such an offer," he said, standing up like a green soldier at attention. "Jasper Bedford's the name."

"Sybille," she answered, pulling out her own pipe and tobacco as she took the seat to his right.

"And do you have a surname?"

She smiled and crossed a boot on her knee, the way a man would. "You think it good form asking a lady to divulge a thing not offered?"

"Quite right," Jasper answered, leaning back. "Forgive me. I presumed an unearned level of familiarity with you, Ms. Sybille. Unearned entirely. I will drink some more of this beer and ponder my impertinence."

Sybille lit a match on her boot and sat the flame in the bowl of her pipe. After a few hefty puffs, she blew out a long cloud of smoke and offered a muffled bit of laughter. "Quite a dance of words, Mr. Bedford."

"I like to think I can dance, but my thinking isn't to be trusted."

"Why's that?"

"Well, to risk running afoul of what one new acquaintance discloses to another, I'll admit that the power of my thinking is generally enervated by spirits."

"You're telling me you're a goddamn drunk."

"Indeed. An apt characterization. Harsh, but apt. I see you prefer a more direct form of communication."

"Yes and no," Sybille said, removing her hat with a shake of her head. More waves of light brown hair spilled down the beaten leather of her jacket. A few passing cowpunchers in the street turned their heads the way men do when sighting a beauty; she acknowledged by smirking and blowing a dense stream of smoke in their direction. "Keep moving, boys. I'm trouble, any and all kinds." She pursed her lips and moved her right hand down near the pistol at her side, waiting to make sure they kept about their own concerns.

"You've taken to protecting yourself with alacrity, Ms. Sybille." Jasper leaned slightly back again, watching her watch the men slink away.

"If you're meaning I've measured up to the world, suppose that's true until it ain't." Sybille relaxed in her chair and shifted her attention to the old man. "But I like the way you're trying to figure me out, Mr. Bedford."

"Only trying to have a conversation. Nothing like a friendly exchange."

Sybille nodded and pulled a rag from her jacket pocket, setting it on the table next to Jasper's beer. It was white, or had been. Now it was covered with streaks of what looked like fresh blood. "My father keeps telling me to get darker gloves."

"Darker gloves?" Jasper didn't know if the question or the rag was more unsettling.

"See, these here are a real light tan," she whispered, placing both hands flat on the table.

"Indeed," Bedford responded, taking a quick drink from his glass, trying to act like his new acquaintance's behavior wasn't off-putting.

"So, I'm always having to wipe them down when they get bloody. In my pa's defense, it would be better to switch to a black set. Then stains wouldn't be much of an issue. Wouldn't have to carry around extra rags."

"Suppose there's something to that," Jasper said, biting down on his pipe and taking in a few drags, still attempting to read the situation.

"Thing is," she continued, "it's not like there's a top glove man just anywhere."

"Is that right?"

"That's right. Right as right gets. Gospel truth, putting it another way. If I was on the hunt for some silk lady gloves, it probably be an easier search. But I'm need'n something sized for a lady, yet still made for more historically manly pursuits."

"Think I'm beginning to apprehend your conundrum."

"I figured you would, Mr. Bedford. Best thing to do would probably just try to find gloves made for a boy near man, but I don't know. There's something about compromising that doesn't properly sit."

"You know what you want. No shame in that."

"Not for something as important as gloves," Sybille said, leaning over the table toward Jasper. He was beginning to grow tired of her manner and choice of topic. It didn't seem to have any destination besides darkness.

He finished the last of his beer and started to get up when she held out her hand and proceeded. "Seriously, Mr. Bedford. I think you could pen one of your fancy stories about the seriousness of having the right gloves."

The old writer didn't know how significant it was that she knew his profession. He pulled the pipe from his mouth and nodded at her with a polite smile that invited her to say what was *really* on her mind. He was stiffening from the cold and the strange aura the young woman gave off. She wasn't unstable, but there was a ferocity in the way her eyes and curved lips tightened when she wasn't speaking.

"It's not like we live in St. Louis or Paris, France. We're in the damn middle of nowhere. You think people back east understand the scarcity involved in living out here?"

"I'm not sure."

"I'm sure you have theories. I'm sure you've even written about it in your Durington newspaper at some point. How border folk can't just go buy solutions to their problems the way they do in the big cities."

"You've read my work, Ms. Sybille?" he asked.

"No, Jasper. I'm only now finding out who you are. Mr. Weaver over at the telegraph office told me that you two spent last night keeping the ladies occupied. That must've been when his machine got fiddled with."

Bedford steadied himself with a heavy, silent breath. He tried to imagine all the alcohol leaving his system; a little wishful thinking couldn't hurt. Jasper first had to maintain himself and consider the nature of *his* answers; not worry about the girl's intentions or her strange ways. He had to lie well and keep everyone involved protected. "I was sorry to hear about his shop. A bit of vandalism can be expected when so many new faces come to town, but it doesn't make the sting of the crime any less severe to the victims."

"But last night. Y'all got after it?"

"I'm afraid so. Wine women and song. I think we both fell to unconscious stupors around the same time."

"You a friend of his?"

"No, not really. Though I'd like to think I'm a friend to all."

"I like that," Sybille said, grabbing the bloody rag. "This here's Mr. Weaver's blood. Some of it, anyway. I had to get a little rough with him."

"Why would you do that?" Jasper asked, feeling she might be about to visit the same fate upon him.

"Because I needed to know if he was lying. A major fugitive escapes and the telegraph goes down in the same night? Something odd about it."

"Hmm."

"What's that you're thinking, Mr. Bedford?"

"A couple things. It seems obvious that the man who escaped was probably the same person that sabotaged the machine. Also, did you ever finish your point about the gloves?"

Sybille smiled. She had little teeth, a bit crooked on the bottom but straight and well-maintained on top. "Mr. Bedford. You're mighty sharp. Yes, it does seem obvious that the *notorious* Brandon Calhoun would disable the telegraph, but there's something a little odd about that."

"What's odd? I'd love to know. Any complications make for a more interesting story."

"Glad to tell ya. If Brandon Calhoun busted into Mr. Weaver's, the place isn't showing signs of it. No broken locks or windows."

"That is interesting. But it might be he just forgot to lock up. Or has an assistant."

"Thought of that. No assistants have keys, and he swears up and down he had it on him all night. I made sure he was telling the truth," she said, clenching her fists to highlight the stains she couldn't get out of her gloves.

"Did you hurt him terribly?"

"Not terribly. An impression, is all. He just got a little big for his britches, said he didn't need to answer questions from a little girl."

"Can see you were nonplussed by that."

"Yep. Anyway, he convinced me he had the key the whole time, or at least thinks he did."

"It's confusing," said Bedford, doing his best to look utterly baffled.

"Any theories?" Sybille asked. "Being a reporter and writer must bump you against this sort of thing all the time."

"Once every so often," he said, "but here I must say I'm stumped."

"One more thing. The thing wasn't smashed."

"What do you mean?"

"I'm no wizard with those contraptions, but the way it was explained, only the essential parts were taken from the telegraph. Neatly done. Only, our Mr. Calhoun was in a hurry. Wouldn't he just smash the thing to bits and move on? It's a funny sort of getaway, this one."

"Yes, it is," Jasper said, looking straight out into the street. He longed for something to break the growing tension. Someone coming in or out of the saloon to touch his forehead to. No one. A terrible time for a drought in foot traffic. Nothing to smoke or drink. His pipe had run out and his glass was desert dry. "I guess you're a lawwoman, then? I know you didn't want me asking after your name, but perhaps you'll at least indulge me your profession."

"Why not. I work unofficially for a man who is, let's just say, he's real official."

"I think I understand what you meant when you sat down."

"Which part?"

"When I commented that you're the kind partial to direct communication, you said, 'yes and no.' Seems you were being direct about your being elliptical."

"Damn, Jasper. That's a fancy way of saying it, but I'll take a helping of fancy where I can get it."

Bedford knew he was being manipulated. It seemed her intent to let him know. How much or to what end, he wasn't sure. It scared the old writer. He grabbed his glass and pipe and stood up, miles away now from caring about etiquette or the need to feel clever. With a few a wrenching questions and a bloody rag, Ms. Sybille had made him feel like she was from another time or place. Somewhere foreign and unknown. His winning ways had been snuffed out and left to disappear in the wind along with his pipe smoke.

"You said two things, Jasper," Sybille said, still maintaining her mannish posture. "Remember?"

"What's that? Oh, yes. I asked for the direction you were headed, about the gloves."

She left the pipe in her mouth and clapped her hands together. "I was making a point about the importance of insubstantial things. Probably would've stumbled to it eventually, though I will admit to having a lot on my mind."

"Insubstantial things?" Bedford was standing over her with his feeble shoulders hunched, mind in three different places. He wanted more than anything to simply remove himself from the young lady's presence. After that, the newspaperman was salivating for a drink of something stronger than beer. Last but certainly just on the heels of his need for intoxicants, he wanted to find out more about the *official* man Ms. Sybille was *unofficially* working for. Asking her straight wasn't going to help strike the target, and more time spent talking only meant more lies he'd have to tell.

Sybille stood up and gave Jasper a slap on his skinny arm. "Insubstantial things, Mr. Bedford. A glove just a hair too tight or too loose can interrupt the pull or the firing of a pistol. Something as big as a shootout, and it's them insubstantial things that come to play more front and center than one might expect."

"Well said," Jasper coughed. "Astute. And philosophical."

Sybille stepped around the little table and stood underneath the old reporter's chin. She put her hands up on each of Bedford's shoulders and spoke into his chest. "Then there's me. Such a small thing."

"I'll be going," Jasper said, retreating from her grasp.

"Enjoy your drinks, Mr. Bedford," she said, spitting and looking out at the town. Her father would be along, but she didn't know how long that would take. *Time for a whisky.* As she tapped her pipe empty against the table, a dirty blonde creature with uneven proportions stepped heavily up the stairs leading to the saloon. "Howdy, ma'am."

She nodded back. He was wearing a badge.

"Name's Sydney Laird."

"Deputy," Sybille said, unclenching her lips to offer a slight smile. "Buy me a drink?"

Sydney took off his saggy-brimmed hat and smiled broad and bold. "Yes ma'am. It's been a day. I might even buy you two."

"Lead on then, Deputy Laird."

CHAPTER 17:
THE BOYS ARE BACK

COX AND KIP PULLED INTO TOWN WITH THE REST OF THE search party a couple hours after nightfall. The street was bustling with activity and a thick fog had settled down upon the valley for the night. Light from the ten working gas lamps along the street was barely enough for a decent cut through the haze. Cox grabbed his rifle and ordered Rooker to fix up the horses in the little stable behind the jail. He thanked the other two men for accompanying them on their fruitless journey to catch Brandon Calhoun. "Come get your pay at the jail tomorrow," he said, wiping his weathered brow with a wash-softened blue bandana. "Appreciate yur time."

Turns out, "Calhoun" had done a good job of hiding the boat. They galloped right by it and none of the others in the posse saw a thing. "Calhoun" gave Cox a wink a mile downstream of the hidden boat, a signal to the sheriff. Not long after, Cox made the executive decision for the posse to head back into town. He cited several reasons sensible enough to the other riders, though from the hard pace the sheriff knew he could've made any excuse; all parties were beat after skirting the rim of the valley.

"Hold up a sec," Cox whispered to Kip, watching Rooker struggle with the horses. "ER, you get some rest tonight. No getting drunk. Probably another long one tomorrow."

"Night, Sheriff," Rooker said. His attitude had been stripped clean by the taxing shift. He fumbled about with three sets of reins, barely enough grip for the task.

"Yep," the lawman said, nodding Kip the other way. "C'mon, son. Let's get to the jail. I want to talk." The sentiment was forced and fragile. Kip had a harder time than usual in the hearing of it. Cox grumbled and nodded forward. "Anyway, think there's still a bottle hiding somewhere in that old rolltop desk."

"Think probably I should lay off the whisky, Sheriff."

"Well you can sit there and watch me drink."

"A chair sounds good enough," Kip said, bowing his head to the wiry older man before they started walking, mostly silent down the side of the street. The gas lamps served for tiny guides in the murky atmosphere. "It's been a day."

Cox answered with a grunt of agreement and nothing more. They continued like that before the door to the jail. A short, middle-aged man was waiting in their way. On account of the fog, they didn't recognize him until a few strides away.

"Easy, Amos. Don't go cockin' that Winchester on account of my presence."

"Hey there, Ike," Kip said, walking in front of the sheriff's barrel to offer a hug.

"Hey yourself," he said, trying in vain to match the intensity of the young churchman's embrace.

"What are you doing here, Trigger?" Cox asked, rolling his slight eyes at Kip's offer of affection. He had no hatred for Ike "Trigger" Teller, but it'd be lying to say he hadn't judged the man to be a damnable pest. Ike was always hanging around the jail, waiting to heap worries about this or that on Cox and his deputies. Until Ike, the sheriff believed women to be the primary purveyors of gossip. Teller was an example to put that claim into dispute.

"Thought you should know, Sheriff Cox."

"What should I know, Trigger?"

"More than a few groups rode out looking for Calhoun after you left. That's not mentioning the bunch that went out while you were still recovering from your tussle this morning."

"Let me guess. Neither hide nor hair."

"Doesn't look as such. I think most of the searchers are back at Trussel's or Romeo's by now. How'd you guess?"

"Because if there'd been news, you would've started with that. Now go on and get, Trigger. I've put in a grind."

Laird smirked at Cox's harsh treatment of the little square-headed man, though he understood its origins. When Ike Teller wasn't rattling off the town's happenings to the law or anyone else who'd listen, he was down at the church, complaining about marital problems. Betsy Teller was a handful, but Ike couldn't wrap his head around the part he might be playing in their ongoing travails.

"How are you doing, Ike?" Kip asked, trying to leave the man with a feeling that someone still cared. "Betsy?"

Cox looked at Kip like he'd just broken the final seal, the one to unleash Hell upon the world for all of time. The lawman's iron chin hit his chest and the barrel of his gun slumped down to the boardwalk.

Teller didn't acknowledge Kip's inquiry directly, choosing instead to dart his eyes at the sheriff. "I don't like that you call me *Trigger*, Amos. It's not right and it does nothing to help my self-regard."

"The hell is self-regard?"

"It's how I see myself."

It took a fair prodding for Cox to string more than a few words, but Ike had a way. "How you see yourself? I can help you out there. You're about up to my shoulders, your cheeks are redder than the fires of Hades, and that nose looks like it's been flattened by more than a few belts from the wife. That cover all?"

"You've always been a difficult man. Honest to a fault."

"Why I never wanted to get married myself."

Teller stepped close. "Never mind what I said about the honesty. That right there. Just a plain lie. You wanted to marry her."

"Okay," Cox snapped. "You've had your fun. Get. And have someone give you something for that eye. Betsy really tagged you, looks like."

Ike stomped one of his little boots, balling up his fists. "Betsy didn't do this. It's all these drovers and haulers that stopped in. The town can't handle it."

"Things will clear out," Cox said, regaining his composure. "You said one of them did that to you?"

"Some brute called Riggs. From outside Durington, I think. Said I spilled beer on him, which I didn't."

"He just up and hit you?" Kip asked. "You didn't provoke?"

"You know me. The last thing I ever want is to cause trouble."

Kip and Cox shared a weary look.

"I'll ask around. Maybe throw him in for disturbing the peace if he's still drunk. Ain't much more to be done over a scuffle."

"Fine," Teller said, looking defeated on all fronts.

"Bear up, now. At least it wasn't Betsy this time."

Ike smiled and kicked at the ground like a petulant boy. Kip gave him a quick hug and sent him off with a blessing. Ike said he was sorry about Ben and that Kip *was about the only one in the world that could care like his father.*

"That's a kind word, Ike," Laird said, watching the town gossip skitter off into the night.

After the pair closed the jail door and finally gained some privacy, they issued respective sighs of relief. Kip plunked down and watched Cox moving faster than he had for most of the day, attempting to excavate whisky from the ancient rolltop in the corner.

"Slow down, Amos. You'll pull something out of socket."

"Ain't nothing left of me that isn't already out of place."

Laird laughed as Cox cried *Eureka* when he finally discovered a dusty old bottle. "This is good stuff, if I remember. Your, uh, dad bought me this. Sorry."

"You're not one for apologies," Kip said. "And there's no need for one."

"Well." Cox sat down in his chair grinning and pulled with all his might to uncork the bottle.

"And I'm not saying it to spare you embarrassment. One doesn't get to see Amos Cox smile all that often. Thunder Hill should have a parade to mark the occasion."

"Whip smart with that tongue," the sheriff said, pushing out of his chair to remove his duster. It fell to the floor by his feet. "Always a whip smart kid."

"I'm sorry, Amos. Being honest, I don't think it's my natural way. More learned. Getting educated by Rufus all those years, arguing with him and my sister. It resembled war more than school."

"Your mother always wanted you and Elsie drilled up real sound. Philosophy of this or that. Whatever the Europeans talk about when they're prancing round. Fact that Doc was the only one in town capable of teaching you was hard for her to reconcile."

"I'm aware. That was an unrelenting feud. Mind you, it never cost my father a finger or his sanity."

"You mean like old Trigger?"

"Exactly. Sheriff," Kip said, reaching across the table for the bottle. He wanted it now. A chance to be close with his father. It was almost like having him in the room while he talked to Cox. Something they never did while Ben was alive. Amos had never been in the forefront of the young man's life; always present, yet, somehow always distant.

"Guess I shouldn't call Ike by that name. Not a lot a Christian charity in it."

"No. Not much at all."

"Labels stick. Man's shooting finger. You know."

"Betsy bit it off. Well aware of what happened. Probably hear about it more than you do. Realize, apprenticing at the church all those years meant I was usually the one to take the regulars."

"Low man on the pole."

"Way of the world."

"It's been almost twenty years since I was low man. Just around the time I first saw you."

"Is this the conversation I was promised?"

"It's not like I can tell you the whole story, son. Elias and Loot are more proper suited to the task. How much did you get from the old newsman?"

Kip started back at the beginning. As they passed the bottle back and forth, he explained how he'd known about being adopted since he could reason proper. How that was dang near all he knew, until just before Ben's death. How his adoptive father told him that he was left by Loot Moreno. How crazy that sounded, until a man bearing the notorious mark showed up shot and shooting in the middle of the street.

"I was the one that shot him," Cox said, almost laughing.

"I was wondering about that. When I came running out…"

"He was fixin' to kill us all. A little bullet wasn't going to stop him. Heck. Ten bullets. Our knowing each other's the only reason that kept him from wiping us all out. Still, them demons were calling. If you hadn't shown your face. Might've got overly bad."

"What do you think got him here in the first place?"

"Respect's a powerful force. Ben and him got pretty close over the years. Me and Elias, too. Moreno's an honest man."

Kip wanted to keep explaining what he knew, the things he learned from Jasper Bedford, but Cox's comment had him on his feet, bubbling over with frustration.

"What? You hear something?" the sheriff asked.

"Just more of the same," Kip said, hands rubbing his temples.

"What's that mean?"

"You say Moreno's honest. He's a killer."

"Not anymore. And you best have an ear for it, son. However it all came to pass, you wouldn't be alive if it weren't for Loot. Wouldn't have nothing and no family. Where's your Jesus and forgiveness and your soul-saving truths? They only apply when it's something distant? Easy to give old Trigger a hug and send him back to Betsy. Grow up and start living life. Too many sacrifices on your behalf, son."

"That isn't fair, Sheriff. Not fair to have the people in your life keeping secrets. Big secrets. I'm all twisted up on it."

Amos rose to his feet sharply and pointed to Kip's chair. "Done with your tantrum?"

"What is this?" the young preacher asked, slinking back down.

"This is me telling you life isn't fair. And you've had a fairer shake than a lot. People that love you."

"People that lie to me."

"You're dumber than I reckoned. We told you why when you snuck up on the jail the other night. Every bit you know puts you in more danger."

"Then why'd Ben say anything?"

"He was too smart for his own good, maybe. Too many ideas or ideals weighing down. I guess we'll never know what prompted it. I've heard a lot of dying words. They cover a range."

Kip was tired of fighting. He could see from Cox's expression that the lawman was in knots the same as he was, clinging on reserves for strength.

"And Loot being a killer. All that darkness? That wasn't what you saw on the street the other day with the Tollier boys. They came looking for Doc over at his place, banging on the door, calling him a cheat at cards."

"What?"

"They broke down the damn door. Loot's in there, trying to hide, only he's a damn colossus. He threw them out into the street. They drew down. He was quicker."

"Shot two before they could get anything off?"

"What?"

"You said the bullet was from your gun."

"Yeah. He's fast. And he *was* a killer. Much as he's shed that skin, there's enough left, I guess. They didn't have a chance. Not once they pulled."

"Jesus, protect their souls."

"And he'd sobered up. Not sure what you heard, but it was them boys that were drunk when the shooting went down. Not Loot. Takes a lot to make him stumble, though I'm pretty sure him and Doc went through damn near a case of whisky."

"I'll testify to that. Rufus, anyway. Thinking back on it, he looked more like a corpse than my dad when I saw him that day."

Cox nodded deliberately and upended the bottle. Kip watched his stubbled throat convulsing as the liquid made the trip down.

"It's a big stack of lying, all this."

"You can't be losing your nerve. Not after what we just pulled. This is serious. Can't let it ride over you."

"Yeah," Kip said, unconsciously biting his fingernails. The constant physical and mental rigor of the last week was taxing him through. He thought maybe it'd be a good idea to ponder on something else. "What was Ike calling you out on?"

"Calling me out? Must've missed that part."

Kip slapped the edge of the desk lightly with the ends of his fingers, smiling crooked in an attempt to lighten the mood. "You don't miss a thing, Amos. Something about a *her*, was it?"

Cox shook his head slowly, keeping his eyes on the kid. "That idiot didn't know what he was talking about."

"Come on, Sheriff. You can confide in me." The preacher was too gentle with his request. It would be swatted away. He was better than that with people, even folks with psyches as impenetrable as Cox's. *You're more tired than you even know, Laird.*

"This ain't the confessional, kid. Leave it."

Kip leaned back into his chair and watched as Cox's cheeks turned a darker shade of red than usual. "Someday I'll hear this story. Must've been quite a girl."

Once again. "Leave it."

Laird's interrogation came to a halt with three raps on the door. "Sheriff Cox? Would you mind opening up if you're in there?"

"Who's that?" Cox hollered, glad for anything to steal him clear of Kip's inquisition.

"It's Jasper Bedford. Quick as you're able, please."

"Jasper?" Kip said, moving quicker than the lawman toward the door. He opened it sharply. The old writer was doing his best to hold up Boon Weaver.

"Ah Master Laird," Bedford grunted. He had one of Weaver's arms over his shoulder as he clung to the telegraph man's waist. "If you'd be so kind, might you lighten the load?"

"Grab him," Cox barked.

"Of course. I'm so sorry." Kip took over for Jasper with ease, helping the struggling man across the room into one of the cells. "Go gently now, Boon," Kip whispered, lowering him slowly into the creaky bed.

While Laird asked Weaver the obligatory questions, the sheriff slammed the door shut and poked his finger into Jasper's bony chest until he was pinned against the wall behind Cox's desk. "What the hell happened?"

"A girl's in town. She did this to him. Asking questions about a *Brandon Calhoun*."

"A girl?" Cox asked.

"A manly witch," Boon cried, holding his ribs and kicking out his feet. Kip surveyed his flabby face along with the girl's handiwork: a few gashes, one pretty good one on the top of his oily head.

"I think I met her," Kip said. "She's got something different, but I wouldn't call her manly. Or a witch."

"What'd you tell her?" Cox asked Weaver, letting Bedford free.

"Nothing, Sheriff. She wanted to know all about last night. Like the telegraph getting tampered with was all my fault."

"What would give her cause to think that?" Kip asked.

Cox was seething. "More than that, why would she care enough to get to beating you? How could she?"

Boon sank deeper into the saggy cell bed and sighed like the pain was threatening to take him. "Can somebody get Doc Rufus? That's if it's not too much trouble."

"In a second," Cox said, crossing his arms in expectation of a heftier explanation from Bedford.

"What? I met the young lady over at the saloon not long ago. It started out as an amicable conversation, but it soon turned into more of an interrogation. An intimidation, actually. That might be the right way to describe it."

Kip left the cell and joined the writer and the sheriff. "Was this girl wearing a fancy rig? Real pretty, flannel shirt. Dressed like a poke, but—"

"A pretty woman," Bedford decided to answer. "Beautiful, in fact. Green eyes. Which is why I was so inclined to talk to her. How did you know what she looked like, young Laird?"

"I saw her earlier. *That's* Fallstead's daughter, I'm betting."

"Oh. Makes sense. She did mention…"

"Wonderful," Cox groaned. "Sounds like she's figured it. Between her and that bearded deadeye, more than likely we're sunk."

"I gave away nothing, Amos," Jasper said, keeping his voice too low for the whining Mr. Weaver to hear. "Nothing."

"Get the doctor!" Weaver cried.

"We need to fetch Elias," Cox said. He needed some heavy thinking. Removing Boon from his presence would go a long way toward the goal.

"Hold up," Kip whispered. He was by the window, looking out a hole in the cheap cotton curtains. "Let's use the backdoor."

"Why?" Cox asked, instinctively moving his hand down near his colt.

"The girl. It's a long look, but I think she's watching us. She smoke a pipe, Jasper?"

"Like a man of fourscore years and more. It's not the most ladylike thing I've seen. Snuff seems a much more feminine choice."

"Yeah, that's her," Kip said.

Cox looked through the hole and squinted for a few seconds. "Damn. Everything that far seems a bunch of nothing."

"The boy's blessed with worldly and otherworldly sight," Jasper said, joking mostly to distract himself from the thought of the mystery woman keeping watch, a specter through the mist.

"You could've done better than bringing Weaver here," Cox said. "She probably told you about hurting him to see what you'd do."

"Oh no," he whispered, looking at the floor. "I've revealed my cohorts."

"Not really," Kip said. "Sheriff's office is a natural enough place to head after a beating. See that justice is meted out and so forth."

"I don't want to keep guessing." Cox gathered up his duster and stepped with purpose for his hat. "But I'd like some privacy, at least. The backdoor sounds like a good plan. Help me with Weaver."

"What the hell are you guys yapping about over there?" asked the beaten man. "Ways to fix my machine? Magical healing solutions? I'm suffering here, gentlemen."

"Let's get you up and over to Doc's," Kip said, negotiating Weaver's stout frame from the bunk. "Sorry about that, Boon. It's been a busy day with the escape and everything. We aren't intentionally ignoring you. Just... we're sorry."

Stepping slowly with Laird carrying most of his weight, they moved out of the cell. "Apologies, son. And you know I'm never coming to that church, being a man of scientific instrumentation."

"I know. You've told me."

"But you've never been anything but a good kid. No right to be snapping. It's not like I got beat up behind anything y'all did."

Kip took more weight from Weaver as he guided him to the backdoor. A paltry, pathetic attempt at recompense to Boon and to God. Their lies were exactly why this man had suffered violence. He looked over his shoulder at Bedford and Cox, water filling his eyes.

CHAPTER 18:
WHAT YOU CAN'T SEE

MORNING CHORES WERE ALMOST DONE. THE SUN HAD JUST risen over the hills and done quick work with the previous night's thick air. It promised to be a warm, dry day in Thunder Hill. Elsie was tending the garden out front while her mother cleaned and swept and cleaned again inside the house. For a few moments, consumed by work, she had let the memory of her father slip to a faraway corner of her mind.

Just a few moments. Then he was back.

Elsie put down her trowel and wiped sweat from her smooth forehead, looking over at the church, glimmering white like it was lit from the inside. "I don't know," she said, talking out loud to the spirit of her father. "I don't know, Papa. Trying to picture you up there with Him takes some doing. She took off her gloves and stood up, face to the sun. "That's better. Didn't think talking to you and God was appropriate, knees down in the manure."

She covered a laugh with the back of her hand and squinted at the sky, knowing how crazy she'd look if Mama or anyone from town came walking by. "Oh, they can think as they please," she went on. "You always said that the church was mostly just a building where people could rest their lazy rears. Talking to God, anywhere was okay for that. We never really touched on the theological intricacies of speaking to the dearly departed. Probably thinking that I'd have more time for asking and education."

Elsie turned toward the house and started to cry, putting a hand over her mouth to stop. "Ah. I've got work to do, Papa." More tears, despite her best efforts to contain them. "Enough already. C'mon now, Elsie. This is a sorry show. Sorry Papa. Give my best to the Creator. Pass on that I'm still mad about Him taking you premature. Guess the rest of eternity wasn't enough time to have you up there."

She picked up her tool and started a ragged walk back to the house, lifting the denim gardening apron over her head and wiping away some remnant tears on a rolled-up sleeve. "Forgive me, Lord. Uncalled for. Expect I'm not the first to be at a loss."

Elsie set the apron on the porch's handrail and walked inside. Her mother was smacking the dining room curtains with a heavy wooden stick, sending particles dancing in the light. "I wonder if that dust doesn't just settle right back down," Elsie said, keeping her head turned away.

"I have the windows open, Else." Mabel noticed her daughter's distress. "Hey, are you okay?"

"I hate gardening."

"Not that much," Mabel said, giving the curtains another go. "Be productive, I say. Keeps the mind off things."

"Right as usual," Elsie said, agreeing to agree and not even thinking about the merits of her mother's advice. "You never miss a beat, Mama. Or a beating. Ask the curtains."

"You going to get back to it?"

"Maybe later. Thinking I'll take Ambrose out for a little jaunt. Dang dog's got enough spirit to run the whole valley."

"Surely does. I'm just glad he didn't bark last night. I needed the rest."

"Ambs, let's go boy. I got your leash. Where you hidin'?" Elsie was eager for Ambrose's simple energy and interacting with her parents living and dead was proving complicated to the point of burdensome. "Ambs!?"

"I thought he was outside with you." Mabel said.

"No, Mama."

Elsie threw down her rag and ran through the house, calling out the dog's name. Upstairs then down again, she found no trace. Mabel hollered out through the open windows to no avail.

"He's probably wandering out back or by the barn. Go and have a look, Else."

Elsie was breathless jumping down the porch steps and around the house, cursing her skirt as it caught her boots every three or four strides. She checked behind the barn and yelled out into the prairie, again, seeing nothing. *Maybe Kip came and fetched him up without telling. If so, I'll tan his hide.*

Her next stop would be Kip's, but first she decided to check inside the barn, just in case the retriever somehow managed to dig his way in. As she opened the door, it took a second for light to seep in and her eyes to adjust. "My God!" she screamed, over and over, fixed in a panicked shiver. In the middle of the structure, between the pen to her left and the stacks of hay to her right, Ambrose's mutilated body was splayed out. Elsie only recognized him by his head. Flies flew around the dead dog in their soulless natural exercise of benefiting from another creature's demise.

Elsie thought to run out screaming, but stopped herself, thinking of her mother. It wasn't a sight she wished on any other soul. "My God," she kept saying, managing tentative steps toward the remains with one hand over her mouth and nose and another engaged in swatting away the insects. For a minute she let herself entertain the notion that it might be the work of coyotes or some other natural predator, but that illusion had a short lifespan. The body had been cut lengthwise from under the head all the way down, then opened up like a book. Biting into her own hand and shaking, Elsie could see that most everything had been removed. There were no organs. The head was bloody. The tongue and eyes gone.

She couldn't stand it another second. Somebody very sick had staged the scene. Elsie stumbled out of the barn trying to imagine what in God's name could compel a person to such horror.

Using the outside of the barn to hold herself up, she stumbled to the side farthest from the house to find a moment for collection. After vomiting breakfast and the previous night's dinner, she slumped against the backdoor of the barn, shivering and sick, scared through to her marrow.

"Else?"

"No," she cried, terrified, attempting to get back to her feet.

"Else, it's Kip. It's Kip! What's wrong, girl?" He helped her up, holding strong while she writhed against his sturdy chest.

"You can't know. You can't know." Over and over she repeated the words, fighting harder and harder with every repetition. The more she struggled, the tighter he squeezed.

"I've got you, Elsie. Whatever it is, we'll deal with it. Hear me?"

"You can't know." She was whispering now, still shaking, but not as violently. "You can't see."

"Okay. We'll figure it out. Hush now, Else."

They stood like that for a few minutes. The shaking started to subside, but it would take a long climb to come down from the shock.

As much as he tried to act the part of calm and composed, seeing Elsie in such a state had Kip more rattled than he'd ever been in his life.

That wouldn't hold up very long.

CHAPTER 19:

SEE YOU AT CHURCH

"I'M COMING, ROOKER. WAIT UP. HERE, TAKE MY BAG." DOC Rufus held out the weighty medical satchel, trying to fix straight his black suit jacket and checkered vest. "It's caught on something back there." He was touchy. Between Loot and Cox, Kip and Weaver, he was patching people up at a higher than average clip. Booze and reading, his two true loves, were suffering neglect.

"You gonna manage, Doc?"

"I want you to tell me what the hell's going on. Wait. Forget it. Big doings at the jail, you can't talk about it. Just hold the case. And don't drop it. Jove, it's a hot one."

Finally, the doctor managed to get his wardrobe situated. He was standing with Rooker on the edge of the street, just in front of the tidy little building that served as his home and medical practice. *Third place from the end. Red, turning brown from the years.* Those were the directions given if asked where he lived and worked. "Lead on, fumbling squire. Exigency, you said."

"I never said that, Doc," ER returned, moving to a brisk pace.

"You said it was important," Rufus said, trailing just behind. He almost had to shout. Another busy day in town. Horses trotting by in both directions. Womenfolk and kids walking to one of the two school-houses from a lunch break. Doc and Rooker went steady without incident, until Elias stopped at the scaffold out in front of Billy Payne's bakery and sweet shop.

"What are you doing up there, Talbot Haas?"

"Hey Doc," the man answered, waving excitedly from the top of the structure. He was big and shaggy, wearing worn-out denim pants, a stained white shirt, and a straw hat that looked fetched from a privy. His boots appeared older than the wearer; they dangled playfully off the top of the scaffolding.

"Hey yourself, Tal." Rufus paused and took his bowler off. Rooker gave him a look meant to urge him on and he returned an expression that put the deputy in his place. "Tal, you wanting to tell me what's going on up there, son?"

"Nothing. Keeping watch, maybe. You know, I'm just waiting to see if they catch the bad guy. If they do, I'll be right here, ready to do my part. Color of law. I heard that from Sheriff Cox. Color of law."

"Son, they haven't found him. No word. Come on down. I'm sure your mama and pop would rather have you around the house, helping with chores and such." Rufus had his hat raised to block the sun and his head tilted back. "Hurry up now. That damn thing's so high it's making me dizzy looking up at you. Let's go, Tal."

"Okay."

Haas didn't bother using the stairs, choosing instead to hop down to the street. He landed like he didn't even notice, then walked with enthu-siasm toward Rooker and Rufus, greeting them both with hugs. "Doctor Elias Rufus," said Talbot. "I forgot. That's what he likes to be called, ER. Doctor Elias Rufus."

"I remember," Elbert said, applying a fake smile to his already corrupted personality.

"Thanks, pal," Rufus answered, returning the big man's embrace warmly. "You know, most people forget."

"I did at first. Sometimes it takes me a few tries at things."

"Not a problem. You gonna go home now and help your folks?"

"Guess I should."

"That's best."

"I'm not really sure, Doc. You know, I built this. Right down to the last nail. Saw a picture in a book and built it to look the spittin' image. Some of those guys down at the diner told me I couldn't do it when I showed them the picture, but that's the spittin' image, alright."

"Really nice," Rooker said. "Doc, we need to be moving on."

"Yeah. Okay. See you, Talbot Haas. And if I come across those peckerwoods, I'll tell them that's the damn spittinest image I've ever slapped eyes on. What the hell do those sons of bitches know, anyway? I'll give them the damn business. Count on it, son."

"Thanks, Doc! Bye, ER!"

As Tal took off running, Elbert said something underneath his breath.

"What was that?" Rufus asked, carefully placing his hat back on his head in its usual carefully crooked position.

"Nothing."

"You said something, Elbert."

"I said the guy's a half-brain short of being a full idiot. Shouldn't be left alone."

"Yeah. Let me see my bag."

The doctor snatched away the satchel before Rooker could hand it over proper. "I'd knock you down with this thing if it wasn't full to busting."

"Take it easy, Doc."

Take it easy, Rufus repeated under his breath. He was upset from the second the deputy knocked on his door, agitated and not willing to say much in the way of specifics. Now, being reminded that innocent Talbot Haas had been used to construct Thunder Hill's monument to medievalism, the physician was positively apoplectic.

"No more talking, Rooker. I need to gather myself for... for whatever the hell it is you're leading me to."

* * *

Despite the warm day, Elsie Laird was still shaking cold. Mabel rubbed her shoulders, making sure the blanket was firm around her daughter's body. Thirty minutes prior, Kip had quietly moved them along the outskirts of town to the jail, where Elbert Rooker was claiming his portion of the watch. After letting the Laird family in, he went and fetched Doc Rufus. Normally, he might've objected, but Kip showed a sterner insistence than the deputy had ever seen.

Now Elias was looking into Elsie's eyes, whispering things Kip couldn't quite hear.

"You're going to be fine, young lady," he said, rubbing her forehead lightly with his strong hands. "A few drops of this to settle those nerves. After that, right as rain." The physician pulled a translucent bottle from the bag at his feet and squeezed two drops of the solution into a small cup of water. Mabel gave him a look that said *you better not be fumbling about with my daughter*. He ignored it, handing Elsie the cup casual as breakfast coffee.

"Thanks Doc, she said, struggling not to spill the liquid. "It's not necessary."

"Neither was the Renaissance, but we can still be glad for it."

Rufus stood up and gave Elsie a kiss through the tangled blonde on top of her head. "Love you, beautiful. Best pupil I ever had, you know."

Rooker was standing in the corner next to the cells, more than a touch confused. He wanted to say something, but the way Kip and Doc were carrying themselves had him caught up and nervous. That, and he was never much settled around proper ladies.

Rufus nodded Kip toward the gun rack nailed to the back wall, rubbing his mustache from the ends and back to his nose with one hand. The gesture served to obscure his words. "What the hell happened, kid? And what's with the six-gun on your hip?"

"She found my dog in the barn. Ripped in half. Like it was meant for someone to come by and see." Kip was leaning against the wall, staring hard at the rifles next to his face.

"Ripped in half. Dissected, you mean? Or just torn up? Maybe her imagination went a little sideways."

"Dissected. Everything was removed. Saw it myself."

"Everything?"

"Doc. Not an organ left. I know what an animal's insides are supposed to look like. Between your lessons and hunting my whole life."

"Barbaric. This refuse mound of a world. Damnable. Barbaric."

"Evil was the word that came to mind." Kip trailed off as he spoke. It was a tough task, trying to describe something while keeping the image of it somewhere on the outskirts of his thoughts.

Rufus seemed to pick up on the personal nature of the situation. "Sorry about the pup. Ambrose was a beauty."

They stood silent for a few a brief seconds before Kip snapped into action. He grabbed a Winchester off the shelf and began loading shells.

Elias put a hand on his former student's shoulder. "Whatever you're thinking, maybe best to put it on hold. I'll go back to my place and get Cox. He doesn't need to be watching over Boon Weaver and that Jasper fella. Take your inclinations to him before doing something stupid."

Kip shrugged off the doctor's hand. "Thanks for looking in on Else." He moved around Elsie and Mabel and stepped with purpose for the door. "Open it up, Rooker."

"Where you going?" the deputy asked. "A little hot, ain't ye?"

"It pains me to agree with ER," Rufus said, still standing by the gun rack, "but running around with loaded guns doesn't seem the wisest of courses."

Laird nodded for Rooker to open the door. The deputy acquiesced, seeing no real alternative. Kip was locked and loaded and possessing the look of man hell-bent on stout endings.

He could barely hear the door slam behind as he walked at an angle out into the street. Two or three people from town tried to stop him for hello, but they were quickly put off by the rigidity in his expression. He had a fixed destination, no getting in his way.

There she was. Sitting out in front of the saloon. The pretty girl. Dressed and heeled like a man. She was smoking a pipe with her hat down low to keep the sun from her eyes. Kip knew she could see him coming, but it didn't seem to concern her in the least. He slowed himself at the foot of the steps and pulled the Winchester tight against his armpit.

"You might want to set the long gun down before somebody gets hurt, Preacher Laird." The girl said it without moving a muscle. She had her feet stretched out, resting on an old rusty bucket. "I know you're loaded by the hammer. Wasn't born yesterday."

He walked up the steps, finger on the trigger. The end of his rifle wasn't more than ten feet from her now. "Maybe I should do the talking, then."

"From what I hear, that's all you do. Man of words, aren't you? Man of *The* Word. If this is your method for saving souls, have to say it's a mite aggressive."

She was smiling underneath the shade of her hat.

"Who are you?"

"I'm the daughter of your riding buddy. Deputy Marshal's daughter. You might've guessed that already."

"I might've," Kip said, keeping the tension in his finger and shoulder. Her hand wasn't down by her gun, but he wasn't taking any chances. From the tortured look of poor Mr. Weaver, the young lady wasn't afraid to court violence. "But I didn't know that beating on the defenseless was under the purview of the law."

"You're talking about the telegraph guy? He'll be fine. *You* might even be fine before this is all over. Besides, I'm more of an unofficial kinda gal. See," she said, sitting sharply up in her chair, "no star on my shirt." The girl's sudden movement was a test, but a dangerous one. Kip almost yanked back on the trigger. "Pa, however, he's a sworn officer. But you knew that."

"I think you and your father should go."

"I think you should put down that rifle before I shoot it out your hands. Gunplay wasn't on my docket; not for the next little while, anyway."

"Seems an unlikely position to be drawing up terms," Kip said, taking a firm step forward. The sound of the wood planks creaking underfoot cut through the high warm air. The people of Thunder Hill were watching, sure enough, from near and far, keeping silent to see what was next to transpire.

"I'll tell you what," she said. "How about these terms? You ease up off that Model 73 and we can talk like adults. Talk about your brother, Sydney, for instance."

"What?" Kip asked. The question was unexpected enough to cause him to reel back ever so slightly, enough for her to draw from her seated position and put a bullet where his right trigger finger met with the knuckle. The 45-caliber round was robust enough to make useless meat of Kip's middle finger as well.

The rifle dropped to the planks before the report from the gun finished echoing its way through the town. Laird staggered, holding the wrist of his wounded hand. It was bleeding fierce, but not quite enough to make him pass out.

"I never said," she continued, "my name's Sybille."

Her Colt was already back in its holster. At this point, Kip was no more threatening than a man on the other side of the world. He dropped to his knees. She walked over and casually leaned on one of the peeling porch banisters, looking around to see if anyone was stupid enough to come running. "See there, Preacher. All the things you've probably done for these folks, and now, in your great time of need, not one about to return the favor."

"Syd." Besides spit and struggle, one syllable was all he could manage.

"Your brother's fine. We have him, but he's alive."

"Why?"

"That's a great question, Preacher Laird. There's a haul of history being unearthed in this little town. Lots of forces at work, you might say. Me and my pa, we're close to pulling it all together."

Kip let out a grunt, trying not to look at his hand.

Sybille walked over and knocked the hat from his head, kneeling down to lock eyes. "I had every right, Mr. Kip. Can't go pointing dangerous weapons at people. It ain't proper, and I'd like to start being treated proper in this town. Never been to a place with so many liars."

Even through blinding agony, he notioned her words held specific purpose.

"How about you talk to your people. We'll meet at the church tonight. Give you and whoever else is involved a chance to think about fetching Loot Moreno back here."

"What?"

"Don't," she whispered, patting him condescendingly on the head. "Told you. The lying's getting me raw."

Walking away, she dropped a blue bandana at Kip's knees. "Sorry about your dog."

Sybille stopped at the top of the stairs and turned back, watching him grab the cloth, curled up like something feeble. "It was for a good cause. And just so you know we mean business, I took care of that tart you were having words with yesterday. She won't be bothering you anymore."

"Where is she? And Syd? Please." If he'd the energy to sound more desperate, his pleas might've struck a more fervent chord. As it was, he was losing control of his eyes. She was walking away. Walking away.

"A pretty thing, Ms. Samuels was, but I could tell yesterday you didn't want her around," Sybille said, tapping her fingers against her pistol's handle. "She parted ways with this world. You'll thank me later." Now with more street between her and the saloon, Sybille was forced to holler. "Before you pass out, remember, we still got your brother! See you at church, Reverend! Go ahead and invite all the liars, if'n you please!"

CHAPTER 20:
THERE ARE THREE

SYBILLE KEPT A STERN EYE ON HER SURROUNDINGS AS SHE LIT out of town to meet up with her father. Her gun hand was shaking. It felt like something was pressing down on her chest, making breathing damn near loud enough to hear over the steed she was spurring.

She'd been fast back in town. A flawless draw. Took hold of the grip at the precise spot to give her pistol true balance. The shot was perfect. Maybe as perfect as she'd ever been. It disabled the preacher just the amount she wanted. Far as the rituals having anything to do with it, she wasn't quite sure. *It takes time* her father said. Over and over he said it, a look in his eyes that made her a little frightened.

Thunder Hill was nothing but a barrel full of deceivers, she told herself. Every person she talked to was hiding something. No doubting it. Still, the more Sybille picked away at the husk of lies covering the town, the less certain she was of her own skin. Truth and identity were hazy notions at present.

An hour's hard ride through the valley brought her to a grove of trees followed by a depression in the land running up against a giant sandstone escarpment. Caves dotted the face of the rock formation. A useful fact provided by their guest. He was a lifetime resident of Thunder Hill and knew the best places for hiding out.

Tying her horse to a felled tree at the foot of the cliff face, she pulled her pipe and tobacco from her saddlebag and walked slowly through the black door which served as the cave opening. The light from her struck match and pipe was just enough to give her a view of Sydney Laird. He was chained to a large boulder near the back of the cave, about thirty feet deep into the cliff.

"I'm thirsty," he growled. The shape of the walls made his words louder and rounder.

"I just got here, and you're already fussing. Come on now, Sydney. You'll never get a proper lady, nagging all the time. Girls don't like taking that off a gent."

"What?" His voice cracked from desiccation and disbelief. "How'd you know what normal people like?" He started to laugh, but it came out sad and weak. "You ain't folks. *Animals*, maybe, but hell, that's too nice a title. All's I'm saying."

"That right?" Sybille asked, walking closer to her captive. Her face took on an orange color and then went black again as she smoked her pipe.

"You heard me, girl. What I saw last night, sitting in circles and chanting next to blood and guts. Do you even know what you're doing? What it's for?"

"Sydney Laird. Are you trying to set me straight? I'd be touched, if you weren't so damn dumb. Before I got you out here, were you really thinking I'd be inclined towards a roll in the hay?"

Scary as the setting was, Syd was momentarily happy for the darkness. It helped him hide his embarrassment. What was he supposed to think? They had drinks. She took him by the hand and stumbled out the back of the saloon after talking him up this way and that. Damn woman was kissing all over his neck, leading him to Case Graham's barn.

Just when it seemed his lucky night, she pulled her gun. The speed of it was something he'd never been witness to. Stories always circulated through frontier towns, especially among lawmen. This bandit or that outlaw being the quickest draw. Syd had always thought it to be a bunch of fool talk. Nerve and aim seemed better servants in a fight. 'Course, that was all stories and supposing. The only person he knew to ever draw down on someone proper was Sheriff Cox, years ago in a confrontation with a reputed crook named Sam Spell. Cox was fast when it came to deciding, and that made the difference. Fast enough so young Mr. Spell didn't have time to clear his holster. No shots were fired, and Sam Spell ended up getting locked away. Whatever notoriety the gunslinger traded on turned to dust after that.

Much as Cox rubbed Sydney wrong, the deputy always admired the obstinate sheriff's stubborn skills. What he saw yesterday, though, that was something different. The kind of fast that didn't seem possible. He'd never have a chance in hell against the girl.

"Saw your brother back in town," Sybille said, kneeling down next to the deputy. She used the pipe as a little torch, checking the ropes around his ankles and wrists. Sydney winced at the nearness of her.

"What'd you do?"

"Yep. Those there are good and tight."

"Answer me, damn you."

Sybille sat down at her prisoner's feet and adopted her usual casual tone. "I'm pretty sure he's got the sand in the family. Boy came barging up on me with a loaded Winchester."

"You're crazy. My brother wouldn't never. He's got his nose in the Bible."

"That's what you said last night at the bar. You said your brother was a damn preacher. You also said y'all didn't get along that well. You also said he wasn't your brother." Sybille sucked in one last good smoke from her pipe and blew it in Sydney's face. He lashed out against the chains and ropes to no effect. "You remember telling me about little orphan Kip and your little town? I feel like part of the community. That was some talking, Deputy Laird."

"Sure. Coming from you. Never heard someone spit more damn words in my life."

"I ask if you remember because of all those whiskeys you were pitching down your throat."

"What happened to Kip?"

"What happened is I shot him."

"I don't believe you."

"Wouldn't blame you, considering our short history. Sure as sunrise though, next time you see him he'll be absent a few fingers. He really liked that dog, turns out."

"Dog?"

"You saw the ritual last night. The insides were from the dog. They're not as useful as human parts, but they still help. Good for practice, if nothing else."

"You're a damn demon," Sydney said, spitting in the direction of Sybille's voice.

"C'mon, now. I was about to let you have a drink."

"Daughter!"

Sybille whipped around and gained her feet. She squinted toward the entrance of the cave. It was the figure of her father, sure enough, all silhouette. "Hey, Pa," she said, leaving Sydney to squirm ineffectually against the rock.

"Fetch the rest of the wood."

Sybille passed her father and walked out into the light. After a few seconds, her eyes took to the change and she spotted the pile of sticks he'd been referring to. By the time she made it back inside the cave, she could see the beginnings of a fire.

"What's this for, Pa?"

No answer. He remained hunched over, focused on his task.

"Marshal," Sydney cried out, terrified by domineering silence. "What the hell kind of Injun shit are you into?"

No answer. The flames grew in height. Sybille gently set down the pile next to her father.

"It's Clayton."

"What?" Sydney asked.

"Not Marshal Holt Fallstead. Dan Clayton."

"Dan Clayton? What's that supposed to mean?" Sydney knew the name as well as anybody else. Dan Clayton was one of the worst killers to ever roam the frontier. *He can't mean the same one. That sick son of a bitch been dead for years. Decades. If he ever existed at all.*

"Pa?" Sybille whispered, stooping down by the fire. "Why you lettin' loose your name?"

Again, her father offered no answer.

"You know what," Sydney said, watching his captors continue to build the fire. "I wouldn't put it passed you to go around thinking you were Dan Clayton. Seeing that crazy shit last night's got me convinced that y'all are playing this here game with less than a full deck."

"Shut your mouth, Sydney!" Sybille darted over to the deputy and grabbed him by his frayed shirt collar. "You're gonna get yourself killed."

She barely had time to finish the words. Clayton had moved up behind his daughter and grabbed her by the throat with both his hands, lifting her off the ground. Sybille kicked and gagged and slapped at his grip until he finally threw her against the cave wall like a half-empty sack of flour.

"Jesus," Sydney said, trying to keep fear and surprise under his breath. His efforts were a failure. The cave amplified even the slightest of noises.

The man calling himself Clayton charged back in his direction, a wild-eyed monster made more sinister by the mixture of firelight and shadow. He grabbed a tuft of Sydney's scraggly hair and whispered in his ear. "It doesn't matter now, but how involved were you?"

"Involved with what?"

"Loot Moreno's escape. Have you known he was alive this whole time?"

"Not this again. You asked me last night. I don't know what you're talking about."

"Fine." Clayton tightened his grip all the way into Sydney's scalp and pulled his head back. With his free hand, he pulled out his Bowie knife and sunk it into the deputy's protruding belly. Laird let out something like a gasp as his eyes went wide from the shock. Clayton kept a firm hold on his captive's hair and whispered into his ear, sawing with upward force into the midsection. Blood began dripping from Sydney's mouth. "You weren't much good in this life, Deputy Laird."

Sydney was dying, but he was still trying to talk. It was no use; every utterance gave up nothing but more blood. His white shirt was a red mess. "Think you've said your last words," Clayton continued. His grip was lighter now. He continued sawing, cutting downward now, toward Sydney's manhood. "Loot Moreno right in front of you, but Cox never let you in. I know you're not brave. Just stupid. Not good enough to be trusted with the secret. They helped to kill you. Die knowing that. And die knowing that you'll serve more purpose being gone from this life."

Runoff from the butchery was everywhere. Ten feet away, Sybille started to regain her senses. She watched as Sydney's head tipped forward against his chest. There was a cut on her forehead from her collision with the cave wall. The dizziness started to subside. As she stood up and staggered toward her father and the pile of meat that was Sydney Laird, a cold she'd never felt sank into her bones, gripping her head to boots.

"Come here."

"Pa."

"Come here and take over. I'll make the circles and tend the fire. You'll do it right this time."

"Pa."

Clayton stood up and swung around to face his daughter. The knife was red all the way to the handle. So was his jacket sleeve. "This is what you wanted," he said. "Isn't it?"

"I'm not—"

"You look scared, Sybille. Ain't you always telling me how you can't get spooked? Ain't you pushing on me to help you be a famous outlaw?"

"I suppose," she said, putting her head down.

"An outlaw isn't made by shooting down a few rustlers or bank robbers. If you want to scare people, you can't be scared. Ever."

"I know."

"You don't know anything. Drawing little circles in the sand. Listening to fool stories your whole life." Clayton held up the knife a few inches from her face. The smell of metal and guts came close to overtaking her. "Take his parts the way I showed you. We'll do this right. Got a lot of killing to do."

"Yes, sir." Her tone was one of childlike obedience.

Sybille pushed away whatever feelings she was having and went to work, telling herself that Sydney was just a deer or elk that needed a quick dressing. She kept her head down, letting her father's words sink in. He was right. This is what she'd been asking for. To know who he was and what he'd done. To know how he did it. The ritual and the words, all of it, just something to get used to. To give her an edge. Make her stronger. Harder. Unafraid.

This is how she spoke to herself while taking Sydney apart one piece at a time.

Dan Clayton walked over and stood next to the stack of guts, breathing heavy over his daughter. "He was big. That's good."

"Yes, sir."

"All my life, I've never put hands on you, Sybille."

She kept her head down and resisted the urge to reach for her aching neck.

"I don't want to do you harm. This here's serious, though. You've always played about, and I've always let you, but that wasn't the hard world. You want to walk in the hard world and survive, playing ain't gonna stand."

"I'm sorry, Pa."

"All right. Let's get started."

Clayton had drawn the circles with the soot from one of the spent sticks and began placing Sydney's innards inside the rims. Looking over his work, he nodded at his daughter, hands dripping. "You told them to meet us at the church?"

"Tonight."

"And you called out Loot Moreno."

"To the preacher. Bout blew his hand off too."

"And his woman? You kill her?"

Sybille almost lied but decided against it. "No, sir. But I had him thinking I did."

"This is what frets me." She could hear the animal grind of his teeth.

"She wasn't worth the trouble, Pa. Turns out she wasn't even his. Besides, seems like lying right back to these liars will at least keep them on their toes. I went with my gut. Besides..."

"What?"

"We said we wouldn't kill this one, and we did. That'll throw another loop their way."

"Good talk, girl. Always with the talk. But if it's fear, you can't be afraid to be beyond it."

"I know, Pa. This wasn't about that."

"Enough. Sit."

They each sat cross-legged, staring out into light pouring through the cave opening. The fire burned at their backsides. As much as her neck hurt and as disturbed as she was at the gutting of an essentially innocent man, Sybille tried clinging to the words. It was like being lassoed to a tree in the midst of a tornado.

"Close your eyes. Repeat after me."

She spit out the taste of ash and dirt and fresh death best she could. "Yes, sir."

These are the words they spoke. First Dan Clayton, and then his daughter:

We fill these symbols of The Three Places with ourselves and our sacrifice. This one may be going to the place of rest or the place of the dark. It is not for us to decide. Only to make an offering. Let the sacrifice give us clarity and power. Power to embrace the rest and embrace the dark while we remain here in this Place. Take the weakness and fear and make us the hammer and the gun. Let us be reminders to the world that there are Three Places, and that this is only one.

After opening her eyes, Sybille grabbed a portion of Sydney's insides and threw them into the fire. She stood silent with her father, watching them hiss in the flames.

"I'm proud," Clayton said, much calmer. "Your mother... Well, enough of that."

"Thanks, Pa," Sybille said, finally rubbing her neck. She watched the last of their sacrifice sink and sizzle into the coals, trying not to look at the macabre husk dripping against the rock.

CHAPTER 21:

OLD FRIEND

THE GIRL'S FINE. SHE'S FINE, KIP. EASY NOW, YOUNGSTER. EASY now. The girl's fine.

Even with eyes wide open, it was hard to see anything.

Easy now.

Finally, the scales started to fall; Kip's vision began to return, along with the other senses. He was flat on his back in Doc Rufus's office. The location wasn't likely to be confused with any other; maps of mighty ancient civilizations lined the walls. Books with fancy bindings and golden filigree were stacked all around. Bottles big and small filled with experimental concoctions covered two long tables opposite the wall where he was lying. Those tables. Memories. Doc standing over him and Elsie, clapping his hands and turning them around to study Latin or the Mongols or Newton. A happier time. *How about you start by knowing something.* One of Rufus's favorite lines whenever one of them began to get out of line or eager for the door. A happier time.

"Lindy's dead."

"No, boy. The girl's fine. She's fine. Amos already went and looked in on her. That perky cowgirl slapped your friend around good, but nothing more." The depth and power of Loot Moreno's voice had resonance enough to shake the walls.

"But Sybille said," Kip moaned, blinking rapidly at the huge man sitting still at his bedside. The man that was supposed to be far away by now. "How long have I been out?"

"Not all that long," he said, moving to pull his hair back and tie it off. "Couple hours."

"But you're here again. Already."

"Something turned me around. Before all this."

"She's dead. Lindy."

Moreno put his massive hand on Kip's chest as he tried in vain to leave the bed. There was no fighting the downward pressure. "You need to gather some calm, boy. I said she's alive. The girl shot them fingers and, best we reckon, decided to leave you thinking dark thoughts just for a whirl. Rufus said that's all you could talk about when they brought you back here. They went and checked on her, son. Hear me when I say it this time."

"So, she's fine? She's fine. This is what I get. Stray from the path. This is what I get."

"Not sure the meaning of that. Vapors and potions are still wearing off, I guess. What you got is two less fingers and no dog. That's as far as it's gone so far. I'd count you lucky."

"Lucky?"

"How long have y'all been taking up?" Loot asked.

Kip looked at the marked face of his guest and scanned the room again to see if anyone else was about. Nobody. He could hear a robust exchange boiling in the main room of Rufus's house, but it seemed a world away from him and the giant outlaw. They were enclosed by an unassailable barrier, it seemed. History and inevitability had them stranded in that office together.

"It's not like that," Kip said, starting to feel the pain in his hand. "What'd Doc give me?"

"Potions, just as I said. Imagine something similar to what he gave me. That first night I met him. The first night he met you."

Kip was still foggy, so he kept himself from following Moreno's comment where it was naturally leading. Ironic to pull back, considering the truth was all he'd been after, but the boy had a sense that there was wisdom in the decision. Doctor Elias Rufus's Famous Elixir wouldn't last forever. "It's not like that," he said, choosing to repeat his pathetic defense. "With her."

Loot sat up a bit but kept the pressure steady on Laird's chest. "No need for defending yourself. Ain't nearing evil to go about with a girl wanting the same."

The conversation was starting to border on the surreal. Kip stopped himself short of looking at his wound. "I'm glad the infamous gunman isn't too judgmental concerning my dalliances." Kip tried moving Moreno's hand, but it didn't budge. It served to keep him from flashing more attitude. "I'm sorry. The medicine, I think. Or maybe it's just the way I am becoming."

Loot realized he was using too much force. It was hard for him to gauge how strong to be around people, physically or otherwise. "Look here, kid. Not saying you need my yes or no on the subject. Maybe I meant that being alone is the evil. Never was much use at talking."

You're not going to that damn church, Amos!

People are getting shot, Doc. There's still a job to do long as I got this star!

Outside the debate was growing loud enough to pierce the veil hanging over Loot and Kip. Moreno smiled. His teeth were surprisingly white, Kip thought, not knowing the reason for his surprise. "Always been like that, them two," Loot said. "Since I can remember. Rare when they don't go at it."

"Seems as if they've managed. Friends most of their lives."

"Imagine you're right. Could be your daddy made it more friendly than it might've been, but I don't know."

He was clearer already. "I'm getting right. Finally tell me what you *do* know. Promises were made."

"Yeah," Loot said, looking around the room and lifting off Kip's chest. He started fishing through his corduroy vest until he came out with a packet of tobacco and a ration of papers. "We'll get to the reminiscing in a sec. You want a smoke?" Loot did his best to roll one for himself. "Borrowed this from Cox. Tried to get some from Elias, but he said that smoking was something or other."

"Barbaric and idiotic."

Loot came near to a smile. "His usual line."

For whatever reason, Kip said yes to the offer. He'd never been one for the taste, but it felt like the thing to do. Something communal about it. Maybe why the Indians were so fixed to it. "Sure. I'll have one."

"Here," Moreno said, passing his cigarette to the kid. As he made himself another, he couldn't help but take in the room. Skulls. Metal tools that looked like they were crafted just to put fear in a man. Jars of dead critters floating in unnatural liquids. The smell and look of progress and study, the Doc would say. Loot would always nod his head and say okay. Far as being a different sort, he wasn't one to go casting judgments.

They sat smoking for a bit, hearing just about half of Cox and Rufus's ongoing argument. "No signs a stopping," Moreno smirked.

"Nope."

"You need to look at your hand, son," Loot said. His big voice had extra weight all of a sudden; Kip could sense the shift.

"I'm working up to it."

"Go on, now."

Kip thought about having just a quick peek, but once his eyes caught sight of the bloody dressings covering the area where his fingers were, he couldn't look away. A billion things he'd never be able to do properly again. Chop wood. Eat steak. Eat anything. Fishing. Hell, playing cards, even. "She got me good," he said, trying his best to show Moreno he could grin casually through it. Anything to show the outlaw that he wasn't a complete joke. "Doesn't hurt like you'd think."

"Probably Rufus's medicine still working on you."

"Yeah."

"You were all done and sleeping by the time I showed up, but Elias said the forefinger was clean off when you got here. He had to take whatever was left of the middle. Leaving that little bit might a made things worse, he said. Sure Doc will tell you more."

It took another minute of staring. "Help me sit up," he said, reaching his arm out to Moreno. Loot placed a pillow behind his back and gently guided him against the wall. Doc's heavy blue ornamental wallpaper felt smooth on the preacher's neck.

"That got you comfortable?" Loot asked.

After a few more subtle shifts, Laird said, "You were adamant. About me looking at my hand."

"Adamant?"

"Do you know what it means?"

"I can venture a guess."

"You couldn't simply let me get used to it? Take my own time?"

Loot stood up from a cargo trunk serving as his seat without a clear reason. His eyes were focused on Kip's, green as grass when the sun hits it just right from high up. "I didn't want anything on top of what I have to say, if'n you're still wanting to hear it."

Kip let out a breath. After a slight nod, he went still as a death.

"It wasn't handled right. The way you got a nibble of the story here and there. Considering the sum of things lately, it hasn't been easy. I told the others that I was the one that needed to give you the truth, but everything happening—"

"Please. Whatever you know. That was the deal. You said when there was time. We have it now."

Loot proceeded to tell the story of that first night in Thunder Hill. How Rufus fixed him up and how Cox and Ben kept him protected. The goodness that "Preach" showed in holding his secret. The friendship that formed over the years, mostly based around the care and raising of one boy. Kip saw and heard what it meant to Moreno as he relayed the story. Every syllable seemed to be chosen with care. The outlaw was loud and imposing, but there was a trueness in his nature that the young man hadn't seen. Trueness born of weight and responsibility he could not yet understand himself.

"It's strange," Kip said, watching Loot sit back down. The big man looked relieved and exhausted all at the same time. "I can't imagine my mother taking kindly to the proposition. A notorious outlaw showing up at the doorstep."

He rolled his dark eyes. "The church step. And she didn't know at first. The notion took some time to find a home with her. Your mama's a fine woman, and she had every right, not wanting anything to do with me or any of my bright ideas."

"She just couldn't resist the sight of you," Doc Rufus said, entering the room with a blood-red face, hot from his verbal war with Cox. "Turns out, young man, there was a time when you weren't the aesthetic monstrosity that lays before me today."

Kip smiled briefly. He couldn't allow Rufus to derail him from getting at more details. "Thanks for fixing my hand."

Elias walked around the bed and felt his patient's head. "Fixed probably isn't the best descriptor, but I appreciate it all the same. Your body seems to be dealing with it," he continued, checking underneath the bandages with a look and a sniff. "The nature of the injury will present us with certain challenges going forward. I shall endeavor to create some sort of contraption to serve as a substitute for your loss."

"I know you'll do your best, Doc," Kip said, trying to sound grateful and dismissive in the same breath.

"I hear that tone, boy," he said, feeling the patient's cheek once more before moving across the office to the long tables opposite the bed. "And despite your unsophisticated attempts to extricate me from the scene, I will reiterate with all of my benevolence: you were quite the little guy."

"Quiet little guy," Loot said.

"Yes. Like a mute. I had to check for a tongue at first."

"Happy."

"Strangely happy. Like you were holding a joke in, ready to take it to the grave. Mabel couldn't resist that. First old Loot here was a dark spirit, next minute she didn't care. To have a new kid around, especially after I'd just told her she wasn't going to have any again."

"What?" Kip asked.

"Oh. Well, probably superfluous. Quite indelicate, actually. Forget what I said. Did you by any chance see this new map?" Rufus pointed to the wall near Loot. "Persia at their pinnacle. Imagine they'd have something for a couple of missing fingers. More than a ramshackle office in the middle of this backwater. Those were the days. Imagine. Remember stone buildings? Me neither. Our dwellings and our lives are similar: subject to a gust."

"What'd you mean, Rufus? My mom. Not all that other nonsense. This is the part where I find things out."

The physician looked down. His face a different shade of red now. "It's better you talk to Mabel about it."

"I'm not stupid. Sounds like it'll be awkward no matter the source."

"Argument well made. I'll finish. She was done bearing children, your mother. Something happened during Elsie's delivery. Of a technical nature, and if you'll excuse me, I need to go finish arguing with our muddleheaded constable." For a moment Rufus seemed able to slow himself down. He came back over and put a hand on Kip's head, wiping away his long brown bangs. After a kiss on the cheek, he skidded out of the room and resumed yelling at the sheriff.

Doc Rufus's behavior had them going in opposite directions; Loot was a stone, but Kip was fuming. "He's worried, kid. And he was scared. You're important, if you hadn't figured."

"So that's what that was?"

"I'd bet on it."

"Okay," Kip said, telling himself to simmer. "Seems the easy parts are over. How about you get to why you were toting me across the countryside in the first place. What happened to my parents?"

"Yeah," Moreno said. His head was hanging low. The strands of hair he hadn't managed to tie back were touching Doc's floor. "Yeah."

"I figure you led with the good stuff. Human nature."

"I ain't of the thinking I deserve anything from you, son, but I'll ask you not to be interrupting me for a bit."

"Got my word."

"Fine," Loot sat up and looked the boy square. "I was with bad people. Raised my whole life with bad people. There were names for us, though I can't say how we ever got names. We never left anyone alive to really tell a tale. I don't know. Everyone's heard some version; most ain't true tellings, but they get to the heart of it. We'd kill anyone we wanted, take what we wanted. Put it under a roof that said it was serving some higher thing, making us higher beings, but it was just dirty. The foulness of our wants."

Each word aloud meant a thousand silent memories for Moreno. His tongue felt like ash. Recounting pained all his portions. As seconds rolled by, Laird thought the reformed outlaw might be done already.

"Mr. Moreno?"

"Thing is, when you're bad from a young age there's no knowing it. Not at first. You sit around the fire thinking on it, but that's as far as the mind goes. Wars, tribal scuffles, killing and more killing. Everybody's been doing it out here since I can remember. When I'd seen about ten years, my mother died. She was a white woman with a son that looked like me. Her for my only protector. Her dying meant I had to survive. Not long after, I lined up behind bent folk. Small stuff at first, but soon I was bigger and stronger than everyone around me. More I did, the more I didn't give a damn. The leader of our gang, bloody as he was, seemed to care about me. *Seemed* is the word, 'cause I was young enough and stupid enough to believe it. He only cared about himself and what he could get from you. One of those. Smart and mean as a dog beat regular. If he wasn't killing or recruiting some down-and-out hoodlum to his cause, he was reading a book. Titus. A name he gave himself. Made us think he was invincible. Made us believe in what he called the Three Places, that we could see into all of them, be in them all at the same time. Never made any sense to me, but I went along, pretending it made me better at doing what we did. It wadn't faith. Just pretend. Years went by, and I started thinking that maybe I was good at killing for simpler reasons, because I had lots of practice. I was bigger and quicker than anyone else. Anyhow, hard to put a finger to what makes a man *do*."

Loot raised his right hand and turned the outside toward Kip. "I carved this. No one else did it. I'm a guilty piece of trash. Walking curse and nothing more. The only good thing I ever managed was you, and that—"

Moreno's voice caught like somebody stuffed a rag down his throat. He was softer on the inside than he realized. Scared of what was coming after.

"Just say it, Mr. Moreno." With his good hand, Kip gripped the end of his blanket. "Is that what I call you? Just realizing, I never asked."

"Joel."

"Your name's Joel?"

"No, kid. That's you. Your name's Joel. Found that out, sometime after."

Except for the dying debate coming from Rufus's house, all went still. Kip needed a moment in order to realize it was going to take a lot more than a moment. "So, I'm Joel. What else?"

"Your folks. They were named Nell and John. You were their only child. They died the day I took you."

Kip pressed the back of his head into the wall and bit down, trying like hell not to let a tear loose. "Did you kill them?"

"No, kid. But it's my fault."

"Keep explaining."

"It's a lot."

"Do your best." He tried to picture their faces. Nell and John. His parents. Nell and John. He imagined a strong man and a loving woman, but no image stuck. How could it. Knowing their names only added to the torture.

"I killed Titus. One day he ordered me to take a wagon train full of women and children that were coming up through this bottleneck canyon the next day. I couldn't do it. The night before, I waited until everyone else covering my side of the canyon had gone to sleep. I did them quiet, one after the other. Used a knife and covered their mouths while they rattled, dead but not quite excepting it. Titus was the last. He woke just in time to get a couple shots off. Wounded me, but I was too strong. Too good at it."

"God."

"God didn't have anything to do with it, but I'll say this: if God is the fella Ben talked about over the years, seems like that was probably one of the only things in my life that would've met with his approval."

"You don't know anything," Kip said, distracted as he kept trying to force Nell and John into his memory.

"That's true. That's true."

"So, you ran from the rest of them, and my parents somehow got in the way."

"You got it just about figured. I never met your folks. Never meant for them to be harmed. They had a place a few miles from a town called Pinewood, down south about a week's hard ride. Just east of the big mountains. It sounded like they put up a fight, but they never would've been able to hold out against Clayton."

"You let them die."

"The fighting was already… I couldn't have done anything. I couldn't."

"Guess I'm supposed to take that on faith."

"It's your choice, kid. And if you want to blame me for getting your ma and pa shot down, that's the right thing." Loot took out his pistol and set it on Kip's outstretched legs. "Be the right thing if you went ahead and pulled that trigger, far as I'm concerned. I won't give you no fuss over it. Be better than I deserve."

The revolver felt heavy on his thighs. He wanted to do it. Only a month ago, he was a boy living an artificial life of peace. A life built on a history of death and pain, covered over with lies and half-truths. A month ago. A month ago, he'd never thought of wishing violence on his worst enemy. Now he was bleeding from one hand and ready to shoot a man with the other. The man who'd saved his life and gotten his parents killed. He tried to think of everything; there was more to the story, obviously, but the knowing and the fact that he'd never known was overwhelming his head. His body and composure were frayed. He went to what he knew and asked

God for strength and guidance, keeping it simple. He waited. If Christ was listening, the message wasn't getting through.

"Maybe that's what you're here for," Kip said, picking up the gun and pointing it steady at Loot's face. "Could be that it's my duty. My *right* to put you down."

"You've got a good claim to it," Moreno said, sitting with his back straight, watching tears stream down the boy's face as he gripped the polished black gun handle tighter and tighter. The weapon started to shake as his finger wrapped around the trigger. Loot was a stationary target, looking off toward the other side of the room. He figured that'd make it easier for the kid, if he decided to go through with it.

"My father trusted you."

"Strange. But yeah. He did."

"None of it makes sense. Amos, Doc Rufus, my... father all deciding to let you go on living your life."

"The situation took a lot of breaking in." Moreno relaxed his stolid expression and looked down with purposeful eyes, like he was recalling something he didn't want to lose. "Maybe we did our best. It felt like it, most of the time. You grew up good and strong."

Kip had dealt with enough confessions to understand that the man before him wasn't looking for forgiveness or punishment in any usual fashion. Moreno had the bearing of someone that had served a sentence. If anything, he simply appeared to be tired. As one second followed the next, the preacher moved back and forth between feeling sorry for himself and feeling pity for Moreno. The gun became heavier in his hand. The shaking more pronounced. He released the hammer and set it back down on his legs.

"I'm not going to shoot you," he said, really starting to smart from his wounded hand. "The truth is, I don't know how I'm supposed to feel about a damn thing anymore."

Loot nodded subtly and sighed, returning the big pistol to his holster. "Probably best you didn't plug me if we're telling the truth. There's some problems coming down the rails and I might be the only type suited for the task."

"What specifically?"

"Sorry, kid. All this. I'm sorry."

As Laird began to ask the outlaw what he meant, Moreno slammed his fist against the side of the boy's head, just above the ear. Kip slumped down against the wall, instantly unconscious. Loot put a hand underneath his nose to make sure he was still breathing. "You'll be okay," he whispered. "Okay."

Moreno rubbed Kip's hair the way he'd seen Rufus do it. Soon after, the doctor was back in the office, hovering over Loot and his now motionless patient. "He went back to sleep?" Rufus asked, eyes sharp with skepticism. "You didn't dose him with my elixir, did you? Too much and there's no returning whence you came."

"No elixir. Put him out the old-fashioned way."

"Fantastic," Elias mumbled, scooting around Loot's brutish figure with agitated hand gestures. "Blows to the head aren't good for a person."

"I've taken my share."

"Not a powerful counter-argument. I'm sure your mountain hermitage is lovely, but most folks prefer more than trees for company. Could be you're not all there."

"Could be none of us are."

Doc grunted but gave no more response. He took a look around Kip's ear and positioned his neck so he'd get the most out of his breathing. "It's gonna be a lump, but I suppose he'll be fine. This is the part when I ask what the hell you're doing, by the way."

Loot turned his head to the sound of new voices coming from Doc's house. Women's voices. And Rooker, the deputy who talked funny and too often.

Moreno stood up and put on his massive sheepskin coat and wide-brim hat, showing Rufus a look that could only be interpreted as an order to be quiet. "I hit the kid because I don't want him trying to put himself in this thing anymore." Loot was quick with his words and whispering; two things he wasn't very tried at. "Amos still in your house?"

"Yeah."

"It's best I go now then. That's the mother and daughter just come in, I imagine. Cox won't leave them, especially if you insist."

"Suppose so. ER was supposed to keep them at the jail."

"That one ain't up for most tasks, let alone corralling womenfolk."

"I'd ask where you're off to, but it seems obvious." Rufus was standing with his hands on his hips at the center of the room, watching his outlaw friend of so many years checking his rifle and pistol. Readying for battle. He didn't want him to go. "This isn't your fault, Loot. Another way, perhaps."

"I appreciate it," Moreno said, smiling subtly. He racked a .45 caliber shell into the chamber of his rifle and gave his hat a little tap on the brim. "But the blame's mine. We both know it."

Heading out the door he offered Doc stern instructions to keep everybody there. He needed to know the sheriff and doctor were watching out for the rest of the Laird family. "Okay, old friend. Time I go meet another old friend."

CHAPTER 22:
THE DAUGHTER

IT WAS DARK WHEN LOOT STARTED FOR THE CHURCH. AT first he skirted the town, but after crouching down the length of four buildings, he gave up on stealth. *This is plumb stupid.* He stood up straight and walked defiantly through the trash-filled alley next to Grimes' General Store. He passed a clutch of youngsters and a few shopkeepers. They scattered like startled birds, one and all. Loot predicted as much. The only one with sand enough to face him was waiting at the end of town. He made the rest of his walk down the center of the road. It wasn't arrogance. He just didn't want to go about lying, like he was afraid for himself. Years of being alone had helped him along in the practice of self-assessment. His own well-being didn't figure in anymore. Only the people he cared about. He feared for *them.* They were all that mattered. The Lairds. Doc and Rufus. Jasper. And so on.

He smiled while passing the telegraph office, thinking how his Thunder Hill friends would react to this course. Amos Cox would be hot as a forge. More than eager to remind him of the time and trouble put into keeping his secret so many years. Rufus was Rufus; he'd offer up some form of agitation that Loot wouldn't nearly understand, then make a joke and say something dark about the state of everything. Ben was always hardest to figure. Moreno imagined a part of the preacher would be relieved to see his friend unchained from years of skulking around, the hiding that had become the bedrock of Loot's life. Ben was always saying *sorry* to Moreno. Apologizing to the outlaw for things that had nothing to do with him. *Sorry you have to live like that. I'm sorry you can't be part of Kip's life. I'm sorry you have to keep so many secrets.*

Moreno was done with secrets. He hoped that somewhere over and around, Ben was having a look at things with a nod and grin. "Guess I'm fixing to invade your church, old friend," he said out loud.

"Go easy now." The order came from a woman not half his age, sitting on the steps of the church with her right leg stretched down to the street. A decent enough position to draw a pistol and fire, assuming the one pulling knew the balance involved in shooting from their rear. Between them was a lit torch, sticking four feet or so out of the muddy road. It gave the little lady a mighty shadow.

Loot could see her hand dangling, gloved and ready. "You must be Sybille," he said. "Plan on going?" Loot halted his progress a few steps from the light. "No? I'll be getting on with it then." Moreno moved quick toward the torch and pulled it from the ground. At the same time, Sybille drew and followed him with her barrel, standing up in measured motion. Loot continued to her right, toward the Laird's house and barn.

"You need to hold it right there, big fella," she said, keeping her nerve with careful footing. The trail of light from the torch wasn't much for maintaining a good view of the ground. *Why isn't he stopping?*

"Pretty good with that draw," Loot said, passing by the house now. "'Course, no matter how it comes off, it ain't never perfect. His voice trailed off softly in the night, like he was called back on a particularly fond memory.

He seemed completely unconcerned with her. Irritating as it was, she was reluctant to let her tongue loose. This wasn't some cowpoke looking to bend her over behind a shitter. Loot Moreno. The scourge that killed Titus the Exile. In her dreams he was different. In the books and illustrations, he was different. *Make believe.* She told herself to forget all that and focus on real life. No more looking ahead. Just now. Sybille shook out the tension in her hands and reset her aim at the huge man ahead. "What are you doing?" she asked, trying to keep any emotion clear of her voice.

"Heading to the barn. I heard something might've got left there."

"That a fact?"

Loot didn't turn, deciding to ignore her last question. He didn't owe the girl anything, and she wasn't gonna be doing any shooting.

Opening the door, he saw the blood-stained straw in the middle of the floor. In the barn where they'd secreted him away from the world so many years ago. In the barn where he'd said his first words to Kip as a young man grown.

Sybille watched as Moreno aimed the torch around the structure before keeping it pointed at a support beam to his right. She wasn't supposed to fire, but she wasn't taking chances. A hair trigger brought to full stop would be the price for any menacing motion put her way. "You or him that left this?" he asked. The torch light danced in front of the symbol on the support beam. The symbol of the Three-in-One painted in dog's blood.

"It was me," she said, backing away just slightly. He was looking at her square now, contempt written on his scarred face.

"Scary tactics. Killing pups. I used to do the same thing with critters, back when Titus first grabbed me up. 'Course, I wasn't even ten at the time, but maybe you're running late to catch the train."

"Let's go to the church."

"Who are you?" Loot asked. With each word, she leaned back a little more. His voice seemed to rise up from the ground when he spoke full-hearted.

"I'm the daughter."

"Your last name's Clayton then," Moreno said, switching the torch to his left hand.

"Like I said. I'm the daughter."

"The daughter who just watched me free up for my gun."

"Maybe you haven't noticed what's pointed at your heart."

"I noticed. Noticed you flinching, too. You're scared, daughter."

"Think you can pull before I fill you with led? Bold as advertised, Mr. Moreno."

"Didn't say you were scared of *me*. Though you are." Loot took one more look at the symbol on the post. "Maybe you're scared of what he'll do if you shoot me before he gets his chance. Scared that being dark and hard ain't what you are. Not like him. Not like me." Moreno spit on the ground between them and started slowly toward her. "Don't be scared, little girl."

"I'm not."

"Just take me to church. Let's give your pa his shot."

CHAPTER 23:

BARBARIC

ELSIE STOOD WITH MABEL IN THE BACK OF DOC RUFUS'S house, waiting to enter his office. Kip was awake again, just minutes after the knock on his head from Loot. To everyone's surprise, he was acting with a full measure of calm. Elbert Rooker was stationed outside the backdoor. Cox was watching the front of the house, sitting on the narrow windowsill. Doc was in the living room, stoking a fire. It was growing colder every night. "Apologies for the draft," he said casually, like the temperature was the prevailing concern weighing everyone down. Cox continued looking through the curtains. Nothing of note. Everyone in Thunder Hill was hunkered down, trying to avoid whatever was going on down at the church. Loot Moreno's reappearance had spread through town fast as Mercury.

"Y'all can come in," Kip said. Mabel and Elsie entered with brave faces, trying not to look at his hand. It only served to make things more awkward, as he was trying in vain to button up his shirt. "One of you is gonna have to get over it. I'm having a drag-out fight getting myself dressed."

"Let me," said Mabel, walking swiftly to the bedside where Kip was standing. "My God." She trembled her way through his top three buttons. "I can't bear it..."

"Thanks, Mama," he whispered, hiding the injury behind his back as he kissed the top of her head. "Else. How about we all sit down for a second? Just family."

"I'd like that," Mabel said, waving her daughter over.

Elsie plopped down on a stool near the bed with tears forming. "Not the best of times, my friend."

"I get it. Has there been a minute in the last week where I wasn't getting beat down or patched up?"

"Don't forget drunk," Elsie said, with a sad little laugh.

"Apparently my name's Joel, by the way."

"Oh yeah. Nice to meet you, Joel. Welcome to Thunder Hill. Peaceful little corner of the world. Think you'll love it here."

"Well," Mabel said, sitting down on the foot of the bed so gently it could've been made of paper. "I never thought the sound of you two squawking back and forth would be a welcome sound."

"Did you know, Mama? My name? The names of my parents?"

Elsie looked at the floor and felt sad once again. *Poor Kip. Poor Mama. I never knew all of it. Didn't want to. I avoided the burden.*

"I never wanted to know," Mabel, brushing the hair from his eyes. "It was a miracle. We thought we were done having children. You came along. That's all I needed." She buried her head into her adopted son's chest. "Please forgive me. Please forgive me for everything."

He wrapped up Mabel tight. "You're forgiven."

"You're not raw?"

"For taking me in, feeding me, giving me a home and a family. Not raw, Mama. You're forgiven."

"Don't be funny."

"I can't help it. Somebody had to entertain you all these years. God knows it couldn't have been Else." He pressed his lips down on Mabel's head once more and leaned over to kiss Elsie on her cheek. It was soft and warm, still a bit wet from tears.

"I love you both," he said, voice instantly at a different pitch. "And we can talk about everything later." Kip started moving around the room quickly. He put on his vest and opened up the bottom drawer of Rufus's desk, pulling out an 1861 Remington pistol and a box of shells. Elsie and Mabel began to object, but he shut them down. "Syd could still be alive. He could be down at that church for all we know."

"Those people could kill you," Elsie said. "Look at your hand. Look at your whole body. You're not made for this."

Kip didn't respond. He went over to the backdoor and gave it a knock. Rooker stuck his head in. "ER."

"Hey there, Preach. Ma'am. Elsie."

"Come in here." Kip's hair fell down over his eyes as he talked and dealt with the surging pain. "I want you inside. Keep a close watch. If you let either of them out of your sight, I'm gonna come back and shoot you in the foot."

"C'mon, Preach."

Kip raised the Remington's barrel and stuck it under the deputy's chin. "Or I could just kill you right now. You think I care about you more than my brother? Or anyone else for that matter?"

"Son," Mabel gasped. She started to say more, but there was just enough admonishment in his bearing to keep her at bay.

"Hey," ER gulped, hands shaking in the air. "Gonna watch, pal. Will do."

"Thanks," Kip said, walking by Elsie and Mabel. "Rooker," he said, not turning, "you keep them put, dammit. Keep them safe."

Sheriff Cox and Rufus were whispering by the window as he came rumbling through the house, feet heavy with intentions.

They turned toward the young man. The whites of his eyes were as red as the bandage covering his right hand. "So, I guess you were lying when you told me you'd calmed down," Rufus said, standing up in front of the door, hands in pockets.

"I guess so," Kip answered. "He didn't hit me that hard. Now get out of the way, Rufus."

"Jesus Christ."

"Easy, Doc. Not asking."

"Calm down, son," Cox said.

"I'm not your son." Kip aimed the big pistol at the sheriff. "I'm going down to that church. Are you just going to leave Sydney to these people? What is it you think you're doing here? Protecting me? I don't want the help of cowards."

"Put down the damn gun," Doc said.

"Sheriff. Don't raise that rifle. I can still shoot with my left."

Cox, who'd been on the windowsill, stood up slowly. "What's the plan here, exactly?"

Kip was blinking at a furious pace, trying to shut out the hurt from his hand. "First you tell me who they are."

"Fallstead and his daughter," Elias said, leaning up against the wall.

"Don't you get it, Doc? I'm not hearing anymore lies today."

"Kip—"

"Enough, Elias." Cox crossed his arms, turning all his attention to the younger man. "You know who it is."

"Dan Clayton," Kip said.

There was no response. The silence was confirmation enough.

Rufus postured up and approached Kip until the barrel of the pistol was sticking in his chest. "Apparently Amos thinks it's time to lay down the cards." He kept coming forward, forcing the gun harder into his skin.

"We didn't know it was Clayton until Loot came back. We told him about Fallstead. Described him. Mentioned the thing with the blasted dog. That was more than enough for him to call it sure."

Laird nodded his head, grinding teeth and breathing roughly through his nose. "All right." He pulled the barrel from Rufus's chest and slammed his left elbow into the doctor's jaw, knocking him to the floor. With the pistol still aimed at Cox, he unlocked the front door. "Sorry about that Rufus. I really am. But the man who murdered my parents is here."

"I'll ask again," Cox said, standing still as a stone. "What's the plan here? More blood?"

The question caught Kip on his heels, but he made little show of it. He hadn't worked out the particulars. "I can walk down there alone, or we can go together, and you can help me end this for good. Suppose shooting me in the back is an option if you're really intent on stopping me."

The sheriff glanced down at Doc. He was propped up against the wall, shaking away the fog from his eyes. "What do you think, Rufus?"

"I think more than likely we all get killed. Damn kid. Patch you up like a gentleman and you knock me down…"

"Don't tell me," Kip said.

"Barbaric," muttered the doctor, checking for loose teeth.

"Help me get him up," Cox said, pushing the end of Kip's pistol in a safer direction with a dismissive roll of the eyes. "If we live, we're gonna have a talk about you pointing guns at people."

"Barbaric," Rufus repeated.

CHAPTER 24:

REVELATIONS

A SET OF HEAVY GREEN DOUBLE DOORS SERVED AS THE
entrance to the church. As he pushed them open, Loot remembered the
smell of fresh paint all that time ago. His first visit to Thunder Hill. Bleeding
and holding a baby. God, what a hopeless night that was.

"Get going," Sybille said. She was four paces behind, gun still trained
on the big man. He barely heard her. Between that night long ago and the
task just ahead, his mind was occupied.

Stopping in the open entranceway, Moreno was surprised how high
the steeple looked and how small and simple everything else was. Eight
tidy pews on either side of the single walkway leading up to the pulpit.
A small raised altar at the back, a couple feet higher than the rest of the
room. A large wooden cross on the far wall. For a moment he saw Preacher
Benjamin Laird up there, making grand statements about hope or help or
some other nonsense, warm, guileless smile on his face. The image quickly
evaporated when he heard the grating call of Dan Clayton. His old cohort
was sitting in a simple little chair in the space between the front pew and
the pulpit, facing sideways toward another unoccupied chair just like it.

The altar and pulpit were covered with burning candles, as was the wooden floor in the space in and around the two chairs.

"This is something of a scene, Dan." Moreno walked slowly down the aisle, turning enough to see that the girl had stopped by the entrance.

"You met my daughter," Clayton said, still looking forward at the empty seat as Loot continued his approach.

"I did," Moreno said. The bass from his voice filled the church. The old mixed breed pointed a thumb back over his shoulder. "See you're starting to teach her the old ways. That's something. I guess."

"Do you want to take a chair?" Clayton asked. He made a slow motion toward his pocket. "I'm gonna have a cigarette. You having one?"

Loot stepped by the last pew and over a few of the candles, taking the seat. It was nothing but right angles and sturdy for its size, barely creaking under his bulk. "Yeah, why not. I don't smoke enough these days."

The next few minutes were slow going. Everything was yellow and flickering, quiet and strange. Loot couldn't believe he was looking at Clayton. His red beard looked a touch violent in the candlelight. Like it was almost on fire. He was calm, as settled in his ways as ever. Always the powder barrel sitting in the corner. The barrel everyone forgets about until it explodes and destroys everything around.

Finally, Clayton tossed him a rough-rolled smoke. "You got a match?" Loot asked, shortening the question. "Forget it," he grunted, leaning down to grab a candle.

The little church was a place of peace as the former compatriots smoked and thought about the things they'd done together and apart. "You look pretty good. *Marshal*. I hear your sense of humor isn't what it used to be, though."

"I was young when you went away," Clayton said, smoke and rasp on the end of every syllable. "It was still a game. Everything's a game when you're young, no matter how good you are."

"Maybe," Loot said, taking in another drag. "I almost don't remember being young.

"It's hard to recall killing my brothers and father, is it?"

Loot waited until his lungs were clear. "They weren't your brothers, Dan. He wasn't your father. Just killers. One and all. Shitty, bad men. I had enough. You'd had enough. I remember *that*. Hell, you agreed with me near the end."

"You took it upon yourself."

"I took my chance when I had it. The way we were taught. And I wasn't going to watch another woman or child or helpless spud get gunned down for another bucket of blood and money."

"It was about more than that. We made sacrifices. We could see the things nobody else could see."

"We couldn't see shit," Loot boomed. "Now I don't believe in this here," he continued, pointing at the cross on the wall, "but at least that's a sacrifice already done. You said we were making sacrifices. The people *we killed* made the sacrifice. You think they gave a damn about the Three Places? Probably not, I'm guessing. Not too many of them rolled over to be slaughtered in the name of Titus's story."

"Don't act like it isn't real."

"It felt real," Moreno said, rubbing out the cigarette on the heel of his boot. "But things get twisted when you're caught up. We was just caught up. Kids. Kids turned murderers."

"You ran. Hid from me. Like a coward."

"If not wanting part in any more killings means I'm a coward, you got me."

"I got you."

"I appreciated the cigarette, *Marshal*."

"Is that right?"

"But I know why you smoke. It's like one of those things folks do to make you look off their failings."

"Meaning what?"

"Means you've turned boring. Bad at conversation. And I'd know, been living in a damn mountain for years." Loot waited for a response, or at least a change in his foe's expression. Nothing came. He let out a breath. "Okay. These candles are starting to run low. You set out the chairs in the old way, so I say we get to blasting."

Clayton leaned forward in his chair, dropping his dying cigarette on the floor. "You've been hiding away. Practicing peace."

Moreno smiled and pushed the long brim of his hat back so Clayton could see his eyes. "Something like that."

"All those years tucked away. What is it? Some way to forget the blood you let?"

"There's no forgetting."

"We agree on that, old friend."

"Okay then."

"Before we draw," Clayton started, pulling the right side of his coat behind his back, "there's one more thing."

"Lotsa words. Reckon you been planning this here situation for some time."

"After I kill you, I'm going to kill the boy. The sheriff. The doctor. The writer. I'm going to kill the family that took the boy in. It might be I have to kill this whole town. Cut them to pieces, all their parts."

"That right?"

"Yeah."

"Think they might snatch that badge from you. Wiping out bakers and such."

Clayton ripped the star from his jacket, throwing it at the wall. "The big lad. He's the one from that farm. We never found a child, but I know he was around. You took him. Brought him here. Your first good deed, was it?"

"I'm gonna take off my coat. You mind?"

Clayton gave a slight nod. "Might be I'm wrong, but my daughter over there got it from that hayseed deputy. The one I gutted just earlier. A child showed up here," he whispered, looking around the church. "Thought you'd want to know that your first benevolent act is the reason all these people are going to meet with my bad side. The way I see it."

Moreno was churning in his bowels now. Keeping planted in the moment was never a passing task before a shooting, but he'd always been able to stay level. Not presently. Now he was thinking about the demise of his friends. How he'd turned away from fighting. How Dan Clayton had kept up with his practice, masquerading as a lawman, putting folks down with that pistol. His massive chest was expanding and contracting. A bead of sweat was running down the big scar over his eye.

Too many thoughts. Clayton was focused. That needed changing. His hand was about to get a mind of its own, but he clenched his muscles and took a chance. "Speaking of your daughter, does she know who her momma is?"

* * *

"I can't hear a damn thing," Rufus whispered, strangling his scatter-gun in dreadful anticipation.

Cox mouthed *keep quiet* from the other side of the steps. They were clear of the door, just in case anyone came out shooting.

"There's just the two in there. All I saw, anyway."

"Oh, I feel a rush of comfort," said Rufus. "Keep your trap shut, Bedford." Jasper had joined the impromptu posse as they were walking down to the church, partially clothed from a night of fornication with

Millie Dee and Stella Ann, shivering beside the doctor with a pistol thick as his arm. Being the only other person in town that wasn't scared of Loot, he'd been watching wide-eyed from the porch of Trussel's saloon and yelled out to Kip what he saw, about Moreno meeting the girl before entering the church. All of this intelligence was spoken in haste as Kip led a march down the street. The doctor and sheriff protested the writer being there but only with half hearts. They had other things on their mind.

So, there they all were.

The plan was to wait for Kip to come back around to the front. There was a little door in the back of the building that opened into a space under the altar platform. Above the space was a trapdoor covered by the altar. Ben had built it that way for storage and for a way out in case of fire. Kip's plan was to get inside and see what he could see. "If you hear shooting before then, make up your own minds," he'd said.

That's fine was Cox's response. *That's fine?* was Rufus's response.

Back out front, Doc was leaning closer and closer to the door, again trying to make out what was transpiring inside. He made an ungraceful motion toward Cox across the stairs, holding up his silver pocket watch.

Once more, the gritty sheriff mouthed *keep quiet*. The doctor couldn't recall seeing a silent communication relayed with such stern emphasis. Rufus leaned away from the door and felt Jasper Bedford press tighter against his body.

"What did he say?" the writer whispered.

Rubbing his forehead against the cold metal of the double-barrel, Rufus whispered, "Sheriff said he's real glad you're here."

"Indeed?"

"No, Jasper. Indeed not."

* * *

"Has he told you, little girl?" Loot asked, turning his head slightly toward the front of the church. Sybille had been sitting quietly in the back row, feet up on the next pew. "You didn't answer, Dan. What'd you tell her about her mother?"

Kip had burrowed his big frame through the little backdoor and now was up on his feet, searching for the latch to the trapdoor with his bloody right hand. He could hear them talking. It was muffled, but clear enough. The boom of Loot's voice. The sandpaper of Dan Clayton's. Finally, the latch. He pulled it back carefully with his ring finger and thumb.

"Stay back there, Sybille," Clayton said, hearing the girl's boots smack flat against the floorboards.

"What's he got to say on the matter?" she asked.

"You do as I tell you. Don't come closer, now."

Moreno had gone fishing and come up with something. He didn't know if his wager had hit the mark or come somewhere close, but all the same it had Clayton on his heels. Good enough.

Kip closed his eyes and lifted the door, praying the hinge wouldn't creak. It let out a little something but didn't draw attention his way. He gave his vision a second to adjust. The embroidered altar cover was hanging almost to the floor, allowing him a few inches to see the candles and the gunmen, sitting in chairs just feet from each other. He was standing just about straight, the door resting on his head. A thousand questions overran him, but he shut them out. *Just wait. Just breathe.*

"Sybille," Clayton said, nails on a chalkboard. "Go outside and have a look. He don't know nothing."

"Mind if I get one more of them cigarettes, Dan? No? Well, thought I'd venture. Anyway, this is turning mighty interesting."

"Enough."

"No need to go outside, little girl. I told you there weren't nobody else coming. I knocked the young preacher out myself. Not as bad as shooting him, but enough to keep him away from this here."

"What was he on about, Pa?"

"He's playing games, Sybille. Check outside like I told you."

"Playing games seems to be more y'all's style. Like when you took off that boy's fingers." Moreno turned his head about a quarter inch in Sybille's direction but kept his eyes fixed on Clayton.

"Man stepped to me with a gun. I didn't see a boy."

"You didn't see your brother, maybe what you mean."

The air in the church got thicker. Sybille stopped her advance, halfway down the aisle. Kip almost dropped the Remington as he was trying to set his aim on Dan Clayton. Loot's right leg was stretched out and stiff. He felt a little like his old self. Dropping all sorts of awful down on folks.

"We're done talking," Clayton said, settling back in his seat. "When the first candle burns out, we go."

"Surely," Loot said. "Sybille. I didn't know until just now, but your daddy's confirmed it. The shot up preacher's your brother. Dan here murdered his father and raped y'all's mama."

"What is this?" she asked, barely audible. Sybille stood motionless and gave a thought to the first time she saw the preacher when they came to Thunder Hill. She remembered being hit with something funny, thinking it was something more than her normal suspicious nature.

The girl was elsewhere. She turned her back and started walking down the aisle the other way.

"Goddamn you," Clayton said.

"Let's not wait for the goddamn candles," Loot answered, throwing the blasphemy back at his foe. It felt like a good way to mock the bloodthirsty gunman's overstretched bluster.

The draw was just about even. Not much in it.

Each man got a shot off. Neither one hit the floor, but through the smoke Kip saw Clayton's pistol slump down by his leg.

He charged up the two steps, flinging the heavy altar up and out of the way to move quickly for Clayton.

Sybille couldn't even turn to see. Her tan skin was whitewashed as she found herself staring into the guns of Cox, Rufus, and Jasper Bedford. They were through the front door and screaming something fierce, trying to get her quick hands stayed. Her speed was known by now and their hollering held fear.

Kip kicked Clayton's pistol away and knocked him on his back with the butt of the loaded and cocked Remington. The murderer was bleeding bad through his shirt and jacket from a wound in the right arm. Kip put a mean knee into Clayton's chest and pressed his boot down onto his free arm, pushing the Remington's barrel into the downed man's forehead hard enough to draw blood. "All that waiting," Kip said. "Can't imagine this is the end you were waiting for."

"What is it you're waiting for?" Clayton growled, almost foaming from the mouth. He pushed his head harder against the metal. "I'm father to your sister, *boy*. The killer of your brother, *boy*."

"You need to die," Laird said. "For the mother and father I can't remember, you need to."

"Your father was a coward. Same as you. Your mother was the fighter, but in the end, she gave herself to me. Stupid, beaten bitch. I killed her the day Sybille was born."

Kip forced his knee deeper into Clayton's chest. He longed to hear bones cracking through skin. A simple bullet didn't seem to match up to the enormity of a devil's crimes.

"Kip! Get away. That ain't for you." It was Moreno, booming at his back. He turned to see Doc Rufus holding a rag against the old outlaw's stomach, shaking his head in frustration.

"Stop the bleeding," Loot moaned.

"I'm trying damn you!" yelled Doc.

"Where—"

"She's over there with Amos and Jasper," Rufus sputtered, cursing something else under his breath as he tried to manage a better look at his friend's guts. "The girl, she didn't even put up a fight. Something wrong with her, I think."

A cascade of blood came pouring out of Moreno's mouth as he tipped forward against the physician. "Stop the bleeding."

"Doing my best, Loot."

Kip checked to make sure his weight was still pushing down on all the right places before turning back to Moreno. The church floor looked like something from a pagan nightmare; the blood and wax mixed strangely underneath the still flickering candles.

One more time: "Stop the bleeding."

Before the doctor could respond, Loot grabbed the back of Doc's silver hair. "Not me, you idiot. Clayton's."

"What about you?"

"Go on, Elias. Kip," he gasped, opening and closing his eyes to stay present, "check him for any more weapons. Be thorough. Then... let the Doc patch him up."

Sheriff Cox had made his way down the aisle. Sybille's fancy rig was slung over his shoulder as he forced her down into a front pew, ordering Jasper to stand away with his gun trained on her. The sheriff's rifle was resting on his other shoulder as he stepped over the blood to pat Doc on the back. "Do as he says, Rufus."

"Hey there, Amos," Moreno whispered, slipping lower in his chair as the moments went hazily by.

"Hey there, Loot. Got banged up I see."

"Just a bit," the outlaw said, nodding ahead.

Cox understood. He pulled Rufus away and directed the physician around the sprawled body of Dan Clayton.

"I'm gonna have to go get my bag," Doc said, tying off the arm wound with a piece of his shirt. "This tore up the bone."

"Go," Cox said, kneeling down next to Kip. The Remington was still flush to the murderer's head. "What do you think, kid?" the lawman asked.

"I have to kill him. It's the only thing to do. Justice."

Amos put a slow and gentle hand on the young man's shoulder. He could feel the heat and hate pulsing under his skin. "I don't know what to say, kid. If you do it, no one here's gonna look askance, but your whole life I've known you. This just ain't what you are."

"He raped and murdered my mother, Sheriff. He killed Sydney."

"I cut them. Sacrificed them for the Sight."

Kip couldn't countenance another word. Not from anyone. He gave Clayton a vicious pistol whip and handed the Remington to a surprised Cox.

The preacher slowly got his feet underneath him and looked at the cross hanging on the back wall. He stared at it for a few seconds, wondering vaguely how he'd get beyond any of what had transpired.

"Kip," Moreno whispered, trying not to tip out of the chair. "Can you wrap your shirt around me?"

Kip turned and looked tiredly at the bleeding outlaw. "I can do that."

"Good. Because my guts are sticking out more than's comfortable. And I got one more idea."

CHAPTER 25:

INTERESTING YOUNG MAN

DAWN WAS STARTING TO BREAK. A WHOLE TOWN WAS IN need of an explanation. Things demanding attention. Still. Kip required a stint of reflection and aimed to have it.

"It's never the end of the world," Jasper said cautiously, standing out in front of the barn built by Ben Laird decades ago. They'd cobbled a fledgling fire together with sticks from the family supply.

"I'm a Christian," Kip said. He was wearing an insufficient wool jacket, standing near the flames alongside the shivering writer.

"Of course you are. Who isn't?" he coughed, trying not to pay attention to the womanly smells of Millie Dee and Stella Ann still stuck to his aging body. "Anyway, damn fine display of charity and self-control back there, not plugging Clayton permanent. You're an authentic practitioner."

"No. You misunderstand. I meant that as a Christian, I believe there's an actual end of the world. Can't hand out specifics, but it's coming, somewhere down the line."

"Well, it's probably not today, young man."

"No." He was tired, voice flat as prairieland. "I reckon not."

Bedford pulled out the cowhide notebook he carried around in his frayed brown vest and set to tearing out pages. By the slow and laborious tempo of the task, Kip knew it to be causing the wordsmith a huge amount of pain.

"Sorry you're having to do this, Jasper."

"Ah. It's nothing. Comparable to incinerating Shakespeare's lost works. Something like that, perhaps."

"You got that pipe handy?"

Bedford finished with the last of his pages and packed a fresh bowl for Kip. "Didn't know you partook."

"Not usually. Just can't seem to get the taste of blood out of my mouth."

Jasper nudged him with a leather-covered flask. "This might help."

"Damn grateful," Kip said, silently using a moment to consider his recent alcohol intake. It was nearing a habit.

Watching the smoke take away all his poignant observations, Bedford smiled. "You're an interesting young man, Mr. Laird."

"Call me Joel. Or Mr. Wilkins."

"See? That's exactly what I'm talking about."

"I'm glad you find me a subject of fascination, Jasper. And not sure if it softens the blow, but I admire the fact that you're not going to write about any of this."

"Who would believe me?"

"Still. A front row view of the legends of the Three-In-One. You'd likely have a hard time printing enough."

"Eh, I know the game, young squire. Every soul in Thunder Hill's going to become a professional author before the week's out. Journalism is a strange thing. With the blasted telegraph shooting nonsense every which way, I don't even want to know where things are going."

Kip smiled slightly and took a puff off the pipe. He was stalling and knew it. The only thing he didn't know was what he was putting off the most. Just one more minute for peace. Maybe two. The morning was cool, the fire warm, the company strange and pleasant. "Jasper," he said, opening his eyes wide for the wind. "It strikes me, I never asked how you knew Loot Moreno. How exactly he found your good graces."

"This was years back. I was travelling from some shit town out past the territory line. Some riders set upon me."

"He intervened?"

"Indeed. It ended up being a pretty slipshod operation as far as armed bandits go. They beat me pretty bad, but he came riding in like a ghost." Bedford wiggled his fingers, asking for a chance to smoke the pipe. "It was all hazy, mind you, but he took care of the situation. Got me close to the next town so I could get patched up."

"So, he killed them, your attackers?" Kip asked, warming his hands on the fire. For a moment he forgot about the lacuna where his fingers once were, interested as he was in Jasper's forthcoming.

"Not a one, squire. Didn't kill one."

"I don't understand."

"He made a few passes. Shot all four of those bastards in one place or another, but he was done killing at that point in the story. Had been for a spell."

"Tough to believe. How anyone could be that good with a gun?"

"A rare talent. Something to see. It's going to be hard." There was a brief pause, then the old man inhaled deeply. "It's going to be hard."

The preacher took a look out at the town and then back over his shoulder. Elsie was sitting next to Mabel on the porch of the Laird house. ER was standing like a well-dressed statue at the open door, staring at something inside. Kip felt a twinge from his hand and shook it out, doing his utmost not to wince or react dramatically. The injury would heal, but the handicap was something he'd carry till his dying breath. Better off just getting on with it, all things considered.

"You saw the talent, of course," Jasper said, calling Kip's attention back to their conversation and the dying fire.

"It was a lot of talking. They drew so fast it was over before I even realized it happened."

"That's how it is. The best shooters, that's how it is. Uncanny to see." Jasper tapped him playfully on the arm. "And you maybe saw the two best. Ever."

"Don't sound so jealous. We're talking about people shooting each other. Violence isn't romance, Jasper."

"Huh. Maybe not in the moment, but don't tell that to most of the poets and writers in history. There'd be a sudden famine of myth and legends."

Laird knew what Bedford was trying to say, and the newsman had a point. Still, he wasn't going to stand there and act appreciative of what he'd witnessed. Kip was glad to be alive. Glad that Elsie and Mabel and Lindy were okay. That was all the good he could allow himself to feel. He extended his left hand to Jasper. "Guess I'll be shaking with this one for a bit," he smiled. "Thanks for helping out, Mr. Bedford."

"Of course," Jasper said, bowing and tapping his spotted forehead with his ready right forefinger. "To more peaceful days, young squire."

"Amen."

Kip turned from the fire and started walking his way over to the family house. He ascended the steps and nodded at Elsie; she was holding Mabel's head against her chest, sharing the pain of Sydney's loss. The scene caused his eyes to water, but he coughed away the impulse before it could take proper hold. "Thanks, Rooker," he said, patting the deputy on the back.

"What are we doing here?" ER asked, pointing into the house. Sybille Clayton was sitting in a chair in the middle of the front room with her arms crossed. Her usually full lips were clenched tight, as were her fists. Rooker nodded at her and continued. "After what these here did, I wouldn't have a problem plugging the little lady in her pretty head. Ceremonials be damned."

Sybille looked ready to spring from her chair, but she stopped when Kip pulled Rooker away from the door. "Nobody's plugging anyone, ER. We're gonna get to working this thing out."

Rooker laughed mockingly and moved his hands from his shiny belt to his fancy vest pockets, like he was settling in. "I know y'all think I'm the dumb one."

"That's not true, Elbert."

The deputy looked up at the much taller Kip and moved in close. "Sydney was my partner. We might a not got long all the time, but who does?" Rooker was talking straight and honest; something that had Laird off guard and a little surprised. ER leaned in closer still. "And don't go on lying to me, Preach. You've been one of the only honest folks I've ever met, since we was kids. Never liked you much, but that's besides the point. All these lies, I'm not sure how much they figure in, but Sydney's killing is at least a little attached. I ain't letter smart, but I ain't dumb enough to let that get away from me."

"Not sure what to say."

"She needs to die." He pushed Kip's sturdy frame with a strong thud as he walked off the porch. "I'm gonna go take a turn around town," he said, voice getting softer as he headed toward the center of Thunder Hill. "Y'all better get this shit sorted."

He allowed Rooker's speech to sink in. It was hard to argue with the man, considering a few hours ago he'd stuck a pistol underneath his chin and *asked* him for a favor. Maybe they'd all taken ER for granted. Maybe he was doing the same thing right now, but there was no time to spend worrying about it at present. Other accounts to settle.

"I'll see about making it up to you," he said under his breath.

CHAPTER 26:

BLOOD

STEPPING THROUGH THE DOOR TO FACE SYBILLE CLAYTON was maybe the single strangest moment in Kip's short life. It seemed each thing trumped the last, but this stood out even in a time of firsts. The sister he'd grown up with was with the mother who'd raised him, just outside. The only blood kin he knew of in the world was sitting before him, perhaps the principle guilty party in the killing of his adoptive brother.

"What test is this?" he said, closing the front door. He tried to take stock of her appearance, but the old straw hat she was wearing obscured the view.

"What?"

He walked stiffly over to the wall and grabbed a footstool, setting it down next to Sybille's chair. With just the two of them in the house, the cool drafts were working their way around. He tightened Ben's jacket to his body and took to sitting.

"I asked what test this is."

"Not sure how to respond to that," she said, looking at him. He was looking down.

"The question wasn't meant for you. I was asking. No matter."

"So, what happens now?" she asked.

"I'm not sure how to respond to *that*, gunfighter."

She looked up. He recognized her eyes. A green that overpowered the rest of her features. "You're cracking wise? Seems a strange thing to do, considering who you are."

"You can't apprehend who I am. Hey. You can give me one joke, considering what you've taken." Kip held up his hand for a reminder of what she'd taken.

"Damn fool thing to do, charging me up like that."

"It's exactly what you wanted."

"A simple tactic. You never stopped to think. Never stopped to think at the church, either. It's a miracle you're still alive."

Kip sat up straight, realizing he'd been leaning over a little too close. "You want some coffee? Smells like my—sister put some on."

"No thanks," Sybille said, dismissing the offer with a quick turn of her head.

"'Course you do. I'll be right back." He stood and moved sharply to the kitchen, keeping a good view of her while he poured two cups from the pot warming on top of the stove. He wasn't afraid of her going for a weapon. They'd taken her guns away and cleared the house of anything remotely dangerous. But still, she needed watching. From her attitude, it was hard to make out if she was more cornered, defeated, or something else entirely.

She was strange. Too strong to be any woman he'd ever met, but it wasn't size. Just a bearing and attitude. Kip thought about her growing up, riding around with a lunatic like Dan Clayton. How could she not turn out to be something wholly different than he was used to? Thinking about it through the lens of her unusual rearing, one might argue that she'd managed to come through rather normal. Kip made an attempt to gather his wandering thoughts and focus on the heart of things: Sydney was dead. Whatever part she played, her hand was in it.

He set down the cups of coffee and pulled a little side table over for her to use before returning to his stool. "I was thinking," he said. "There's no way I'm gonna understand you. Blood or no blood."

"'Cause we got similar faces don't make things easier," she said, drinking down the hot beverage without flinching. Kip looked at his cup and couldn't help being set on his heels from her apparent lack of feeling. He wondered if it was a demonstration for his benefit. "I'll say this. I didn't know who you were when we got here. We came for Moreno. It's plain as that. And your brother, he wasn't supposed to die. That wasn't the plan."

Laird leaned his big frame forward. "You're a silly girl, aren't you?"

Sybille met his hard demeanor with equal severity. "We grew up the way we did. No sense in it. I learned my ways and you yours. If you want me to say I'm sorry, I'll say it. I'm finished, either way."

"So that's what you want? Everything to be over?"

Sybille sat back and once again crossed her arms. "I keep thinking about all the things that led us here. Revenge and loyalty…"

"Hate," Kip said, covering his eyes. "Hate, black as coal. Beliefs that spur people to take lives. It's a damn waste. The world is cruel enough. People don't want to see…"

Sybille could tell he was crying. "I think we're both silly, Preacher. So, get done wailing and let's walk this out to the end."

Kip put up a fight with his emotions until they burned themselves out. No matter what Doc or Moreno said, he'd lived his life high on the notion that a man could make the right choice. That all seemed like the dream of a boy. Sybille had thrown his words back in his face, and maybe she was right. *A silly boy.*

"I'm tired," he said, wiping away the last of his tears.

"Me too, Preacher. Say we go on with it."

CHAPTER 27:

SOLUTIONS

AS THE MORNING SUN ROSE TO WARM THE TOWN OF THUNDER Hill, the residents gathered enough sand to emerge from their respective holes. Word had spread that the danger was over. All manner of nonsense was working its way around the rumor mill, but a majority of the townsfolk were about their business, eager for the big event. There was gonna be a hanging. Justice would finally have its day.

The jail was a bloody mess. Doc Rufus had to apply every bit of his skill to keep Dan Clayton's wound from killing him. He was weak and pale, shackled to the bars of the cell.

"We best get to," Loot said, speaking softly in pained syllables to Rufus and Cox.

"You have to let us try again," Cox said, standing by the door. "We need to get that bullet out of you."

Rufus was kneeling next to Moreno, applying a fresh set of bandages to his stomach. They had the big man sprawled out on the desk. Doc gave the sheriff a look of defeat before returning to his work. Wherever the slug had ended up, the physician couldn't find it. It was hiding, continuing to shred apart the old outlaw's insides something wicked.

"Son of a bitch," Rufus gritted, hands slipping from sweat and the bloody afters of a killing wound.

"Doc don't seem to share your sentiment, Cox," Moreno said. "Just patch me up good enough to get the job done."

Outside, Jasper Bedford watched as a whispering crowd started to gather around the gallows. He took a drink from his flask and dabbed sweat from his tired head. Mr. Weaver walked up and stopped next to the newspaperman, talking erratically about the state of his telegraph office. How his face might never heal right. Jasper, the man who spent a lifetime listening to everyone and remembering everything, barely heard a thing. He couldn't help but blame himself. If he hadn't gone to Loot and told him about Ben Laird, none of this would've happened. Moreno would be safely hidden away, as always. He wouldn't have come to Thunder Hill and gotten in a fracas. Gotten shot.

And on and on.

Weaver wearied of being ignored and eventually moved on, leaving Jasper to stare at the platform and the nooses that hung from the cross-beam. A big ungainly lad was standing at the top of the stairs waving a dirty old hat, keeping people from disturbing the setup. He was smiling strangely and repeating something that Jasper couldn't hear; the grumbling crowd was growing in volume as the minutes rolled by. Clogging up the street was a wagon that looked like it had gone 'round the world. As it passed by, the driver yelled out at Jasper, "What's going on?"

Bedford didn't want to be rude, so he chose to point at the scaffold rather than say anything out loud. The young man driving the wagon was bone thin and carting around his meager possessions, plus a wife and little girl that looked like they'd seen nothing but the hard side of life. "Sorry to be interrupting," the scrawny newcomer said. "We'll be on our way. Don't want any part of those doings."

Jasper touched his forehead to the youngster's wife as they moved along. He wished more were like them, wanting nothing to do with the sad business to come. Unfortunately, that wasn't the case. A town of people that cowered at the thought of a few men with guns were all too ready to cheer violence from behind a wall of law and order. He felt sick in his guts. Sick to be a human being. "You're taking this personally, Bedford," he said out loud, dumping more liquor down his throat.

Back inside, Doc Rufus touched foreheads with Loot Moreno. "It's not bleeding for the moment, but it's only a matter of time."

"Won't matter by then," Loot said, trying not to gasp. "And don't look so pale. You neither, Cox. We're finally closing the book on this thing."

The sheriff looked around the room. Clayton was cold and trembling from blood loss on the floor. So be it. His old friend dying, on the other hand, was not something he was ready to lay down.

A knock at the backdoor. Cox snapped a round ready in his rifle and walked over the blood and used bandages littering the jailhouse. "Who's there?"

"Kip. The girl's with me."

The sheriff opened up and took two quick steps back, almost tripping on the outstretched legs of Dan Clayton. His rifle was pointed firmly at her chest and Kip had a pistol at her back, but the guns didn't seem to have any control over her. Sybille walked casually and moved as she liked. You could shoot her, but she wasn't going out dancing to anyone else's tune.

"Ah shit," she said, dropping down to her knees. "Pa. These bastards got you all chained up." She turned and looked at Rufus. "Thought you people were supposed to be civilized. The hell is this?"

Doc left his post next to Moreno and stood over the girl and her father. "I won't be having it, young lady. Not today. Not today. He got the best I could give. The best I could do." Rufus's voice was loud but tremulous, and as he spoke, he waved his hands around, casting Moreno's and Clayton's blood about the jail. "The best I could do."

She turned away from Doc, wiping her face to address her pallid father. While they whispered, Moreno grunted an order for Kip to help him up. "Have you decided?" he asked, holding out an arm for the young man to take.

"I have."

Moreno coughed as he transferred weight to his feet. "You're predictable as your pa. But there's things left unfinished."

"I know. I'm willing to take a risk. Thing is, I was given a real chance," Kip said, looking down at Sybille. "Think she should get one too."

Moreno ran a hand through Kip's shaggy mane. "You need to see the barber."

"Things have been a little busy."

"I suppose they have," Loot said, nodding at Cox. "Let's get this done."

Kip gave Moreno a gentle hug. "Thank you."

The old outlaw clenched his jaw and walked out into the light for the very last time, Cox's gun at his back. Not long and the sheriff was back to fetch Dan Clayton. It took the work of a few of the townsfolk to get him up the steep stairs of the gallows.

As the noise outside rose steadily, Kip and his half-sister were left alone in the jail. "He tell you anything important?"

"He was crossing to one of the Places. Nothing much to say."

"You better get going," Laird said. A large portion of him still wanted her dead. He breathed in the smell of blood coming from almost every surface of the jail.

Enough.

"Every eye in town is going to be focused on one place."

"Can I have my guns?" she asked. "Okay, fine."

"Be careful out there."

"Yeah," she said, putting her thumbs inside the waist of her pants. "They wanted me dead, right? They had to."

Kip sighed and looked down at his only remaining kin. "They wanted what I wanted. And for anyone else, you escaped. I'd ride a bit before getting comfortable."

"Never been comfortable, Preacher," she said, stopping by the door. "Brother."

"Stay out of trouble. Maybe start by picking up a Bible."

"And you better pick up a gun. Three hours a day with that left hand after prayers or whatever the hell it is you do."

"That's a deal."

The growing sound of the crowd made it impossible to say more without distraction. She was out the backdoor, away from her big brother. Kip rubbed his eyes and made for the front. This was a show. Parts to play. The sunlight hit him hard. The bustle of the citizenry, eager to see the display in which he still had a role.

From the back end of the crowd, Jasper Bedford watched Kip Laird rising the stairs of the scaffolding. "Damn," he said, pulling out a little spare notebook and pencil from his pocket. "Can't help it," he mumbled, elbowing for enough space to write his account.

The citizens of Thunder Hill clapped and clamored, ready to receive their entertainment. At the top of the high structure stood a young man named Kip Laird, the newly-minted leader of the Thunder Hill congregation, along with the noble Sheriff Amos Cox. The sun was high enough to beam down the backsides of the prisoners as they stood on unsteady feet, nooses cinched around their necks, blood trickling down various wounds in their bodies. Minutes earlier, this humble reporter was witness to an extraordinary revelation: We learned that Marshal Holt Fallstead was actually the outlaw Dan Clayton, evidenced by the infamous Three-in-One symbol carved into his back. Readers may be reticent to believe me, but mine eyes and unimpeachable honor testify to the veracity of it. Be warned, fair readers, the surprises didn't end there. Just previous, we had already learned that the fugitive Brandon Calhoun was in fact Loot Moreno, villainous cutthroat and bandit of legend and yore. He confessed his crimes voluntarily, asking forgiveness for himself and peace to those who he might've wronged, though he seemed to expect neither.

Dan Clayton had nothing for the crowd. He looked on at Moreno with Lucifer's contempt as the young preacher bestowed upon the citizenry a few emotional and poignant words that would've done old Martin Luther himself proud.

Clayton was the first to go. Sheriff Cox pulled the release on the trapdoor and the crowd went eerily silent when the splitting sound of a broken neck reverberated down the busy thoroughfare. I myself admit to jumping in my boots ever so slightly, as if a cosmic tremble that started far away only just reached the tip of its finger out to give me a shock. A few cries of 'good riddance' and 'to hell with you' bounced around the pool of onlookers. I have to admit that these earthly sentiments brought me back to realm of the present. Dan Clayton had been a remorseless killer, after all, and any metaphysical grievance I might have at his execution could be saved for another day.

Next to come was Moreno. With his former gang associate swinging dead down below, the crowd went silent. His gut wound started to pour more blood as he stood up straight, saying once more that he wished he could take back all the bad. The young preacher said a few more words. The sheriff's hand seemed paralyzed on the lever. Loot Moreno repeated something a few times. It sounded like goodbye.

Finally, the trapdoor gave way. Despite the lengthy drop, Moreno didn't die instantly. He struggled and kicked until his dark skin turned a shade of purple too ghastly for human eyes to behold. Twenty seconds went by. Perhaps a minute. The writhing stopped. His fight was over. Justice was done. Justice was done.

Jasper stopped writing and touched his forehead to the pendulous corpse of Loot Moreno. "Goodbye old friend," he said, not giving a fig for any around who might've heard him. Pushing a path through the crowd, he found an opening to an alley where he decided to take rest. After imbibing the remainder of his flask, he doubled over, trying to breathe. On some level, Moreno deserved to be swinging. Bedford could see that plain enough. "Isn't it the sum of a man?" he whispered to himself, reading through his notes. "Isn't it the sum of a man?"

Perhaps fate had called Moreno's number. Bedford didn't like it, but he'd learn to live with it. What he couldn't stomach was the sight of Loot swinging next to Clayton. They weren't the same. One, a brutal, confused coward. The other, a troubled, flawed, deeply sorry man. A hero to some. They didn't belong on the scaffold together. Nor on the page. Jasper ripped the notes and threw them into the mud. He adjusted his coat and countenance, ready to make for the bar. He would drink to the bad man he only ever knew as noble while listening to saloon sages offering expert versions of characters they could never begin to understand.

CHAPTER 28:

PICTURES

IT WAS SIX MONTHS SINCE THE HANGING AT THUNDER HILL. March meant the snows were receding enough to try for a long journey. The nights were still cold but moving south made it easier on everyone. Kip stood inside the orderly little lobby of the Pinewood Hotel and asked about the land east of town. He asked about John and Nell Wilkins and Mr. Trent, the man Moreno said to look up.

"Those names," the hotel owner said. He had a shiny head with ten or so hairs combed over. Short but dignified, he stood soldierly, ready for action in case one of the little bells behind him sounded off. A wide and thick ledger was opened flat on the counter, resting under his meaty elbows. Kip gave it a glance: the spacious pages could hardly contain the words. Handwriting looked ready to burst from every edge. "John was just about my age. Nell, a few years younger. They kept their own company, mind you, being out beyond the township line. It's gotten a little more populated since. The line has pushed out."

"Then you had a decent measure of them," Kip smiled, looking up from the ledger. "It's none of my business, but it seems you take a robust accounting of most things."

"My wife says it's a condition."

"If it is, I'd say it fits your line."

"Oh yes. I write down everything my guests do, from the time they check in to the time they ride away. Nothing worse than being a derelict servant. Can you imagine? It goes against the entire idea of the profession. That's what I tell my wife."

Kip smiled again, this time wide enough for the hotel owner to see the dimples in his cheeks. The younger man was a head taller than him. Very respectful. Handsome and freshly shaved. Asking about John and Nell. His hand fought the urge to write down everything he was noting in his head. Better to wait a minute. "My name is Cliff Rudolph. I'm the owner and operator of the establishment." The short hotelier set down his pen and shot a stubby hand in Kip's direction.

"Forgive me," Kip said, meeting Mr. Rudolph's gesture with his left hand. It was a motion he was still trying to adjust to—being polite without trying to make the other fella feel awkward about his maimed fingers. "Anyway, I appreciate the rooms. Real nice. Been a few days since we had a proper roof."

"It was late when you arrived," Mr. Rudolph coughed, releasing the strange grip he had with the guest's wrong hand, "so I didn't want to bother." He coughed again, flattening the precious hairs on top of his head. "But, you're not the usual sort of people that come through."

"Is that right?"

"It's mostly a trading stop. We get a goodly number of travelers, mind you, but you don't seem to be on business."

A similar line of questioning from someone else might've put Laird off, but he saw no guile or malice in the little brown eyes of Cliff Rudolph. He wondered if the man lacked a measure of intelligence or if it was simply a case of one of those enigmatic creatures you find manning little posts on the frontier.

"Call it family business," Kip said, robust in his tone. "Nothing that'll cause you or anyone else trouble."

"I knew that," Rudolph said, waving his hand a little too dismissively to be good form. "I could tell right away that y'all were straight, upright folks. Good Christian types."

The last comment caused Kip to look down for a moment. Behind him on the carpeted stairs, he could hear descending footsteps. He turned and nodded his head, glad to see Elsie. She was wearing a long denim skirt and boots with a functional but tight-fitting flannel shirt that made it hard to ignore her figure. A cowboy hat hung from a strap and rested on her back; the last few months had seen her adopt a style of clothing that some in feminine circles might've smirked at. It made no matter; she was doing a lot more riding and work around the house with Syd and Pa gone. Sitting around drinking tea in a dress seemed somewhere in the realm of ridiculous. Maybe she'd change her mind and go back to her old ways. Maybe not. Kip didn't seem to mind. *It's hard to mess up pretty.*

"Gentlemen," she nodded, taking out a little of the refinement from her voice. "What are y'all getting on about?"

"Mr. Rudolph, this is Elsie. My fiancé."

Cliff picked up his pen and resumed his sentinel posture. "A pleasure to meet you. I would've introduced myself last night, but—as I explained to the gentleman."

She hopped the last two steps and put her little hand over the owner's thumb and wrist, reaching from her toes to deliver Kip a quick kiss. "That's quite all right, Mr. Rudolph. Don't worry, either. I stayed put in that big room with my mother. Nothing untoward will be happening in your fine establishment." Elsie gave Kip a punch on the arm. "All right, fellas. Quit with the blushing. I just thought to have it out. Morning's too fresh to see grown men embarrassing themselves."

"Yes, ma'am," Cliff said, snapping back to attention.

"Mr. Rudolph knew John and Nell," Kip said, pushing away the tedium of morning pleasantries for good.

"Well that's fortunate," Elsie said flatly. "Eureka, right from the jump. Did he know them well?"

He decided to answer for Mr. Rudolph. The owner's face showed relief as he started to write down the details of the morning, beginning with the time. "They weren't kin close," Kip said, leaning up against the high-set reception desk. "But you're right in saying that Cliff is a fortunate find. A man of detail and memory."

Rudolph looked up for a mere second from his writing and offered a short smile.

"We'll get out of your hair," Elsie said, detecting a sense of fraying nerves from the proprietor. She gave her fiancé's boots a little kick with one of hers. "Did you ask about Mr. Trent?"

"I did, although we haven't a chance to finish up. You interrupted *menfolk* going on about important things. What have I told you about that?"

Elsie let him have that one. Humor was necessary. Their old ways. Old patterns. It was vital to what one might be inclined to call *getting on with things*.

She could support Kip as much as possible and make the journey alongside him, but this final burden was ultimately his to shoulder. They'd weathered so much together since Ben's death, but here it seemed like he was a little out on his own. In doing her best with him, the young woman was learning the canyon between understanding and *being* understanding.

"If you mean Tobias Trent," Mr. Rudolph said, breaking up a loaded look between Kip and Elsie, "he lives in the house that sits crooked to the street. All the way down. Red shutters. Couldn't miss it if you tried."

"Might we miss him?" Elsie asked. "Could it be he's already about his work?"

"Oh no," said Cliff. "Mr. Trent doesn't work much anymore. He takes in some rents, but he's well set. Sits on his life's earnings."

"Older gentleman?" Kip asked.

"Quite old," the proprietor said. The tone of his voice went up, like speaking of Mr. Trent was a source of distress. "But that hasn't dwindled his capacity to be prickly. I'd appreciate it if you didn't mention me sending you his way."

"So noted," Kip said. "We'll leave you to it, then."

"Nice meeting you both," Mr. Rudolph said, looking around Kip's expansive frame to see Mabel descending the stairs. The Laird matriarch was meticulously accoutered in a dark blue dress and black shawl. Her face was stoic as she nodded toward the front desk. "Don't tarry on my account," she said, walking out the front door into the warming morning air.

* * *

Tobias Trent was rough in manner as he let them into his home, grumbling under every breath and with each motion of his withering body. The old man took to a cushioned chair near his stone fireplace like it was the only place in the world where he wasn't bitterly uncomfortable. "Sorry to call on you so early, Mr. Trent," Kip said.

"Eh, never mind that, boy. My feeble bones yank me from sleep hours before the sun rises. It's worse every day, I think." As he spoke, he looked at the ground, presumably hunched over by a weakened back. "What was it you wanted, again? Sit down, already."

Furniture was crookedly placed around the room. The guests hurried to find anything strong enough to hold their weight. Kip sought out a simple wooden chair near Mr. Trent as the ladies resigned themselves to a dusty cloth sofa near the door.

Creaking upright to survey his guests, the host waited no more. His voice was predictably fragile, but it had its intended effect. "You should already be in the midst of why you're here, not trying to get cozy. Life isn't cozy."

Laird smiled as he came to rest in his chair, but quickly realized that Mr. Trent was definitively unimpressed with his expression.

"Grinning, are you?" the old man barked.

"No, sir," he said humbly, aiming his eyes toward his feet. As he did so, Mr. Trent seemed to gain a certain vitality. Enough to straighten up his frail posture. The longtime Pinewood resident wiggled his toes and dug them into the rug. The motion was almost undetectable, as he was wearing five pairs of socks.

"Pretty ladies," he said, turning his attention away from Kip and his reddening cheeks. "Come by way of Clifford Rudolph, you said?"

"That's correct, sir," Elsie offered, fighting the lumpy cushions to adopt her customary ladylike refinement. "We're staying over at the Pinewood Hotel. I should also say that we're not to divulge the fact that he was the source of our directions."

Mr. Trent was not too old to detect the playfulness in Elsie's tone. He looked at the pretty girl and then again at the young man to his left. As he smiled, Kip noticed that he was near toothless and had one eye that held no color. "I'm liking her a lot more than you so far, son."

"I can see that," he quickly responded.

"You have a lovely home," Mabel said. It was the perfectly nice thing to say, and thus, perfectly Mabel.

"And this one," Mr. Trent said. "A captivating creature as well." Now the old man was smiling fully. Though his attention was warmly directed at the ladies, he seemed to be addressing all of his comments to Kip. "Call me Colonel. Everybody does around these parts."

The women nodded politely. Kip began to think that coming to Mr. Trent's had been a mistake.

"Relax there, tenderfoot," the host said, smacking the floor with a cane that had been furtively hanging from the arm of his chair. "And thank you so much, my dear. My only regret is that it's in a state of disrepair. Two lovelier faces I can't recall ever gracing this humble domicile. You deserve a more appropriate setting. Dusted and swept, ornaments shining."

"You're something else," the preacher couldn't help but say.

"I am. Something else entirely, greenhorn. Please," he said, pointing the cane at Kip, "allow the rest of us to be acquainted. So. You've had the displeasure of meeting the busybody over at the hotel."

"We have," Mabel answered matter-of-factly, like Rudolph's name was now *Busybody* and that was the end of that particular discussion. "And we're looking for information about some people that used to live near here."

"Well," Colonel Trent coughed. "I'll be happy to help, assuming I can."

"Nell and John Wilkins," Kip interjected. "You knew them."

"I did."

"I'm their son."

Kip was terse to the point of rudeness, but there was no staying himself. Enough with roads, hardship and stories. He leaned back in the little chair and waited for a response. "What can you tell us?"

Colonel Trent tapped his cane on the floor twice, still smiling his cavernous smile at Mabel and Elsie. "Could you help me up, young lady?" he asked Elsie. She paused for a moment and then came across the room, allowing Trent to take her arm. "You can call me Tobias," he said, winking his colorless eye before unclasping his grip to set off toward the back of the house. Kip put up his hands as Elsie resumed the seat adjacent to Mabel.

A series of loud noises reverberated through the house. It was enough to make them wonder how such an ineffectual old man could cause such a ruckus. "This is pointless."

"Be patient," Mabel told her son.

"I know," he answered, standing up to pace around the scattered furnishings. "Sorry, Mama. Just be ready to duck. For all we know, he's rummaging through an ancient armory back there."

"I like him," Elsie said, offsetting his tension with a casual tone.

"Of course you do, Else. Can't believe the dusty old peacock hasn't offered to make you an honest woman yet."

"There's still time."

"Enough," Mabel said, voice raised and stern. "You two are unceasing. I'm tired."

He watched his mother rub her temples and was instantly awash in shame. There was no way to imagine the feelings she was having to negotiate, losing a husband to sickness and a son to murder. Now, having to see her daughter betrothed to the boy she'd raised as her own. After a winter of mourning and taking stock, ultimately it had been Elsie's resilience that steered the ship, slowly warming Mabel to the idea of her marriage to Kip.

I love you, Else. But mom doesn't need another burden.

I love you, Kip. And it's not like this will be news to her. Mama's not oblivious.

Of course not. But I'm the cause of her heartbreak. It's in my head.

You can be a guilty ruin, or you can live your life. Live it well.

Elsie was right. Capitulation to the wreckage that had befallen their family was unmanly. It took a good woman to help him pick up his head and look forward. He'd made one condition. A trip to his birthplace. Hearing about the journey, Mabel insisted on taking part. Kip wasn't about to leave his mother alone back in Thunder Hill while they backtracked the frontier, so of course he consented. Things would work out, he knew, but the work wasn't always smooth.

"I apologize, Mama," he said, remembering his duty to be worthy of the gifts still at hand. "Sincerely."

"Me too," Elsie said, patting Mabel on the knee.

When Trent reemerged, Kip was actually glad. He was in need of a tension break. "You called yourself Kip Laird when you sauntered in, greenhorn." The colonel was holding a metal box overcome by rust. It looked heavy in his veiny hands.

"I did," he answered. "It was the only name I knew until recently."

"And what changed?"

"I found out where I came from."

"Seems to have taken you a long time to figure it out."

"A long time," Kip said, eyes fixated on the box. "And a hard time. I won't burden you with details."

"Good, 'cause I'm burdened with a lifetime of details. Rough and sad ain't gonna set my heart to stir." He sat back down and let the box rest on his legs, pointing to his colorless eye. "Faint of heart don't do."

"A lesson I'm learning."

"If you ain't learned it by now..." Trent said, nodding at his guest's bad hand. "Tell me your name, son."

"Joel Wilkins."

Colonel Trent went from intractable to agreeable in a heartbeat's time. "I've got a wagon and horses out back. Get it hitched and we'll head out to where you were born."

* * *

"We're coming up on it in a bit," said Colonel Trent, holding the reins of his two-horse team with surprising strength. "But like I said, it ain't gonna be much."

The journey from town was strange. Kip and Trent rode in the open carriage while the ladies trailed behind on their horses.

And so they traveled.

"Why did you want me to ride with you?" the younger man asked. He'd been too engaged with the contents of the box to direct his attentions anywhere else. Faded pictures of his mother and father. A few shots of a town social gathering. His father's army papers and regimental patches. Little books of his mother's writings with her initials sewn on the covers. Mostly diary entries. Some poetry sprinkled in. Correspondence between a young couple still hopeful in a hard world.

"So you could ask what you needed to ask. That's why you're riding with me."

"Did you know them well?"

"I'm the reason they came," Trent said, urging his horses over a patch of unsteady road. He didn't look at Kip. "That's right. Came at my prodding. John was my best junior officer in the War. We were friends. I came out here just after the fighting, bought up some land. Offered him some on the cheap. To be friendly."

"It wasn't your fault," Kip said, closing the box. "Not sure that's what you're getting at."

"Saying your pa was a brave soldier. And I ain't telling tales. Damned if you don't look like him. Chin like boxers, both."

"Is that why you believe I'm their son?"

"Can't say how or why you'd show up saying you were Joel Wilkins if you weren't. Be a damn strange thing to do."

"I suppose."

"But yes," he continued, steering the horses off the road through an uncultivated field. "A lot of it has to do with your looks."

"My mother was beautiful," Kip said. He'd spent half the ride looking at her likeness.

"Nell was a real special one," Trent said. "Like a daughter to me. Real special to all."

Sadness was catching up to the old colonel—he was done talking for a time. Kip waved to Mabel and Elsie, riding on their right flank as they started to slow down.

It was as Trent said. Not much. There was an outline of two simple structures that had long ago succumbed to the elements. The only discernable remnant of the house was the fireplace. Kip wanted more from it. Where memory was failing, he tried imagination. Nothing came. No echoes from the past.

"The land is still good," Kip observed. "River access. Good dirt." He jumped down and picked up a handful of the soil. It was dark brown and healthy.

"It's yours if you want it," he said. "I bought it back after... after what happened. No descendants. But there you go."

"I'm gonna have a walk around if you don't mind."

"Take your time, son." He held out his hands flat and up, like serving an offering.

"Y'all tie off to the carriage and have a stroll with me," Kip said, nodding toward Mabel and Elsie. They were soon off their mounts, stepping through tall grass and the meager vestiges of the Wilkins house.

Elsie was at his left, their arms tightly interlocked. "You see inside that box?" she asked.

"I did."

"And did old Colonel Cad tell you anything?"

Kip listened to the river running close by and closed his eyes like soaking in his beginnings. "He told me enough. My father was a good man. My mother was a good woman. Somehow, I always knew that, but it's nice to hear it from somewhere outside my head."

With his right arm, he beckoned Mabel over. "Mama," he whispered, squeezing her little body against his. "Love you."

She tightened up inside his embrace for reciprocation. "Is it what you thought it'd be?"

"It's pretty land," he said, "and I'll admit to thinking coming here would spur a memory or two. A happy image. Something."

"You were so young," Mabel answered.

"I know. Dumb wishful thinking."

"Not dumb," Elsie said, leaving it at that.

"How about we go home?" Kip gently patted his mother and fiancé on their backs and walked toward the carriage and Colonel Trent.

"You thinking you want to take the place?" he asked.

"How much money do you have on you?"

"Two or three dollars. Why you asking?"

"I want you to take it off my hands. Two or three dollars sounds good."

"Youngster, this land fetches a good ransom. I've been holding it against all comers for years on end. You might want to be doing some rethinking, son."

"I appreciate it, Colonel Trent," Kip said, climbing back up into the carriage. "And I'm not just talking. I really do. It's obvious you cared a lot about my folks."

"I just don't understand. Take what's yours, Joel. Hell, at least sell it off for something reasonable."

He gave the old soldier his warm smile. "Profit from it wouldn't feel right. And home's somewhere else."

"I won't keep on about it then, Joel."

"Thanks again." They shook hands and nodded. There'd be no more on the matter of money and land. "Colonel?"

"What is it, son?"

"If you don't mind, call me Kip."

The End